He stood on a dirt ro
with no wind to give
ture of red, yellow, and orange. From somewhere close by, he
smelled something burning.

As he surveyed his surroundings, his vision seemed to blur
to the consistency of water. His clothes were heavy on his body.
The sun was hot, yet he didn't sweat.

Something appeared in front of him, becoming clearer as he
approached. A church, its stone structure tall and reaching up
to the sky. God's house.

And yet, he stopped as if struck. Fear swirled in his belly, a
whirlpool that made his senses spin. His fingers trembled and
his armpits felt damp. Sweat from his forehead began to run
down into his eyes, caressing them like tiny needles.

He knew before the door of the church opened what would
appear.

He knows it only as the beast, appearing more loathsome
and frightening each time he sees it. Its hair is dark and matted
in some places, distended in others. Its face remains in perpetual shadow, but the eyes are clear, burning like charcoal, and he
acknowledges the madness residing there. He hears the thing's
harsh breathing as it confronts him, carrying something in its
arms.

"You've come back," it says in a voice like sandpaper grating
on metal. "Good. I have something for you. For us."

The beast places its load down on the ground and kneels
before it. The body of a girl no older than his daughter, her eyes
closed, her face composed and unblemished.

"Beautiful, isn't she?" the beast says. "One of God's perfect
creations, you would think. But she's tainted, like all of them."
The beast looks at him. "She's yours if you want her."

Blake steps back, too horrified by the notion to speak.

The thing's eyes darken. "Why do you refuse my offering?
If you are not here to partake, why come?" It pauses, then says,
"It's very simple. Watch." Still kneeling, the beast bows its mas-
sive head in prayer, holding in tableau for a moment.

Then it begins

BLOOD WORK

BY JEFF JOHNSTON

PART ONE

CHAPTER ONE

The woman held the razor to the baby's throat. "Get me the preacher!" she screamed again.

Blake heard her from the back of the patrol car as it came to a stop, and the answering reply, "He's coming!" amplified by a bullhorn.

The world outside the police cruiser was chaos. Police crouching behind cars. Snipers in hiding waiting for a chance to take a shot. Bystanders watching the show from behind barricades.

"Do you need a moment to pray or something, Reverend?" the young cop driving asked. He looked young enough to be his daughter's age, though Bethany was only fifteen.

Ten minutes ago, he'd been home putting the finishing touches on the next day's sermon, hoping his daughter would be home soon. As usual, worrying about her. Then the knock came at the door.

"No," he said. "Let's go." Exiting the car, he felt the eyes of the crowd on him. And, for a moment, sensed what Jesus must have felt entering Jerusalem on a simple mule.

Two plainclothes officers approached him. "Frank," he said, acknowledging the one he knew.

The other cop, holding the bullhorn, stepped forward. "I'm Captain Allen Guthrie. Thank you for coming Reverend Hardesty."

"What's going on?" Hardesty asked. It seemed like as many cars as the Allenside police force owned were here, cordoning off this section of the street.

"I believe she's a member of your church," Guthrie said.

"Margaret Haas? Brief him, Frank."

Frank Torrance stepped forward. "She took the neighbor's baby son out of his stroller while the mother was inside for a minute. She's been asking for you."

"How old's the child?"

"Three months," Guthrie said. "Reverend, if she's a member of your church, maybe she's said something or given you some indication she was going to pull something like this?"

"No."

"It's just that we all know her down at the station. She phones the station once a week with her stories about Satanists trying to get her."

"She's a good woman," Blake said. "Just troubled. She's had a lot of hardship in her life."

"Is he here yet?" they heard her scream, and, from this distance, the baby looked like a doll crooked in the woman's arm.

Guthrie lifted the bullhorn. "He's here, Mrs. Haas."

"Send him in here!"

Guthrie started to respond, but Blake cut him off. "It's all right. I'll go."

"No way, Reverend," the captain said. "We can't allow that."

"Is Kenny in there with her?"

"We think so," Torrance said.

"If she hasn't killed him," Guthrie growled.

"She wouldn't hurt him," Blake said. Kenny was her handicapped son. "Where's her husband?"

"We don't know."

Blake nodded. "Let's go then."

"Damn it, I said no."

"If I'm going to talk to her, it has to be in private."

"This isn't confession, Reverend. She might have a gun in there. Even if she doesn't, she's still extremely dangerous. To you and her hostage. I've got enough trouble—"

"Get him in here now!" Margaret Haas raised her prisoner above her head and seemed about to dash the baby to the ground. People in the crowd gasped and pointed.

Then she relented, still holding the razor blade close.

"What would you rather do?" Hardesty asked. "Wait until

she's killed him, then move in? If I talk to her, inside, alone, maybe I can convince her to give the baby to me."

After a moment, Guthrie sighed. "All right. See what you can do. Stall her; distract her. Give the snipers a chance to line up a good shot. If she ends up giving you the baby, she'll be distracted."

"No shooting."

"What?"

"No shooting, Captain, or I won't do it."

Guthrie stared at him. "Then don't." He shrugged. "Stay out here. She's a member of your church, but she's nothing to me. Whatever I have to do to save that baby, I'll do it, and I'll sleep fine tonight. You can stay or you can go in. But either way, my snipers' orders stand."

The two stared at each other. "I just don't want anyone to get hurt," Blake said finally.

"Neither do I. That includes you." The captain extended the bullhorn. Hardesty took it and faced the house, catching sight of the crowd. The look in their eyes now more like Romans watching as the Christians were about to be fed to the lions.

He raised the instrument to his mouth. "It's me, Margaret. Reverend Hardesty. I'm coming in."

"Hurry!" she shouted back. "I'm not sure how much longer I can hold out."

He gave the horn back to the captain then turned to Torrance. "Walk with me part of the way, Frank?"

The air was stifling as the two men advanced. "How's Martha?" Blake asked, referring to the other man's wife.

"She's fine."

"And your daughter?"

"She's fine, too."

"I haven't seen you in church lately."

"We've been busy..."

"You've found another church. I know. You're not the only one. You'd better stop here."

They stood not far from the open doorway. Margaret Haas had moved back out of view.

"Have you noticed the baby's not making a sound?" Blake asked.

"Yeah, we've noticed."

"If I pull this off, maybe you'll consider coming back."

Blake felt Frank pat him on the shoulder then move away. For a moment, he did not move. He may have sounded flippant with the detective but only because he was scared shitless. They didn't teach you how to deal with this in seminary. He was sweating freely, his hands slick and useless. Was it possible he could have foreseen her doing something like this?

He was about to take a step when he thought he caught movement in the periphery of his vision. Felt a touch on his shoulder. The touch of God, maybe, giving him His blessing? Or maybe it was Barbara. His dead wife waiting for him to join her on the other side if he screwed this up.

"Reverend?"

Margaret had returned to the doorway, the baby cradled in her arms, wrapped so tightly in the blanket Blake couldn't see him clearly. For the moment, she seemed vulnerable and very needy. If he backed up, would she follow him out, eyes on him, hand him the baby while giving the snipers a clear shot?

He moved forward, and she gave him room to enter.

Once inside, Hardesty found one of his worst fears confirmed. Margaret Haas's husband sat in his favorite easy chair facing the TV. For all intents and purposes, he could have been watching one of the television evangelists his wife loved so much if not for the knife sticking out of his right eye. His good eye was open and still showed the surprise the man must have felt before his wife killed him.

Her son sat in his wheelchair, not moving, not talking. Staring straight ahead, as he'd been doing for most of his twenty-eight years of life.

His mother still held the razor above the bundle she carried, the bundle showing no telltale rustle of cloth, no sign of movement.

"Margaret," the minister said, trying not to sound accusatory.

"You going to tell me I should give myself up?" she said. Her eyes slits, her breathing heavy. The razor blade ready. Margaret Haas, who claimed to love God with all her heart and soul.

"I'm here for you." What else should Blake say? He was playing it by ear. Depending on inspiration, divine or otherwise. Had she heard him? She nuzzled the baby, who still didn't move, but shouldn't he be? Shouldn't he be crying, screaming? Blake didn't want to think why the baby wasn't, why she was making such an obvious effort to prevent Blake from seeing him.

"Let me look at him," Hardesty said, chancing a step toward her.

"Why?"

"So, I know he's okay. Then we can talk."

"I'm tired of talking," she said. "Everybody's always talking. 'Take your pills, Margaret. Remember what the doctor said, Margaret. Rest. Stay calm. Everything's going to be all right.' But it never is, and nobody ever listens. I flush the pills down the toilet. Two a day when my husband thinks I'm taking them. I watch them go around and around and away. Let the alligators in the sewers have them. I need a clear head."

Blake's hand went to the small silver cross he wore around his neck, the last gift his wife had given him before she died. "Why did you ask them to bring me here?"

She brought her face down to the tiny form, the razor blade at her side for the moment, where a braver man than he might have made a grab for it. "I used to hold Kenny like this," she said. "When he was little. Tried to make him smile. He never smiled, never made a sound. Even then God was preparing him."

He'd heard variations on this theme before.

Her mood changed as quickly as it took for her to bring the razor up again, shaking it as she would a fist, her lip curling into something grotesque. "I wanted you to see what they've done to him! To my Kenny!"

"Who's they?" Blake said. Though he knew the answer. The Satanists, as she always claimed.

"They're hurting him again. Just because he's different." Tears streamed down her face. "God's Chosen One, made to bear our sins."

"I would have come if you'd asked, Margaret. You know that. You didn't have to do this."

"Not just you. Everyone. I want everyone to see what's been done to my son."

She talked about the Satanists a lot. The Satanists who she said were coming after her, though none had ever been identified. The Satanists, who were coming after her son because he was the only one who could recognize them. The only one who could stop them. When the time was right, she claimed, her son, Kenny—who hadn't spoken or barely moved in twenty-eight years—would rise up and smite them, and anyone who blasphemed God. This was what she was waiting for. This was her purpose for living. And until that day arrived, she had to protect him.

Blake wasn't sure how he felt about this poor, disillusioned woman who had created this elaborate fantasy to justify her son's extreme handicap. Sometimes he envied her passion, her desire. Stronger than anyone else's in his congregation, who mostly watched with blank stares every Sunday as he preached his sermon.

But she was living a lie. Fabricated to help her accept a son who could not reciprocate the love she so willingly gave and so desperately desired from both him and a husband who was pulling further and further away from her.

"She's driving me crazy with her talk, Reverend," he remembered her husband, Bill, telling him one rainy after-noon in the minister's office at the downtown Seventh Street Disciple's Church Blake Hardesty served. "I don't think she's giving Kenny his medicine the way he's supposed to be getting it. Not that I know how to talk to a son who don't know how to talk back. But she does or claims she does. Claims he answers her too, though I never hear him. It's like they got something going on between them the rest of us ain't allowed to see. But, Reverend, I tell you, there's nothing there. The boy's mind's as blank as a new chalkboard, forgive me for saying so. All those people saying hi to him at church, they're just doing that to please Margaret. He hasn't talked or barely moved since he was a baby. If it was up to me, they'd put him away, that's what's best for him. And for us. Do you know this is the third house we've lived in the past four years? We keep moving 'cause the Satanists keep finding us, you see. They're after us 'cause of our son, that's what she says. But that boy does nothing more than eat and shit in his diapers all day."

"Go look at him, Reverend," Margaret now said, breaking through his thoughts. Her voice low, the bundle now resting on her hip.

"Margaret—"

"Look at what they've done."

Kenny did not register his approach. A narrow face, impassive eyes, slack jaw. A faint odor of wet diaper. He had a thin frame to go with thin arms and legs. His upper torso was twisted in the chair, his legs bent against the leg rest. Except for an occasional blink of the eyes, he did not move.

"Look at his nose."

Hardesty had been through this ritual with her before.

"They're using their spells on him to change it," she declared. "It's gotten bigger. He used to have such a beautiful nose. So delicate.

"He gets nosebleeds regularly now," she stated. "His teeth are still moving, too. Look. Look!" Carefully, he opened the handicapped man's mouth. "And his ribcage. It's shifting." He'd developed scoliosis when he was ten, a side effect of his cerebral palsy. "How can they do that to such a beautiful boy?"

The minister heard her mutter something under her breath. A prayer, perhaps.

What am I doing? Surveying the room, Blake saw Kenny, silent and oblivious. His father, dead and bloody. His mother, eyes glazed, rocking back and forth. The baby hidden among the blankets. As unmoving now as it had been when the preacher entered. Because the child was dead. She'd killed it right away then held off the entire Allentown police force with a corpse. Too late. They were all too late. How much longer before Captain Guthrie got tired of waiting and ordered the police to move in? While he stood here doing nothing.

Blake took a step forward. "Give me the child, Margaret. I promise I will do everything I can for you. But you have to give him to me now."

"No." She stepped back, holding her captive close. "I don't want to hurt him, Reverend."

"You can't, Margaret," he whispered. "He's already dead."

The look on her face confirmed his fear. He extended a hand. "I can still help you, if you come out with me now."

"No," she insisted. The razor blade remained ready to strike.

"Come on, Margaret," he said, advancing on her slowly. "Let me have him. Give this whole thing up."

She kept shaking her head. "You don't understand."

"Margaret—"

"It's more than just the way they torture him. They've changed him. Turned him into something else. I thought God would protect him, but I was wrong. God has abandoned us."

Blake was close. All he had to do was reach out.

The sound from one of the back bedrooms stopped him. Piercing through the moment.

The sound of a baby crying.

Margaret let the bundle fall.

Hardesty reached for it, almost catching it before the wrapped form came loose from the blankets and hit the floor.

A doll. A plastic doll. Staring up at him with painted eyes.

The baby in the back room screamed louder.

"Kenny, no!" he heard. Looking up, he saw Margaret Haas staring past him. "Not now. Please, not now! Reverend, look what they've done to my son!"

Blake turned to look behind him.

And saw the wheelchair.

The empty wheelchair.

He swung around the room once, quickly. And saw something in the farthest corner of the room. Something that was moving, shifting. Kenny Haas, but with eyes that seemed to burn like charcoal.

Later, Hardesty would look back and still not be sure what he saw, or even explain what happened exactly. Kenny, who had never walked in his twenty-eight years coming at him much too fast. Hardesty twisting his body away from the onslaught as something sharp cut his sleeve, ripping flesh.

Crying out, Blake lost his balance and bounced against the wheelchair before hitting the floor, his attacker going with him, landing on top of him. Teeth turned his defending hands into ribbons. The snapping mouth pulled back, then lunged again, and pain as hot as flame shot through the minister's chest, his shoulders, blinding him with agony, blood bathing him and the face above him, oh God, now it was coming for him again.

What happened next Blake would only make sense of long after he had come out of the coma in the hospital, long after the terrible events that were to come. The face above him rising again with something in its mouth—flesh, his flesh, along with the silver cross Blake wore, swallowing it all whole. Then the great mouth descending again, this time for the killing blow, but stopping short as his attacker suddenly reared back. Reached for its throat. Then fell backward, the body writhing as if from a seizure. Twisting once, twice. Followed by a rush of blood from its mouth.

Managing one plaintive cry.

Before the writhing stopped. And Blake's attacker lay still.

For one long moment, Hardesty lay on his back, in shock. Feeling something warm and wet on his chest and arms.

Then Margaret Haas appeared above her son's body. Whispering, "Kenny." Then louder, "Kenny!" Then, "Kenny!" shouting the name over and over.

She turned to Hardesty, her lips stretched back to reveal uneven teeth, the razor still in her hand, coming up, as somewhere in the background the baby cried bloody murder.

"You killed him," she hissed. "You killed my son!" And there was nothing he could do as she lifted the tiny weapon up higher then brought it down toward his throat to finish what her son had started.

He heard a gunshot, and the razor missed its mark as blood sprayed from Margaret Haas's back, and she landed on top of him, her glazed eyes inches from his own.

As figures leaned over them, lifting her off him, and as Detective Frank Torrance said Blake's name over and over, he felt a warm darkness overtake him.

And, thankful for its intervention, he went away for a while.

CHAPTER TWO

He expected a tunnel. With a light at the end and someone waiting for him.

What Blake got was memories. Painful memories.

Seven years old. It was the first time he'd been allowed to stay overnight at a friend's house, and he felt grown up and important as he ate Cap'n Crunch cereal and watched morning cartoons. Later, he and his friend planned to go out to shoot baskets, something he'd never done before. They laughed and giggled and threw little pieces of cereal at each other when his friend's mother wasn't looking.

He barely acknowledged the ring of the doorbell or his friend's mom giving them a warning stare as her foot crushed a stray piece of cereal on her way to the front hall. On TV, Shaggy and Scooby Doo were falling over each other trying to get away from the latest so-called ghost Mystery Inc. was investigating.

"Blake." Turning, he saw his friend's mother back in the kitchen, crying, while a policeman shifted uncomfortably behind her. "Honey," she said, "I have some very bad news…"

A fire had gutted his house during the night, killing his mother and father. The fire department would blame it on faulty wiring. Just like that, his life irrevocably changed.

Next memory: A scream. His own. In the middle of the night. His Aunt Ruth's approaching footsteps. He'd been living with his mother's sister a little over a month. The nightmares that had started two weeks ago were occurring now with terrifying frequency.

She entered his room and immediately hugged him. Her breasts warm, soft.

Pulling away, he rubbed his eyes. "It wants to kill me."

"The monster?"

"Uh huh."

"Why does it want to kill you?"

"It says I've been a bad boy."

"But you're a good boy. A very good boy."

"It wants to eat me."

His aunt had been a smart woman. Well-read on the psy-
chology of children and the impact and meaning of dreams,
especially the dreams of a troubled seven-year-old who'd lost
his parents.

She held the boy's hands firmly, but lovingly, and looked at
him. "I want you to listen to me, Blake. I think I know how to
help you with these nightmares. But you have to be willing to
do what I tell you."

He waited, frightened.

"God gives us a way to make the dream monster go away.
Do you know what angels are, Blake?"

"God's helpers?" the boy whispered.

"That's right. These are special friends we can call on for
help when we sleep. If you want the angel God has chosen to be
your helper, all you need to do is call her.

"From now on, every night, as you fall asleep, call to your
angel. Do it over and over in your mind. If she doesn't come the
first night, do it again on the second. And the third if necessary.
Keep calling, every night, and she will appear. I promise."

After a few nights, the angel did come, made up of the
best parts of Aunt Ruth and his mother, and she chased away
the monster with charcoal eyes and claws for hands that represented his fears and feelings of guilt. Soon his sleep grew
peaceful again. And even as he grew older, his savior continued
to appear to him in dreams. But even the angel wasn't strong
enough to keep his aunt from dying of a heart attack one week
before his graduation from the seminary. She'd been so proud
of him the day he announced his plans to go into the ministry.
As he'd walked up to get his diploma, with no family members
in the crowd to applaud him, he used the memory of her smiling face to get him through.

Another memory: Was that Barbara he saw, adorned in

her wedding gown? Was that him at the front of the sanctuary waiting for her, looking so damn scared? It had been a small wedding, a few friends. Now, was that their daughter, Bethany, being born, crying as she came into the world?

More memories: Their move to Allenside, located in Pennsylvania about seventy-five miles north of Philadelphia, where he took over ministry of the Seventh Street Disciple's Church.

Whether a large town or small city, depending on who you spoke to, Allenside had been dealing with a gradual increase in crime, its residents worried that their home might soon rival American cities ten times its size. Just a few blocks from Blake's church, prostitutes walked the streets, drug dealers worked their corners, and two members of his own church had been mugged. But that hadn't stopped him from approaching his new ministry filled with hope and the power of God in his soul.

Next, Blake found himself standing in a room of cold steel and bodies. Made to stare down once again at the lifeless eyes of his wife on a metal table. Lying naked and exposed from the waist up because nobody had bothered to place the sheet in a respectable manner before he was asked to identify her.

"I'm sorry, Reverend," Detective Frank Torrance said, standing next to him, looking away. "If it's any consolation, we think she was one of the first to be shot, so she probably didn't see it coming. All indications are she died quickly."

She'd gone to the bank to withdraw the cash he'd forgotten to get for himself earlier. Because he preferred paying with the cash in hand rather than use a card. And the money machine had been down for repairs, so she'd gone inside. Followed by two men who entered not even a minute later, who, according to Frank had been kind enough to kill Barbara first, and ended up killing five people and wounding seven others. They were killed by the police during a shootout a half hour after the massacre.

"Barbara, no." The darkness came for him again. "Barbara!"

The memories stopped. What came next was the recurring dream, the nightmare that had started torturing his sleep sometime after his wife's death—a dark, terrifying variation on the nightmare that had caused his child self to call out to his aunt at night.

He stood on a dirt road, the air around him deathly still, with no wind to give it life. The sky carried a strange mixture of red, yellow, and orange. From somewhere close by, he smelled something burning.

As he surveyed his surroundings, his vision seemed to blur to the consistency of water. His clothes were heavy on his body. The sun was hot, yet he didn't sweat.

Something appeared in front of him, becoming clearer as he approached.

A church, its stone structure tall and reaching up to the sky. God's house.

And yet, he stopped as if struck. Fear swirled in his belly, a whirlpool that made his senses spin. His fingers trembled and his armpits felt damp. Sweat from his forehead began to run down into his eyes, caressing them like tiny needles.

He knew before the door of the church opened what would appear.

He knows it only as the beast, appearing more loathsome and frightening each time he sees it. Its hair is dark and matted in some places, distended in others. Its face remains in perpetual shadow, but the eyes are clear, burning like charcoal, and he acknowledges the madness residing there. He hears the thing's harsh breathing as it confronts him, carrying something in its arms.

"You've come back," it says in a voice like sandpaper grating on metal. "Good. I have something for you. For us."

The beast places its load down on the ground and kneels before it. The body of a girl no older than his daughter, her eyes closed, her face composed and unblemished.

"Beautiful, isn't she?" the beast says. "One of God's perfect creations, you would think. But she's tainted, like all of them." The beast looks at him. "She's yours if you want her."

Blake steps back, too horrified by the notion to speak.

The thing's eyes darken. "Why do you refuse my offering? If you are not here to partake, why come?" It pauses, then says, "It's very simple. Watch." Still kneeling, the beast bows its massive head in prayer, holding in tableau for a moment.

Then it begins.

Using its razor-sharp claws, the creature first cuts a piece of flesh out of the side, lifting it up as it intones, "This is His body, which is given for you." After placing the meat on its tongue and swallowing, it moves again, parting the soft flesh of the throat as easily as cheese, reciting, "This is His blood, shed for many for the remission of sins," before it leans forward, as if to kiss a lover, and drinks from the newly formed mouth.

Then the beast slices the body up the middle, revealing blood, bone and viscera. It is halted temporarily by the rib cage until it snaps the bones with its huge hands, proceeding all the way up to the bloody neck. Then it plunges its animal-like hands into the rift, coming up with the inner parts, shoving them into its mouth, chewing, swallowing...

"My... God..."

...until it has had its fill and turns to him. "Your turn," it says, gesturing toward the remains.

"No." The minister steps back.

"It's not enough to watch. Why do you think God has let you live? He killed your parents, your wife. But not you because you have a purpose." Holding forth the bloody entrails, it pronounces, "This will give you strength. Power. His power!" It grabs hold of the head and rips it loose from the body, then presents it to Blake with the neck turned up. "Drink."

"No."

"This is His blood..." Advancing on him.

"I can't..."

"...shed for many, for the remission of sins." Closer.

"Stay away!"

"Coward. You need this."

"Please..."

"How dare you talk this way to me! Leach! Fucking parasite!"

It flings the offering to the side, and, just as swiftly, grabs his arm, digging its claws into the skin, and pulls him stumbling and whimpering toward the ruined form. He is made to look down into what is left of the kidneys, liver, bladder, intestines.

Then his face is forced into the cavernous mouth formed by

the opened chest, his own cries turning to screams as the beast laughs...

...then screams. The angel, Blake's savior, has come, and, falling back, Blake watches angel and beast do battle.

The scene shifts abruptly, and Blake finds himself on the barren hill of Calvary, looking up at three crosses, and on the center one hangs his nightmare beast, crucified with nails driven through its hands and feet. The angel stands at the base of the cross holding the hammer she used to force them through its flesh.

He is surprised by the sympathy he feels for the beast as it hangs, helpless. Dying. "How can you do this?" it says, staring at him. "You need me. You need me!"

The angel, sheathed in white, hands him the hammer for the final blow. He approaches the cross then finds himself lifted up until he is level with the beast, staring into those haunting, disbelieving eyes. "Why have you forsaken me?" it whispers.

He lifts the heavy weapon.

And suddenly he is on the cross, confronting a figure bearing his own face, the mallet poised to pierce his flesh with the final nail. "No!" he pleads, his voice now the sandpaper growl of the beast, and he screams in pain as blood spews forth, showering his executioner, while the angel, still beautiful, watches him dying.

His eyes close. Darkness surrounds him.

Opening them again, he finds himself in a hospital room. Looking up at doctors, nurses. Familiar faces, such as his daughter's, Bethany. Frank Torrance. The chairman of the church board, Paul Blackburn. Louise Calabrese, the church sexton. Faces spinning, turning, a blur of images, his mouth so pasty dry he finally said to a surprised nurse hovering over him, "I'm thirsty."

But he passed out again before the precious liquid could touch his lips.

He was in a coma for ten days. Now, a day after waking up, lying in his hospital bed with all the bandages removed from his hands and chest where Kenny Haas had mauled him, he felt stronger.

"Can you believe it?" Frank Torrance was saying. "She was carrying a doll the whole time. Of course, she did kill her husband. But she'll never stand trial for it."

"Her wounds...?"

"She was shot in the back of the shoulder. She's okay. Physically."

"Kenny...?" Blake asked, knowing the answer.

"He choked to death. On that silver cross of yours. I guess when he attacked you... Blake, what happened? I'm supposed to ask..."

Hardesty thought for a moment. "Margaret and I were talking. I thought ... I could get her to give me the child. Then I heard the baby cry from a back room ... and I realized... But then he came after me..."

"You mean Kenny?"

"Yes. He was out of his wheelchair. I couldn't find him at first. Then, suddenly, there he was."

"But I thought he couldn't—"

"I did, too. Maybe... I don't know."

"Your wounds... The doctor said it was as if you were ravaged by a wild animal. It's hard to believe human teeth could do that."

"He wasn't..."

"What?"

"Nothing." He looked at Torrance. "Where is Margaret?"

"At the state hospital."

"I should see her..."

"You'll do nothing of the sort. You need to get some rest. And I should go."

"Is Bethany all right?"

"Louise is staying with her at your house while you recover. Your daughter's a tough cookie."

"The congregation?"

"Paul Blackburn's been running things. Some of the members came to visit you while you were in a coma. I'll be back to see you again." Torrance turned to leave.

"There's something else you're not telling me, isn't there?" Blake said.

The detective hesitated at the door.

"I can see it in your eyes, Frank."

"Not now." Torrance looked at him. "Tomorrow."

Hardesty held the other's gaze. "All right. Tomorrow then."

"I'm sorry..."

"No, you're right. I should rest. Whatever it is can wait until morning." He smiled. "I'll see you then?"

"I'll be here."

The unspoken thing came out the next morning, with Frank Torrance watching from the farthest corner of the room as the doctor talked.

An MRI to check for head trauma while Hardesty was still in a coma had found a tumor. A type of brain cancer known as glioblastoma. The tumor already in stage four, which meant cancer had already spread to other parts of the body. They should perform surgery right away, followed by a major course of chemotherapy.

"No," Blake said.

Both men stared at him.

"How much time would I have without surgery or chemo?"

"Six months to a year. Treating it might give you more."

"'Might.' Meantime, I'd be dealing with the side effects of the treatment. Until the cancer finally gets me."

"Side effects can be different with different patients," the doctor said.

"Without treatment, how much time till I start feeling sick?"

"You've been asymptomatic up to this point. It happens that way sometimes. It's probably why you didn't know anything was wrong. My guess is you'd be fine for a couple months, maybe a little tired at times, weak, experiencing head-aches now and then. After that, the full symptoms could come any time. And when they do, it'll be bad. You won't be able to function on your own. You'll go downhill pretty fast after that."

"A couple of months at least?"

"Probably. Until then, nobody should be able to tell you're

sick."

"And that's the way I want it," the minister emphasized. "Tell nobody."

"What about Bethany?" Frank asked.

"I'll tell her when I'm ready."

Both men stared, then nodded. "I'm sorry, Blake," Frank said.

After Frank and the doctor left, he lay in bed, wondering why he felt relief instead of sadness. As if a weight had been lifted. Maybe because his life had been filled with too much sadness, had been too much of a damn struggle. But now he'd been given a blessing. He knew how much time he had left. It was up to him to make each minute count.

As he lay back, he became aware of the small clock by his bedside someone must have brought him from home.

Ticking.

CHAPTER THREE

Two weeks later. Saturday night. Five days since his release from the hospital. The timer of his life started and counting.

He sat behind his desk in his office at the church, the pages of his sermon spread out in front of him, still insisting on writing by hand instead of typing on a computer.

"You should go home," he heard and looked up to see Louise Calabrese, the church sexton, standing in the doorway.

"I could say the same for you."

"I'm finished cleaning and ready to go, believe me. But I don't have a fifteen-year-old waiting for me."

"She's hardly waiting for me." He studied her. "I didn't even hear you."

"You usually don't. I could walk off with the place." Louise entered the office, bringing with her the aroma of tobacco. Already, she had the crumpled pack of generic cigarettes in her grasp, rough fingers digging deep for another one. Sitting down in the chair in front of his desk, she lit up using a cheap throwaway lighter. He pushed forward the ashtray he kept on his desk especially for her.

"Do you want to talk?" she asked, her low, gravelly voice reflecting the abuse her vocal cords had taken over the years.

"What about?"

"How you're feeling about entering the lion's den tomorrow."

"I feel fine."

"Then let's talk about why you almost got yourself killed; how upset I would have been if you'd died in that hospital. Shit, Blake, who the hell made you God?"

Her profanity didn't shock him. Louise Calabrese, church sexton, was so much more. A friend and, yes, a confidante. For the little money her job paid, he didn't know how she got by. Probably the insurance money from her husband's death. She didn't talk much about her past. She was one of those people you ended up sharing all your secrets with while she managed to keep hers to herself.

"I'm sorry for worrying you," Blake said.

"What were you doing going into her house like that? Unprotected. And for what? The woman was batshit crazy."

"The baby—"

"Was a doll. The real baby was fine."

"I didn't know that. And I ... I thought I could help Margaret."

"Yeah? Well, sometimes you have to pick your battles. You can't help everyone, Blake."

"I don't feel like arguing, Louise."

She opened her mouth then hesitated. Maybe reconsidering what she was about to say. Finally, she sighed and said, "You look tired."

He was. But he wasn't ready to go home. Not yet.

Listening to her, Hardesty was reminded, yet again, how much he valued Louise Calabrese. At fifty-four, ten years older than Blake, and dressed in the jeans and flannel shirt from her latest Goodwill thrift store purchase, she seemed worn and leathery and was as tough as anyone he knew. But, also, in her way, quite caring and giving. The fact that she was even alive was a miracle in and of itself. Her husband had beaten her regularly for years until he died from a heart attack. Officially, he was dead before he hit the floor. Unofficially, or so the rumor went, he might have lived had she been a little quicker to dial 911. He'd been in the process of beating her yet again when it happened, so it was understandable if her injuries had slowed her down. But maybe she'd seen that moment as her way out. God finally paying her back for what she'd been made to suffer all those years.

When it came to running the church, Blake and Louise made a good team. But the congregation, which had always been small, was getting smaller. Who wanted to be a member of a church in a bad part of town where the minister was jinxed?

His parents dead from a fire, his wife killed during a bank robbery. Now they could add Margaret Haas to the latest—

"Stop it!" Louise snapped, cutting off his thoughts.

"What?" he responded.

"Feeling sorry for yourself. Feeling guilty. Sometimes things happen. We don't always know why."

"I should have done more to help Margaret."

"Well, aren't you just a saint, Blake Hardesty? If Jesus Christ himself came back at this moment, he'd have nothing on you."

"That's enough."

"No, it's not enough. Do you think Barbara would want you sitting around feeling sorry for yourself?"

"I'm not feeling sorry for myself."

"Then what is it, Blake? You tell me."

"I want to do more. What's wrong with that?" He took a breath. "I'm tired of just standing behind a pulpit, offering words that mean nothing. I became a minister because I wanted my life to have meaning; I wanted to have some impact. It's not enough for me to talk about God's love and expect them to feel something just because I say they should. I want people to open their eyes and realize that what they do every day has meaning. I want to know that what I do has meaning..." He stopped, suddenly embarrassed by his outburst.

"Go home," Louise said, sticking the last cigarette from the pack into her mouth. "Stop torturing yourself. You have enough to do. Barbara's only been dead a year. Just two weeks ago you almost got yourself killed. You should be taking care of yourself. Staying home with your daughter."

"She doesn't need me. She doesn't even want to talk to me."

"That's a stupid thing to say. Bethany's a fifteen-year-old girl who lost her mother. You don't have to have all the answers. Just be there for her."

Barbara had been the one who did that. They'd spent so much time together. Mother and daughter, sharing special times that a father couldn't understand. An older woman to help Bethany deal with her fears of burgeoning womanhood. Barbara was the one with the answers, not him. And in the time since his wife's death, he saw the look of betrayal in the teenager's eyes, as if he was the one who'd pulled the trigger and took her mother away just when she needed her most. So much anger and nowhere to place it except on him. Especially since he was so bad at giving her what she needed.

Or did he avoid her because she reminded him too much of Barbara? In her eyes, in some of her expressions, even in the tilt of her head? The truth was, sometimes it hurt to be around Bethany. His own daughter.

"She won't talk to me," he said.

"She's rebelling. It's natural."

"She says there's no God."

"What better way for a minister's daughter to rebel?"

"I'm beginning to wonder if maybe she's right."

"What?"

"Do you think she blames me? For what happened to Barbara?"

"Why don't you ask her?" Louise said, her expression softening. "She may be afraid to tell you how much she needs you right now."

"Maybe," he said, looking down at the pages in front of him. Feeling inadequate.

"Go home," Louise said, rising. "I sure as hell need to." She threw the empty pack away. "You can finish your sermon there, can't you?"

"I'm almost finished."

"Give Bethany a hug for me. I liked staying with her when you were in the hospital. She's a good kid. Stronger than she wants to give herself credit for." She crossed to the door. "You're really something, Blake Hardesty. You know that?"

He looked at her and saw beauty and dignity behind that rough exterior. And in that moment, he almost told her about his illness. The secret of it weighing on him, begging to be shared with someone.

Instead, he said, "Thank you, Louise. For listening."

She shrugged. "No charge."

"I love you, you know."

He watched her hesitate, her smile dropping for just a second before turning away. But not fast enough to mask the look in her eyes. "Goodbye, Blake," she said. Then she was through the door and out of sight.

Stupid, he thought. What a stupid thing to say. He'd meant it as love between friends, and God knew he needed her friendship.

And yet, how many times had he noticed the way she watched him when her guard was down? Did he only imagine it, or was there something more she wanted from their relationship, something he couldn't even hope to return?

He decided not to think about it anymore tonight. He was too tired, and he really should go home. His sermon had been difficult to write, but it was almost completed. There was no need to hang around here.

And yet he took the time to sit in the sanctuary a while before he left. He always found solace in the quiet of this room. Peace. The space a true sanctuary from the outside world.

But how much longer could his church last with the membership dwindling like it was? It had started gradually, after his wife's murder. Everyone so supportive at first. Casseroles brought to the home. Offers of help. Money collected. But in their eyes: fear. A need for distance. Getting too close meant acknowledging such a thing could happen to them. After an appropriate time had passed, people began transferring their memberships to other churches. Others just stopped coming. And no new members were showing up to take their place.

He wondered if he cared. Maybe it was better to let this place die a peaceful death rather than delay the inevitable. Maybe he could find better things to do with the time he had left.

He rubbed his sore hands together. The wounds there had healed, but small scars remained. And sometimes they still hurt, though the pain was probably more memory than actual physical pain.

They were hurting now, and he closed his eyes. And felt the cool touch of someone's fingers on his face. The filmy cloth of the angel's robes brushing his shoulders.

Ever since he'd left the hospital, he felt as if someone was watching him. If he closed his eyes, he could imagine it was the angel born in his childhood dreams.

He continued to rub his hands, pressing harder until they came away wet, and when Blake opened his eyes, he saw blood pooling in the center of each palm. Ragged holes where there had been scarred flesh before.

But he didn't cry out. Instead, his eyes were drawn to the front of the sanctuary, where he saw her, wearing a flowing gown of gossamer white, her face pure, perfect. He had no name for her, had never needed one. Had only called her "angel," since he was seven years old.

He started to speak, but she held up her hand.

"No," she said. "Just listen. You need to prepare yourself."

"For what?" he said. Suddenly frightened, he asked, "Is it my time? Have you come for me?"

"No. I've come to warn you. It has returned."

"It?"

"You know what I mean. The beast."

"Will you help me?"

She smiled. "Haven't I always?"

This is my body, which is given for you.

The voice. Low, menacing. He turned but saw nothing. Still, he was sure he'd heard it.

This is my blood, shed for many for the remission of sins.

"All we can do is wait."

"Wait for what?"

He felt the pain in his hands again, saw blood flowing freely, dripping onto the pew. Then from somewhere came the sound of laughter, and he almost saw it, the creature of his childhood nightmares. Facing him with its sacrifice, a human body, in its arms.

This is my body...

He thought he might scream then realized he was sitting in an empty room. The beast, if it had been there at all, was gone. As was the angel. He was alone, with only the cross hanging above the communion table and the portrait of Jesus watching the empty sanctuary to keep him company.

His hands were unblemished but for the scars from Kenny's attack. He felt no pain.

It was time to go. Feeling shaky, he rose and walked out of

the church, stopping at his office to gather the pages of his sermon. Still feeling as if something was watching him. Maybe it was God, placing His holy hand on his soul, offering guidance. If there was a God. But, of course, there was. How could he be an effective minister and not believe that God existed and was always near, a definite presence in each person's life?

God did not have charcoal eyes, however, and that's what he thought he felt watching him as he finally exited the church, remembering to lock the main door before starting his four-block walk home.

CHAPTER FOUR

The morning broke bright and clear, but Stan Marles barely noticed. The police detective had arrived at the station while it was still dark. As the dawn broke, he was involved in the work before him. Grotesque crime-scene photos spread out on his desk.

A lot of things made Marles nervous, yet he was blessed with a strong stomach when it came to this kind of thing. Or not blessed, depending on how you looked at it. The photos showed what had once been a family of four. They horrified him, angered him. But he knew he needed to take in every little detail if he was going to discover who had done this. And why.

He hadn't wanted this case. Captain Guthrie had forced it on him because of his previous experience working homicide in Philadelphia, where it was assumed that he might know more about dealing with this kind of "big city" crime. Not too long before his arrival two men had shot up an Allenside bank, killing five people and wounding seven. As had been explained to Marles, one had to go back fifty years to find a crime as bloody as that one around here, and people were worried about what was a definite uptick in crime.

And now, less than a year later, this awful thing had happened. An even more horrendous act of violence, the aftermath of which was shown by the photos in front of him. An entire family butchered. Allenside residents reeling from its impact. Afraid now that their large town or small city, depending on who you spoke to, might not be a safe place to live in anymore.

Nothing in his five years in Philadelphia Homicide had prepared him for something like this, though, strong stomach or not. And now everyone was watching him. His first big case since coming here. He wondered how soon it would be before he became the scapegoat if he didn't solve this case fast enough. He looked at his watch. The church closest to where the murders had occurred wouldn't have started its Sunday morning service yet, so he had several hours until he planned to head over to the minister's house. He could try to catch the pastor at the church right after service ended, but then he might have to go inside the church building itself. Where there'd be a cross and pictures of Jesus. No thank you. He'd wait until later.

The detective began studying the photos again, hoping this time he'd find something he missed, something that would help him find the monsters who did this.

An entire family. Christ.

Blake waited to begin the service, hoping that a few more people might enter the sanctuary. But he knew that the less than twenty people settling down in front of him would probably be it. The total membership had dropped to below seventy, but how many just hadn't bothered to tell him they weren't coming anymore?

Earlier, he had been in his office, telling himself he needed to go over his sermon, but really avoiding the members of his congregation.

Now he noticed the empty space where Margaret Haas always sat. As if the congregation had left it vacant by common consent.

Louise sat in the back row on the left, probably craving a cigarette. Lasting through the entire service without a smoke was her own little sacrifice to God. On the other side of the room in the back sat his daughter, Bethany. Arms folded, head down. Her usual pout. When Barbara was alive, the teenager hadn't seemed to mind coming to church. That had changed since her death. Still, it was the one thing he managed to be firm with her about. A reverend's daughter attended church every Sunday. That was just the way it was. Since his return from the hospital, though, they hadn't talked much. When they did, they were usually at odds.

Paul Blackburn, the chairman of the board, sat front and

center next to his mousy wife. His eyes dark, brooding. One or two others gave Blake an uneasy smile.

The room felt too warm. Blake's palms were wet, but, thankfully, not from blood. He closed his eyes, but not to pray.

Joe Gilmeyer, the organist, began a labored version of "Onward Christian Soldiers," and the service began.

Louise rose with the rest of the congregation. It pissed her off to see such a sparse crowd. On today of all days. These people should have been rallying around their pastor after what happened, offering support.

Joe Gilmeyer finished the opening hymn on a missed chord that even made Louise wince. The congregation sat and waited, a hushed sense of expectation in the air. Wondering what their pastor would say. What had happened to Margaret Haas shocked everyone, but truth be told, most of them were probably relieved they didn't have to pretend around her anymore.

But now members of the church were buzzing over what had happened to the Rheman family two nights ago, not members of their church, but they lived just two blocks away. The news of what happened had been splashed across every news outlet imaginable.

Blake rose from his seat, and, as always, Louise Calabrese's heart began to beat a little faster.

For a period of time after her husband died, she'd sworn off men, had promised she'd never again put herself in such a vulnerable position. The emotional scars from her marriage were too fresh. The easiest thing to do was stay away from all men. She had even experimented with women for a time.

Then along came Blake Hardesty. She had been working here for over a year—free of her husband for two years—when he and Barbara arrived, following the retirement of the previous minister. At first, she'd kept her distance, refusing to admit her attraction. He was a man, after all, and in charge.

But over time, her resolve began to soften. He was different from other men. Sensitive, and not afraid to show it. Honest. Caring. Vulnerable. Perhaps too vulnerable. She began fantasizing about him and envied Barbara. But she felt safe around him and so did her fantasy. He was a happily married man after all. Then Barbara was killed during that bank robbery, and suddenly the fantasy took on new dimensions, frightening her. She grieved for Barbara, and she supported Blake as best she could. But, after the grieving, she was left with these other feelings. Feelings she had not experienced since the time she thought she'd loved her husband. She didn't want to trust it, or believe it was possible. But it lingered, and grew, and remained hidden behind her gruff exterior.

What the hell kind of woman lusted after a man grieving the loss of his wife? She hated feeling this way, like a flighty teenager. Hated herself for being so selfish and for letting her defenses down like this.

And she was especially angry that, after finally feeling this way about someone after so much time, it should be so damned inconvenient.

As he'd laid in the coma, Louise wondered if she had blown her chance, and she'd promised herself that, if he came out of it alive, she was going to tell him how she felt. But since his return, she'd had second thoughts. He certainly didn't seem to notice how she felt.

Or did he?

Blake finished the opening scripture, and the congregation stood for the next hymn.

God, he was sexy, she thought, like Jesus himself sent down to turn a few heads. Eyes a deep chocolate brown. A smile that was small, but genuine. Thick, dark hair. A face with hardly a wrinkle. The body and grace of an athlete. Forty-four years old, but he easily looked ten years younger.

Christ, what a pair the two of them would make if they were ever to get together. A ten-year difference between them already, but with him looking so much younger than his years, and she, a tough war horse, looking much older and making the age gap seem even broader.

Life was so unfair.

Shit.

Louise needed a cigarette. But she had too much respect for this place to sneak out. Pushing her thoughts aside, she joined in with the singing, smiling to herself as she noticed a few people who still frowned at her loud and out-of-tune voice.

Which only made her sing louder.

Blake thought the service was running smoothly. During announcements, he thanked them for the cards and visits while he'd been in the hospital. He felt his usual sense of unease during the communion service but performed the ritual without showing his nervousness.

Following the offering, he listened as the church's six-person choir attacked today's anthem in a workmanlike fashion.

Then, slowly, he rose, moved behind the altar and looked out over the small crowd. How much longer could this church survive its dwindling membership? Afraid of its own minister. The jonah pastor.

They stared back at him, and, suddenly, he felt on display. See the minister who'd been in a coma. Come one, come all!

Who were these people? What did they expect of him? He was supposed to lead them, but the truth was he'd never felt connected here. When Barbara was alive, she'd served as a buffer. Everybody had loved Barbara. But after her death, the gap between him and his congregation had become apparent. Had always been apparent, except to him. How had he been so blind?

He looked down at his notes, then back up at the expectant faces.

"Tragedy," he started, "is a part of life. If we're lucky, we don't get to feel its touch too deeply. It doesn't get too personal, or too close. And yet the world is full of violence. We see it or hear about it every day of our lives, slapping us in the face, demanding our attention. Sometimes we feel as if we've lost control. As if God has left us to fend for ourselves."

Barbara!

"But if we are all part of the family of God, then how do we understand violence when it strikes? How do we get our minds around tragedies of such horrifying magnitude?"

My God, Barbara! No!

"And yet, tragedy is a part of life. It affects us all one way or another. It's affected me personally. It's affected us in this

congregation more than once. My wife. Bethany's mother."
Blake glanced at his daughter, her head still down, and found
himself looking away before she might raise it. "Most recently,
Margaret Haas, her husband, Bill, and their son, Kenny. We feel
the gap these people leave. We try to understand why it happened. But how can we? Does anger help? Maybe. But what do
we do with our anger? How do we deal with the deep anguish
we feel?"

Was he sweating? Were his hands really this clammy? "And
yet, we're told we should go on with our lives. Grieve, and then
move on. God has a plan, we're told. I've said it myself, right up
here at this pulpit, about how we should accept God's mission
for us. But what mission could that possibly be, we ask? What
plan could include such horror?"

He remembered how angry he was that they hadn't bothered to cover his wife's body before letting him see her, laying
there naked for Frank Torrance and anyone to see.

And then had come Blake's realization that this wasn't his
wife at all, it couldn't be, not these lifeless, soulless eyes which
had held so much life before.

Thank God this wasn't her, he'd told himself, even as he'd
begun to cry and realized that he would have to go home and
tell their daughter that her mother was dead.

The congregation stared at him with what seemed a stunned,
silent attention. Even Bethany watched him now.

"If we are to believe in the existence of a loving God, then
how can we accept such things? How can we bring that image
of God back to us? Every Sunday we stand before Him at the
communion table and ask for His forgiveness. But what about
the times we think He should be asking us for forgiveness? I'm
sure we've all felt that way before. So how do we learn to forgive
God and go on with our lives?"

And then, from somewhere deep in his brain, he heard
a voice shout, *You don't forgive the bastard!* and he stopped. It
sounded like the voice of the beast from his dream. Growling.
Screaming in his head.

*You don't turn back to God; you turn your back on God! Get rid of
Him! We don't need Him. He needs us! Toss the prick away.*

Stop it, he told himself, unaware of the congregation for the moment, aware only of this presence invading his being. It seemed so loud in his mind, how could anyone else not hear it? *I say to hell with God! Who needs His sanctimonious bullshit? He's worthless! Dated. Fuck God!*

And with the shouts of horror and outrage rising from the congregation, led by Paul Blackburn as he stood and pointed at the pulpit, Blake realized they had heard the rasping voice of the beast, and it had issued from his own mouth.

He screamed aloud for it to stop then felt his knees give way, as the voice, thank God, began drifting away in his head. As did the world around him. Louise Calabrese kneeling over him. His daughter staring down in horror. Other faces of the congregation—ugly, twisted, crying. He didn't understand what was happening and was only too glad to see everything go away, as he allowed himself, once again, to be wrapped in another blanket of darkness.

CHAPTER FIVE

Bluejay was always talking. Most of it bullshit, Scott Draven usually letting it go in one ear and out the other. But some of it was worth listening to, and made Scott think of his father, now spending time in prison for rape. The tricks his old man used to play on him with the glowing end of a cigarette. Testing him. Be strong, boy. Always. Toughening him up. Don't ever let them see the pain.

Scott stood at the mouth of the alley, dawn having long since broken, watching the few Sunday morning people passing by. Some of them abruptly picking up their pace upon noticing him. He was a big man—huge, in fact—with short-cropped blond hair, eyes that were too small for his face, and a thin line of a mouth. He'd only slept a couple of hours. He rarely needed more.

After a while, he moved back into the alley and opened the first door on his right. Below, he heard the rest of Bluejay's "vampire" crew moving in their sleep.

"Each person dies," Bluejay loved to say. "It's inevitable. What we do is help speed up the process. The world is full of boring, stupid people leading stupid, boring lives in stupid, boring homes. If someone doesn't want to use the power God gave them, why shouldn't they give it up to us, allow us to do something meaningful with it?

"Cannibals believe that eating another human being infuses them with that person's spirit and strength. It's a holy worship. An honor to be eaten by a friend after death. The people we choose should thank us for making their lives meaningful."

Yeah, a lot of it was bullshit. But some of it made Draven think.

Especially after last night.

Walking down the stairs, he re-entered the basement that was their current base of operations. Stepping around old newspapers, torn cardboard boxes, remnants of food gone bad, and his sleeping companions, his body still hummed from the previous night's activities.

It had been invigorating. Especially the show the guy put on for them with his wife while Jimbo and Bobby held knives to their two kids' throats. Not to mention what they had done to the son while the parents watched. Once they were finished with the other three, they'd brought the sixteen-year-old daughter back here with them. A good choice for their grand experiment, Bluejay proclaimed. Dead and propped up against the wall the way she was now, she didn't look like such a great choice anymore.

All at once, Bluejay got up and kicked Jimbo in the side. "Wake up, asshole!" Leaning over Bobby next. "You too, shitface." Both men groaned while Bluejay nodded a greeting to Draven.

What a stupid name. Bluejay. He hoped the guy wouldn't be talking reincarnation again. Claiming he was a bird in a previous life, hence the reason for his name. The jerk was full of stories.

The subject of his thoughts asked him, "Did you sleep at all?"

"Some."

Jimbo got to his feet. "What are we gonna do with her?" Indicating the teenager.

Bluejay crossed to her, the disappointment clear on his face. "I was sure she was the one."

"We're not done with her, are we?" Bobby said.

"Shut up," Bluejay admonished in a soft voice.

"So, we're just gonna leave her?" Jimbo asked.

Bluejay said nothing. He seemed to be thinking. That was something else Bluejay was always doing. The man claimed to be a prophet. Which was enough to convince the other two. Ass-kissers, both of them.

Skinny, wiry Bobby, always talking too loud—the kind who

thought farting was the funniest thing in the world. His face angular, the texture of pizza—extra cheese. Jimbo, meanwhile, had probably been a hell-raiser in his day, when he'd had muscles, not the fat he carried around now. His teeth had gone bad, and his eyes were always red-rimmed and wet.

To them, Bluejay's shit was just the latest kick, the new high. Scott didn't think for a minute they understood most of what their leader was talking about. But they went along, like lap dogs. Draven, meanwhile, was no disciple but at least he took time to think about the parts of Bluejay's so-called lessons worth considering. Bluejay, tall, gangly, and muscular, was not as big as Scott, but was certainly dangerous. Someone to watch out for. Pronounced features, a mean face, ravaged from hard living. Not sure what to make yet of his newest disciple, he offered Scott wary friendship. But Scott knew this tinhorn savior would just as easily cut off his balls as look at him if the situation warranted.

Bluejay continued to stare at the girl. "Such a shame," he declared. He shook his head, then said, "We'll leave her here."

"Jesus, Bluejay!" Bobby said. "There's a lot left to eat." Jimbo ran over with a knife, ready to cut off another piece of her, but Bluejay shoved him, and the heavy man lost his balance, falling on a pile of loose newspapers. He immediately struggled to his feet, embarrassed.

Scott felt a sermon coming on and kept his expression neutral.

"Remember what I taught you. We're vampires!" Bluejay proclaimed, long black hair flying as he swung his head, something admittedly attractive in the way he delivered his message. "But we take more than blood. We take everything the victim has to offer. Until there's nothing left to take. Until the victim is us and we are the victim. That's what makes the meal holy. It has to mean something."

Looking at the dead girl again, he said, softly, "This one was supposed to be special. The one that would take us to the next level. But she didn't last. The experiment failed. Whatever power she had before is gone. It wouldn't do us any good to eat her now." Turning back to his flock, he added, "But don't worry, we will get another chance. And we're smarter now. Sharper. When the next chance comes, we will be ready. We will not fail."

The look of rapture in Bobby's and Jimbo's eyes made Scott sick. They had no idea what their master was talking about but nodded their heads anyway. Anything you say, boss. You want us to eat flesh? We'll eat flesh. You want us to piss in your hand? We'll piss in your hand.

"But last night was not a total loss. You feel better this morning after last night's offering, don't you?" Bluejay was on a roll now, as good as any Bible-thumping preacher.

"Yeah!" From Jimbo.

"Fucking A!" Bobby, trying to outdo him.

"All right, then! Let's do something with that power!"

"Yeah!" Both of them together.

"But first, go steal us some doughnuts."

"Yeah ... huh?"

"For breakfast, you morons. I'm hungry. And I want real doughnuts this time, not fucking sweet rolls. With the white cream inside."

The two looked at each other, shrugged, and ran out like two knights after the Holy Grail. Scott remained silent as Bluejay walked over to the dead girl again, lifted her up under her chin, and muttered, "Too bad. I liked her." Letting the head drop, he walked away as she fell to the side. Sitting next to Draven, not looking at him, Bluejay said, "You haven't said much since we woke up. That's what I like about you. When you do talk, it means something." He turned his gaze on Scott. "How are you feeling? Good?"

Draven nodded.

"Did you have fun last night?"

Scott allowed himself a smile. "Yeah."

"Good. Thought you would. Even with the girl not working out." He shrugged and started to clap the bigger man on the shoulder, then seemed to think better of it. "Have you thought about what we talked about?"

"Some."

"Come to a decision yet?"

"No."

"We've hit two houses, so I figure we can hit one more. Not tonight, though, tomorrow night. Then we'll move on before this shitty town becomes too small to hide out in. You should go with us."

Scott's stomach grumbled, which surprised him, considering last night's feed.

"I like you, Scott. You're not like those other two. I need someone who truly understands what the hell I'm talking about. A real disciple. Someone with brains. Like you. If I had you traveling with me..." He let his words trail off, as if expecting an answer.

Scott said nothing.

"You travel with me I promise you a lot more nights like last night. Even better. Too many people out there wasting what they've got. We put it to good use. We're different, Scott, because we're free. We ride a different kind of life stream than anybody else."

A user, Draven thought. That's what this guy is. Easy enough to convince stupid men with no sense of direction like Bobby and Jimbo. But what would Bluejay be like against someone with real backbone, someone perfectly capable of standing on his own two feet? He'd probably fold. But Scott had decided it was worth hanging around a little longer.

"I'll keep thinking about it."

"That's all I ask." Bluejay smiled, then turned away. "Now where the hell are those assholes with the doughnuts?"

"Right here, Bluejay!" Jimbo shouted from the entranceway, holding a bag and leading Bobby in behind him.

Watching the white cream slide down the corners of their mouths as the others stuffed their faces with pastry reminded Scott of the soft contents he'd found last night after cracking the man's skull. His senses were buzzing. He felt strong. Bobby offered him a doughnut, but he shook his head no.

Once they were finished, they shoved the dead girl into one of the bigger boxes that littered the room, then headed into the late morning light.

Scott watched the people they passed. Common people with common faces. What kind of secrets did they hold? What knowledge was there to be gained from them?

They passed the 7th Street Disciples Church as it was letting out—a small group, many of the people talking excitedly. Something dramatic must have happened inside there this morning. Maybe God Himself made an appearance, and Draven took an extra moment to stare at the small crowd before moving to catch up with his companions.

CHAPTER SIX

Hardesty spent the early afternoon sitting in his living room, listening to the room's single clock ticking.

He wished he could call what had happened at the service this morning a dream. But it wasn't. It was real. He'd seek help, except what would be the point if he had so little time left. What good did trying to heal his mental state do for him as this stage of the game?

Maybe he was going crazy, though. Or it was a side effect of the brain tumor? What other excuse did he have for why that voice had come out of him? Bethany had remained in her room since they'd gotten home. What kind of thoughts was she having about her father?

Blake glanced at the clock. Two minutes had passed since he'd last looked. He'd carried the small hope that some of his church members would call—someone other than Louise—with words of concern, asking if he was all right, if he needed anything. But there'd been nothing. It was probably only a matter of time now until … what? They fired him? Or maybe with the membership dwindling and the pastor one step away from institutionalization, they'd just go ahead and close the church for good.

Perhaps closing the church was for the best. He'd have more time to spend with Bethany before time ran out on him. Maybe he could get to know her again. Mend the wounds between them that Barbara's death had created.

Barbara had been the one who'd known how to talk to their daughter. One woman to another. There was something special about the mother-daughter bond. Formed during the nine months the baby spent growing in the mother's womb. A bond that put the father at a disadvantage right from the start.

No, he shouldn't think that way. Maybe Bethany wanted to talk. He had found a joint in the pocket of his daughter's jeans when he was doing the laundry; subconsciously, had she left it there for him to find? Had it been a cry for help? A desperate plea for limits to be set? And yet he said nothing. The conversations they did have were bland and meaningless, except for the times they fought about stupid, unimportant things. Clumsy attempts at connection.

Then there were the phone calls. Men's voices, not boys, asking for Bethany, never identifying themselves. He knew he should be doing something about it, but he was too afraid to confront her. He didn't want to risk losing someone else he loved.

And he did love his daughter, even though he felt he didn't know her. He cared for her so much sometimes it hurt. It frightened him how much she reminded him of Barbara. It even angered him at times.

The phone rang. He let it ring two more times before answering it.

"Hello?" he said and heard silence on the line. "Hello? Is—?"

"Rot in hell, you disgusting prick!" He heard an abrupt click, then the drone of the dial tone. He'd been unable to tell if the voice was male or female.

He put the receiver down slowly then bowed his head.

He heard the ticking again. Earlier, he'd considered removing the clock from the room, but decided he preferred to leave it close by as a reminder not to waste precious time. As he was doing now, feeling sorry for himself. With his daughter upstairs probably frightened. Needing a parent. Someone to help her.

Remember how He suffered. He looked up. Was that Bethany on the stairs? No, there was no one. Except the voice. *They hated His son despite all he had done for them, the miracles He performed.* Or was there something there, across the room? *They worshiped Him, and still they hung Him. Killed Him.*

You must prepare yourself.

"Prepare…?" His palms began to hurt, and he rubbed them together.

They don't understand. You frighten them. They'll try to hurt you. And then the beast will come. When it does, you must accept it with an open heart.

"What do you mean?" Blake said. Was there something forming in front of him? His angel, maybe? Becoming clearer?

They hung Him up by nails for the world to see. They continue to eat His body, drink His blood. He still suffers. You must learn to suffer, too.

"I don't understand. Please—"

The phone rang again. He looked at it, then returned his gaze to the spot where he thought he'd seen something forming. He now saw nothing. He listened for the voice. And heard nothing.

Except the damn phone. "Hello?" he answered. Wondering why he bothered.

He heard harsh breathing. "Whoever this is, would you please—?"

"Reverend?" A pause. "It's Margaret Haas."

Something cold ran the length of his spine. His fingers tightened on the receiver.

"Reverend … I haven't got much time. They're going to find me. Listen."

He waited. Heard the clock ticking.

"I want you to know … I understand now. You didn't want to hurt my son. You couldn't help…" More harsh breathing.

"Margaret," he said. "What can I—?"

"I didn't know you were one of the chosen ones. But Kenny did. My good, sweet Kenny. He knew."

"What can I do to help?"

"Just one thing. When it comes, be ready." A pause.

"When what comes?" Blake asked.

"The beast."

The same feeling of cold pierced him and grabbed his heart. "What … did you say?"

"The beast, Reverend Hardesty. It's coming…"

Sudden pain in both hands caused him to drop the receiver. Something wet and dripping—

He stared in disbelief at the bloody holes in the palms of his hands.

"Dad? What are you doing?"

Bethany stood on the stairs, staring at him. Her crazy father. "Nothing," he said. "Just talking on the phone. Dropped the receiver when I tried to hang it up. Clumsy of me." He looked back at his hands.

They were whole again. No sign of blood.

Giving his daughter a weak smile, he picked the receiver off the floor and returned it to its base. Beautiful Bethany. So much of her mother in her. The wave of her black hair as it hung past her shoulders. The intense gaze in her eyes. Fifteen years old, but she seemed older. Much too big, certainly, to bounce her on his knee the way he used to when she was little. He still remembered how much she'd idolized her daddy back then.

"I'm going out," she said as if that was all he needed to know. Her dark eyes daring him to challenge her. She was almost five-six. A couple of inches short of her mother.

"Where are you going?" he asked, trying to keep his voice casual.

"Just out."

"Who with?"

"Friends. They're picking me up."

"Do I know these friends?"

"Please, Dad. Don't start."

"Bethany, I want to talk to you about what happened this morning."

A look of sudden terror crossed her face. "Can't it wait?" she asked, edging toward the door. "They're picking me up any minute." As if on cue, the blare of a car horn sounded.

"Bethany, I just—"

And then the phone rang again, followed by the car horn's invasive cry, and he felt that overwhelming sense of helplessness again as if Heaven and Earth were conspiring against him. He wanted her to stay, needed for her to stay. Just for a moment. But Bethany had reached the door, refusing to look at him, and he noticed how cheaply she was dressed. A filmy blouse and tight jeans left little to the imagination.

He heard the voice before realizing it was coming from him again, just as it had this morning at church. Too late to stop the words from spewing forth. *Don't you dare go out looking like that, you ungrateful bitch!*

They both stared at each other in shocked silence as the phone continued to ring. Bethany staring at him with an expression he would give anything not to have caused.

The voice was gone, as was the rage that had accompanied it. In its place a horrible emptiness.

"I'm sorry," he whispered. "I don't know how—" The car horn sounded again.

She opened the door. "I've gotta go."

"Bethany, please. I don't understand what's happening."

"I'll be back tonight. Okay?"

"Bethany..."

Almost pleading. "Okay?"

Then she was out, the door closing behind her.

The damn phone was still ringing. "What?" he said into the receiver.

"Blake. It's Paul Blackburn." The chairman of the church board. "We've got to talk. I think you know what about. I've called an emergency board meeting for tonight. At my home. We want you to be there."

"Tonight? Paul, I understand your concern. But tonight ... I think you and I should talk first."

"No time for that. And I'm not going to talk about this over the phone. The meeting goes on tonight whether you're there or not."

There was no love lost between these two men. But he had never understood the man's animosity toward him. Or why it had gotten worse after Barbara's death.

He sighed. "At the church?" He parted the living room's front curtains and saw Bethany getting into the back seat of a car between two boys. No, not boys. Young men. Easily four or five years older than her. Another girl, dressed in almost the identical style of his daughter, sat up front, next to the male driver. One of the men in the back slid his arm behind Bethany's shoulders as the automobile drove off with a belch of smoke and thunder.

"No, my home. Are you listening to me?"

Hardesty closed the curtain.

Prepare yourself, the angel had said.

"Blake..."

You must learn to suffer too.

The front doorbell rang. Now who the hell was that?

"Blake, are you still there? For God's sake—!"

"I'll be there," Blake said abruptly, then hung up before realizing he hadn't asked what time the meeting was.

He crossed to the door. Hesitated a moment. The doorbell rang once again.

It was probably the rest of the church congregation outside with a hangman's noose.

He didn't recognize the man standing in the doorway. "Can I help you?" he asked, not bothering to disguise the irritation he felt.

The short man spoke nervously, licking sweat off his upper lip. "Reverend Hardesty? I'm Stan Marles." He showed him a police detective's badge.

"What can I do for you?" Blake asked, his hands and stomach clenched tight. He had had too many bad experiences with cops coming to his door.

"I was wondering if maybe you could help me."

"Help you? How?" He hesitated again, then stepped back to allow him to enter.

"Thank you." Marles walked in carefully, as if expecting something to jump out at him. "May I trouble you for a glass of water?"

"Okay. Would you rather have something else? Iced tea?"

"Water's fine."

He was standing awkwardly in the center of the living room when Hardesty returned. "Why don't you sit down?" Blake offered. "Anywhere's fine." He handed him the glass and watched his visitor drink it gratefully. The detective had short blond hair, clear blue eyes, and a chubby baby face. On another day, Blake would find the man's shyness amusing.

"How can I help you?" he asked, indicating an armchair when the detective still hadn't moved.

"Thank you," the other said, finally sitting and placing the glass on a coaster. "Please excuse my nervousness. I don't know why, but I get this way around anything to do with religion. It sounds silly, I know. This is just your home, after all." He shrugged, his eyes apologetic. "I haven't been inside a church in years. I guess you could say I'm an atheist out of necessity. Or is it agnostic?" He looked away, then back. "I hope you don't mind."

"Why would I mind?"

"Oh. Well..." He looked around the room. "Nice house."

"Detective Marles—"

"Yes, I'm babbling. I do that when I'm nervous. Sorry." His leg began shaking, but he didn't seem to notice. "I'm working on a case. A very disturbing one. I'm sure you've heard about it. It happened a few days ago. The Rheman family. They lived two blocks from your church. I thought maybe they might be members?"

"An awful thing," Blake said. "No, they weren't. And I didn't know them. A few in my congregation did, though."

"I've talked to some of their neighbors, and I thought ... with your church in that neighborhood and you being a leader in the community... I'm grasping at straws, can you tell?"

"I'm afraid I don't know anything more than what was in the news."

"An entire family wiped out. Husband and wife. Two boys, eleven and eight. I've never seen anything like it. There are certain ... aspects of this case that are ... particularly bizarre. No, more than that. Grotesque. Do you have a strong stomach, Father?"

"Reverend."

"What?'

"You called me Father. I'm not a priest. I'm not even Catholic."

"God, I'm sorry. I didn't mean to insult you."

"It's hardly an insult. Why don't you call me Blake?"

"Are you sure? Is it all right?"

"I'll make an exception." He smiled, but the detective didn't seem to catch the humor.

"Thank you. Uh, why don't you call me Stan?"

"All right, Stan." He paused. "If you don't mind me asking,

are you as young as you look?"

The detective smiled this time. "I hear that a lot. Well, I don't mean people ask me that exact question. Other cops ask how I got to be detective so young, and I'm not that young... Actually, I'm thirty-five."

He looked like he could still be in college. "You were saying before about the Rheman family?"

"Yes. I..." He let out a rush of air. "I'm finding it hard to talk about this with you. It's so disgusting..."

"Don't worry," Hardesty said. "I can take it."

"Of course, you can." Was this strange little man blushing? The detective turned away and reached for his empty glass. "May I have some more water? No, of course not. I've taken too long getting to the point as it is." His features hardened as he concentrated. "The things they did to this family... I'm not going to go into details. But I will tell you ... when they were done ... they ate them."

"What?"

"Cannibalism, Father. Some of the body parts they cooked in the stove. Some they ate raw. The wife and husband... Did I say there was a husband, wife, two children? These monsters cracked the parents' heads open and ate part of their brains."

"My God," Blake whispered.

"I wondered if there might be some connection ... you know, between this and the communion service. You know how the service goes. The bread is referred to as the body, the wine is called the blood..."

This is my body given for you.

"Reverend? Blake...?"

This is my blood—

"Are you all right? Can I get you something?"

Blake realized he was sweating and wiped his forehead. "I'm sorry, I... It's just so horrible. I can't imagine anyone..."

"Are you sure you're all right? You went all white there for a moment."

"I'm fine." Blake took a breath. "Do you have any idea who did it?"

"I'm afraid not. We think there were several... Four or five anyway. They might be nomads. A group that lives on the road and just traveled in here, maybe they're planning to stay only a few days before moving on. It's been shown in the past that a surprisingly few number of people—wanderers like these guys maybe—have been responsible for a lot of the disappearances that occur, missing children, that sort of thing. Brutal crimes. Assholes." His face turned suddenly red. "Sorry."

"I could think of a stronger word or two myself." Blake noticed his own hand trembling.

"I'm sorry this has upset you." The man seemed genuinely alarmed. "Of course, it would upset anybody. It upset me and I'm a cop."

A ringing sound came from inside the detective's jacket, and he pulled out a cell phone. "Please excuse me a moment."

"Certainly."

Marles rose and crossed to the other side of the room, speaking into the phone. "Marles here." Hardesty watched him listen then turn suddenly pale. "I'm on my way."

"What is it?" Hardesty asked.

"I have to go," Marles said. "I ... I'm afraid there's been another one."

"Another...?"

"Another family."

"My God. Where?"

"In the same general area."

"I'll go with you."

The detective looked at him, surprised. "You can't do that."

"Why not?"

"You're not a policeman."

"You said you wanted my help. If I can offer you a unique angle on this, help you in some way to stop these ... nomads."

"But you don't necessarily need to be there to do that."

"I want to."

"Why?"

Why indeed? Maybe because, up to now, he'd lived a life delivering empty words to congregants who listened to him with deaf ears. Or because fate, it seemed, had affected his life so arbitrarily over the years, from his parents' death to Barbara's murder, to the violence of several weeks ago in Margaret Haas's house, that, maybe, this time, he could meet the violence face to face, and, somehow, get control of it.

"I want to help," was all he could think to say.

"You may feel differently if this is anything like the last time," Marles said.

As the minister followed him out the front door, the feeling of something watching him returned. He resisted the urge to turn around and look, closing the door quickly behind him.

Every pastor, in the course of his or her ministry, wrestles with their own definition of Hell. It is part of scripture, part of a preacher's job to come to terms with it and help lead a congregation on a path that offers some answers.

Blake Hardesty's own life had made him face the prospect of evil more often than most. It had been a struggle for him to hold on to his faith in God after the events in that bank a year ago. To accept tragedy of such magnitude did not mean that God had no plan, or that life was simply chaos. There was order in the world, and God was still the One that a person could depend on.

But what Blake observed in the household of the Holder family had to be the result of evil in its purest form, with no hope of redemption, and no place for a loving God. Because if there was, then the Supreme Being had to be both God and Devil, and the world was nothing but His plaything, His children merely puppets to do with as He pleased.

Marles tried to block Hardesty's entrance, telling him he'd go in first then call Blake in later. But by the time Hardesty had arrived, his need to see what was in there was too great to allow him to wait any longer.

And see it he did.

The first thing he noticed was Mrs. Holder's body nailed to the wall, crucifixion-style. Both of her eyes had been plucked out. Her tongue had been yanked from her mouth. Not only had nails been driven through her hands but two had been driven through her heart. Both of her nipples had been cut off, and holes carved into the tips of each breast.

Someone had used this method to drink her blood.

At her feet lay a boy's body. No more than eight or nine years old. It had been eviscerated, the organs spread out around the body Jack-The-Ripper style.

The greatest amount of cannibalism had been committed on Mr. Holder's body. Both arms and both legs had been ripped from the corpse then cleaned to the bone. The chest was laid open. The heart and other organs were in pieces. The penis had been removed and the scrotal sac slit. The head, like the boy's, had been cracked open.

Blood bathed the room, the walls, was soaked into the furniture, the rug. Bloody handprints were on a door.

Time seemed to slow down as he stood in that room, taking in the destruction of a family, etching it indelibly into his brain where nothing would ever be able to remove it, not prayer, not the kind word of a friend. Not even the promise of a loving God. His teachers had lied. Hell was not a place waiting for sinners in the hereafter. Nor was it something for philosophical discussion. Hell was right here on Earth. Able to manifest itself anywhere.

Expressions on the police officials working around the remains showed how hard it was to perform their jobs. The fact they could do them at all in these conditions was something Blake found obscene. Perhaps, later, they would drown the horror they were feeling in booze or in the arms of a loved one, but, for now, they went about their business as best they could. But how could anyone function in this place where there was such disdain for the value of human life?

He could not stay here any longer. Turning, he ran out of the house on weakened legs that finally gave way as he fell to his knees on the front lawn.

Then he vomited, not caring as he spewed the ground with thick, acid bile, only praying that by doing so he might expel all memory of what he had witnessed here today.

Finally, he sat back, feeling lightheaded, disgusted, and tainted. He heard someone walk up behind him and looked back to see Stan Marles, appearing pale and worried, squatting next to him.

"I'm sorry," he said, a hand on the minister's shoulder. "I'm so sorry you saw that. I tried to tell you—"

"How could…?" He fought to breathe. "How could someone do that to other human beings…?" He gasped for air.

"I don't know. I wish I did. Are you going to be all right? I've got to talk to some people. There's a teenage daughter missing. Maybe she wasn't here, or maybe whoever did this took her."

"A daughter…?"

"Is there anything I can do for you?"

He grabbed the detective's arm. "I can't stay. You can't expect me to…"

"Of course not. Maybe I can get you a ride—"

"No, I … it's not far."

"Where? So, I can talk to you later."

"Home. No! The church. I'll be at the church."

"All right. I'll see you later."

The detective rose and walked back to the house. Hardesty's breathing came in short, shallow bursts. But he had to move, had to get himself to somewhere pure, some place where he could cleanse himself of the stench, the poison that had affected his soul.

He rose before he knew what he was doing. Then he ran, past a surprised police officer, out into the street. Away from Hell, toward a place where the air was good, and he hoped he could feel clean again.

CHAPTER SEVEN

"Cal, I don't want to." Bethany pushed the grappling hands away from her blouse.

"Come on," Cal slurred, "why not?"

"You're drunk."

"Actually, I'm high and drunk." He giggled. "Why don't you join me?" He handed her the last of his joint. "It'll make you feel so much better."

"I don't feel like it today."

"You don't feel like doing a lot of things today, do you?" Cal leaned in, his rough face almost grazing her cheek, his breath a rancid mixture of marijuana and whiskey. "Brandon told me you were high when you did it with him."

Bethany glared over at Brandon, but he wasn't paying attention, busy as he was working his hand under Angela's blouse while taking another hit off his own joint and giggling.

"It seems to me," Cal continued, "that if ole pimply-face is good enough for you, then I certainly should be." His hand went to cup her breasts through her clothes.

"I said no, Cal! Not today!"

"Jesus, bitch—"

"Hey, Cal, come over here!" He turned to the third guy who held something in his hands. "I got something for you."

Bethany breathed a sigh of relief as he walked away, weaving as he did. Ed would keep him busy for a while. Ed didn't care about sex or booze. Only drugs.

She'd leave, or maybe make a call on her cell, if she only knew where the hell she was. Some warehouse was all she knew. And whom would she call? Certainly not her father.

She watched Angela and Brandon for a moment. His hand

was in her blouse, massaging her breasts. Then he lay back with a stupid grin on his face as she pulled down his zipper and reached in for his penis.

Bethany turned away in disgust. What had Brandon been telling Cal, or anyone else for that matter? Yeah, she'd "done it" with Brandon, if you could call it that. A hurried act, her pants pulled down around her knees. Painful, rough, his sperm soaking the inside of her leg. He'd been drunk; she'd had some beer and a few tokes. Enough to make her think it was what she wanted. Until that moment she'd played around mostly, allowed him to touch her here and there, one time jerking him off until he'd come. That had been messy too, but daring, fun. Still, what did it amount to? What had she expected? Mom had said the first time should be special, with someone you care about. She'd let her mother down. Now, with Brandon all over Angela, Cal would expect her to perform with him. Unless he got too buzzed to care, which she prayed would happen.

She took a drink from her beer and set it back on the floor. Wondering what her mother would think if she could see her daughter. Wondering if she was watching her right now, from above.

The thought of it made her feel ashamed. Angela had introduced her to these guys, told her they'd be fun, not like the typical high school geeks. She went along a couple of times because being with them made her feel like an adult. And it got her away from the house, and from Dad. The hurt in his eyes, the way he looked at her, so sad, and something more, as if he thought it was her fault Mom had been killed.

It was Mom who had always been there for her if the teenager needed to talk. Dad was a distant figure who took care of church business. That was his job, being there for others first. Mom had understood, she'd claimed, and had tried to explain it to her. If his wife could deal with it, then his daughter could too, Bethany had told herself, until the teenager passed her parents' room one night and heard her mother crying, alone. The girl had been too afraid to do anything more than just keep on going. She didn't ask what was wrong or even offer to listen, the way the woman had always done for her.

Dad had tried to spare her the details of her death, but Bethany understood how her mother had died, had constant nightmares of her mother lying in a pool of blood, slowly dying, reaching for her only daughter, who merely walked by and did nothing.

Her mother was gone. Forever.

And she was left with a stranger.

She knew her father was also in pain. She saw it in his manner, his posture. His eyes. Trying to hide it from her out of some misguided idea that to be strong for her meant not showing his feelings, when what she needed most was someone willing to be open enough to share emotions that were real and honest.

She supposed she'd been looking for something like that with this group of people here with her now. But they hid their feelings as much as her father did, maybe even more so, behind booze and drugs. But she didn't feel she could just stop seeing them. If she did, then what would she do? Who could she turn to?

A giggle made her look over at Brandon and Angela. She had him in her mouth, and he sighed and rubbed his hand through her hair, and Bethany turned away, sickened. The room seemed suddenly close, and she found it difficult to breathe. Dare she just stand up and leave, even if it meant finding her own way home?

Afraid, she remained where she was, still thinking. What if she just acted on her own initiative and told Dad how she felt? Her real feelings. The time he'd been in the hospital, not knowing if she was going to lose another parent, had felt almost as bad as her father telling her her mother was dead. Even with Louise Calabrese staying at the house with her, she had never felt more alone. But it was more than the idea that she'd have no one if he died. It was the realization that despite her anger and hurt, she did love him.

Sometimes, the way he looked, the way he suffered, silent with his despair, she wanted to throw her arms around him and tell him everything was going to be all right. Like he was the child and she the parent. And other times she couldn't stand to be in the same room with him, the pain was so great.

What would her dad say if she just tried talking to him? About something. Anything. What had happened to him this morning in front of the entire congregation scared her. Calling her a bitch before she left the house later had hurt her more than she wanted to admit. And yet a part of her wondered if it was true. By hooking up with Cal and his friends, hadn't she'd betrayed her mother? Betrayed the faith the woman had put in her to make the right choices? Made the betrayal worse because she had done it after her mother was dead?

Would she be able to talk to her father? Would he even listen? Could she make him listen? No proclamation, no laying down of boundaries or rules that were not followed anyway. Just the two of them sharing their pain, breaking down the wall between them.

Tonight, she thought. Maybe tonight. Once she got out of here.

It gave her something to hope for.

"Hey, Bethany." Cal was stumbling toward her. "I got something for you." He held up a clear plastic bag containing some white powder. "Maybe you don't wanna get high, but I bet you'll like this. This'll make you fly."

"Cal, I told you—"

"I know what you told me!" he snapped, making her rear back. "Don't be such a tight cunt now!"

She noticed the others watching her silently, their faces suddenly sober. She had never done cocaine before, only grass, and that only a couple times. She felt herself shudder.

"Cal," she whispered.

"You'll like it, baby, I promise," he said in what he probably considered a sweet tone, his grin a death's head. "All of us here have tried it." His smile broadened. "You're not saying you're better than the rest of us, now, are you, little preacher's daughter?"

Everyone watched her, waiting for her answer. Cal standing over her with the bag in his upraised hand.

"Please," she tried.

"Damn it, Bethany! You're not going to just sit there! This is a party!" His face had turned purple with rage.

She stared at that ugly face. God, what was it she had seen in him? "I'll do anything else. But not that."

"Anything" Grinning again, he put the bag down and began unbuckling his pants. "Only one other way, baby." They dropped down around his knees.

She heard Angela giggle. Ed said, "Come on, Cal."

"Shut up and enjoy the show." Cal stood in front of Bethany. "You've got a nice-looking mouth, baby." Pulled down his underpants. "Show me how good it is."

He got her by the back of the neck, and Bethany began to whimper. "Pretty minister's daughter doesn't like to put her lips on a real man's cock, huh?" He let her go and pushed her back. "That's all right. We got time. She's not gonna party with the rest of us, she's gotta find some other way to fit in." He began undoing the buttons on her blouse. She felt herself begin to cry. His hands were rough as he reached in, worked his palm under her bra to the flesh beneath.

"I'll do it," she whispered.

He stopped, looked at her. "What did you say?"

"I'll do it. I'll try some..." She pointed to the bag of white powder.

She'd have given anything not to see the look of triumph on his face as he carefully closed her blouse then patted the side of her face. "That's my good girl."

Cal pulled his clothes back on and picked up the bag, showing it to her as if it was a valued prize. "Watch Ed."

Ed stepped forward. He had two lines already formed on a piece of old cardboard. Leaning forward with a straw, he placed one end delicately on his end of the line of powder.

Then he breathed in quickly through his nose, and the line disappeared.

"Your turn," Cal said. He picked up the piece of cardboard, brought it over and placed it in front of her, handing her another straw. She leaned forward, shaking, and tried her best to duplicate what she had seen.

Instead of breathing in, she mostly gave a loud snort, and while some of it entered her nose, most of it went flying into the air. Still, it was enough to make her sinuses tingle with fire while the others laughed. She heard Angela say, "God, Bethany."

"It's all right," Cal declared magnanimously. "Not bad for the first time. You'll do better." He reached for the bag.

"No," she said. "I don't need anymore."

"Aw, come on, babe, you hardly got any. Most of it went in the air."

"No, really, Cal, I mean it."

"You're saying you're better than the rest of us?"

"No. I just don't—"

She didn't see it coming, so she didn't have time to tense up before he hit her. Her head snapping back, she fell like a rag doll. Lying on the floor, she waited for the world to stop spinning until the sound of Cal moving toward her caused her to push herself up. "Hey, Cal," Brandon said from somewhere distant.

"Don't ever think you're better than me, girl!" Cal hissed. "Not ever! You understand me?"

She stared at him, not daring to move, though the right half of her face ached. She had never felt so scared in her life.

"Not ever...!"

"Cal..."

"You stuck up whore..."

"Cal." It was Ed. "It's wasted if they don't want it. It just makes more for the rest of us."

Silence. No one moved.

"Cal?"

"What the fuck," he said finally, turning away and walking toward Ed. The other two eyed Bethany for a moment, then followed. Soon they were all doing lines and laughing, ignoring her, even Angela, who, at one point, glanced over at her before Cal yanked her back.

Miserably, Bethany watched them, wondering how she was going to hide the bruise she knew was already beginning to form under her right eye from her dad, sure that this was something the man would notice. Even after Brandon and Cal began fooling around with Angela, clothes falling off between them as Ed watched from his drug-induced haze, she didn't move.

A little girl lost with no place to go.

CHAPTER EIGHT

Sitting alone in the quiet of the sanctuary, Blake found it possible to believe that, as vast a being as God was, with the responsibility of the entire world on His shoulders, He still had time to listen to this one man in this one room. So, he sat with his eyes closed and prayed, working desperately, to blot out the vision of what he had seen in that house earlier today. He tried filling his mind with positive images. Signs of God's love. People who represented that love to him. Like his Aunt Ruth. Charged with the responsibility of raising her nephew after his parents' deaths. She'd never had children of her own, but she'd been more than willing to take in a troubled seven-year-old boy and talk him through his nightmares.

She had been the model of a good Christian woman. As influential as she had been in his life, choosing the ministry had seemed totally natural to him. Seeing his aunt's delight at his decision made him sure it was the right thing to do.

When she died a week before his graduation from the seminary, it felt like another of God's tests as he went out into the world alone.

Well, not totally alone. God was with him. Blake had felt Him as a tangible force.

Looking back now, had he been a fool to believe that?

Letting out a sigh, he leaned back in the pew and perused the room he held so sacred.

The small sanctuary had wooden pews, divided by a center aisle, going twelve rows back. The room was decorated simply, the wooden communion table in front draped with a red cloth, the cross, also wooden, hanging above it. To the right of it, from where Blake sat in the third row on the right side of the sanctuary, was the space reserved for the small choir, where the members tried their best every Sunday. To the left of the communion table stood the pulpit from which Blake preached.

It was a small, simple church, destined to be small, despite the hopes of some of its members. People like board chair Paul Blackburn, who pushed the idea of expansion, even as the membership dwindled. Wasn't it enough that these people came together here once a week to draw strength from each other, to pray, to worship? Why did size have to matter? Who demanded it? Surely not God. It was enough that this place be kept serene, a space where people could find peace. Sanctuary. Without the outside world pressing in.

He wished he could call his angel now, and, closing his eyes, he began, again, to pray. And, suddenly, he felt her nearby, so close he dared not open his eyes for fear she would vanish. In his mind's eye he saw her wearing a beautiful white, flowing gown. Her delicate hands reaching out for him in a loving gesture as he heard her whisper, I'm here.

"Help me," Blake responded. In his mind, or out loud, he wasn't sure.

He felt her touch him. Warm, soothing. Felt her caress his shoulders, his back. Surely, this was God's touch she brought him. Blessed, all-knowing. "Help me," he said again.

Help yourself.

"How?"

Use the power that called you to me. The power He has given you. Her touch so comforting. Empowering. *The power to change your life and the lives of others around you.*

"Yes."

Welcome it into you. Accept it.

"Yes."

It is lonely.

"It?" He almost opened his eyes. "What do you mean it is lonely?"

Accept it. Was her touch changing? Becoming rougher? Hurting? *Embrace it.* Now her voice was low, harsh.

He cried out. Pictured the face of the beast from his

nightmare where hers had been before. Pieces of meat and blood dripping from its jaws.

He pulled away, opened his eyes inadvertently.

And saw it. The beast. Eyes charcoal-red, staring at him. The sandpaper-against-metal voice speaking. *I have something for you. An offering.*

Blake turned, ran to the front of the church, spun back. The monster was still there, its face in shadow. It began to advance toward him.

With Hardesty pressed against the communion table, he felt the tray containing the communion wafers prodding him in the back, and, reacting intuitively, he grabbed a handful of them, symbolic of the bread Jesus served at the Last Supper, and threw them at the creature.

He expected the "bread" to strike the beast like holy water splashing a vampire, showering it with the power of God, the righteous fire of Jesus pushing back the evil of Satan from which this monster must surely have spawned.

But the thing in front of him reared back its massive head in ecstasy as the wafers pelted its body and, catching some of the small pieces in its great paws, it shoved them into its mouth. More, it growled. Looked at Blake. Give me more!

All at once, the thing ran toward him, and, screaming, Hardesty threw his arms up in front of his face.

Nothing happened. Slowly, he brought his arms down. The room was empty. Wafers littered the aisle.

His hands started to bleed. From holes newly formed in his palms.

"What's happening to me!" he whispered harshly. "What's—"

"Hello? Blake, are you in here? Reverend Hardesty?"

He checked his hands and found whole flesh.

"Blake?"

He looked up and saw Stan Marles coming slowly down the aisle. "I didn't mean to interrupt your praying, Father."

"I wasn't praying. I was... I had an accident. Spilled some..." He crouched down and began picking the wafers off the floor. "And it's Reverend."

"Pardon me?"

"You called me Father again. I'm not Catholic, remember?"
He took one more uneasy look around the room.

"I'm sorry," Marles said. "You know how I get in a place like
this. Nervous. I told you that, didn't I?"

"An atheist out of necessity."

The detective grinned sheepishly. "Right. Here, let me help
you." He moved forward.

"No, that's all right. See, I'm finished." He brushed the
wafers onto the communion tray. He would need to throw them
away and get fresh ones before the next service.

Detective Marles was looking around the room. "Have you
been here all afternoon?"

"What time is it?" For the first time, he noticed the shadows
sneaking into the sanctuary.

"After six, I think."

"Oh. I guess I should…" Dizziness made his knees buckle,
and the detective rushed to his side to steady him.

"Here, Reverend, let's sit down." He guided Blake over to
the front pew closest to them. "Can I get you anything? Water?
It's dark in here; can I turn a light on for you?"

"I'm all right. And would you please call me Blake?" He
pointed. "There's a light switch over there." By the time Marles
had returned, he felt better.

"Were you praying? I didn't mean to interrupt."

"I told you I wasn't… I was contemplating. It's been a rough
day."

"Yes, it has." Stan sat next to him. "I don't know if I could
take too many like it." Looking at the minister, he said, "I'm
sorry you saw that. I should never have let you."

"I chose to. You didn't make me."

"Still…" He let it go, looking forward. Both men sat in
silence for a moment. The artificial light in the room now hurt
the minister's eyes.

"I thought you might want to know … we've identified
three of the men responsible. From fingerprints. There were
some good ones this time. In the blood on the wall and door. I
guess they didn't care." Marles paused. "Transients, just like we

thought. Robert Henneman, James Gresham, Kenneth Beltmore. Beltmore calls himself Bluejay. They've all got criminal records. Last-known addresses have them living in three different states, so they must have hooked up somewhere along the way. Probably just passing through. Who knows what else they've been planning? But a city this small, they might figure it's best now to just get out of town. Out of the state, even. They may have left already. We've got APBs out on them along the entire East Coast."

"There were three you said?"

"Actually, there's a fourth. We just don't know who it is. His fingerprints aren't on file anywhere, which means he's never been arrested, never been in the armed forces or had a government job, never had any reason to have his prints taken. He might even be from around here."

"What about the daughter?"

Marles sighed. "We found her body in the basement of an abandoned building not too far from the scene of the crime. Probably their hideout, though it's empty now. I guess they weren't finished with her."

Hardesty closed his eyes. "How do you stand it?"

"I used to work in Philadelphia," Marles said after another sigh. "I've seen some bad stuff. It's why my boss gave me this case. But I've never seen anything as bad as what happened to those two families."

"It doesn't seem to have ... affected you."

"I don't know about that. You learn to distance yourself, I guess. Otherwise, the shit can get to you." He blushed. "I'm sorry."

Hardesty looked at him. "After what we've witnessed today, cursing in front of a minister still makes you blush?"

"Oh, believe me, I curse. I mean, not when... Well..." He blushed again.

"Don't worry about it. God will forgive you. Considering the circumstances."

"Did I tell you I'm an atheist?"

"Out of necessity, yes."

"I was raised Catholic. But all that ritual stuff scared the hel ... scared me. In the church I was raised in, there was this picture of Jesus in the front of the sanctuary, much larger than the one you have here. Wherever you stood in the room, it seemed to stare at you. Like He was condemning you. I grew up feeling like He was always around somewhere watching me, judging me."

Blake just listened.

"When I was a kid, I had to go to church when my mom told me to. Even as I got older, I wasn't strong enough to refuse. I used to have nightmares. Just the other night I had one, first time in years. The face of Jesus watching me. Telling me to get these ... creeps ... and get 'em good. It's silly, I guess."

"Why didn't you just choose another religion after you became an adult?"

"I considered that. But what if switching meant I was condemned to Hell? Our priest used to tell us things like that. It was easier to believe God just didn't exist at all. Besides, by the time I was old enough to make a decision like that, I was already too scared. Just entering a church... any church... makes me nervous. You can't imagine the flip-flops my stomach is doing right now." He paused. "Actually, I'm not really sure I am an atheist. Maybe I do believe in God. I figure there's got to be something out there. The problem is, whatever God is, He terrifies me." He looked at the minister. "I hope that doesn't offend you."

"It's not for me to judge."

Marles continued to stare a moment. "You know, Blake, something about you... I could almost try church again ... if you were the minister... Well, maybe we can talk about that later. There's something else I want to discuss... Can we talk here? Would you rather...? We could go for coffee. My treat."

"I should probably be getting home soon. My daughter—"

"A daughter? I didn't know. You're married?"

"I was. My wife died a year ago."

"I'm sorry. I really am."

"It's all right."

Silence again. Then Hardesty asked, "Would you rather go somewhere else? Considering—"

"This is fine," Marles said, "I'll be quick. The way we found

Mrs. Holder ... the way they left her on the wall ... didn't that make you think of ... crucifixion?"

The pastor hesitated then nodded slowly. Of course, he had noticed it.

"These monsters are..." Marles faltered. "They're eating their victims after they're dead. I was wondering if ... cannibalism ... if there was some religious connection ... in a perverted sort of way, of course, I don't mean to suggest... Well, I thought there might be a connection between that and the communion service. I've been reading about cannibal tribes ... how it's almost a religion."

"They believe that they ingest the power of the ones they eat," Blake said.

"Yeah, that's what I read. And, you know, I've never really understood the significance of the Last Supper."

Blake bristled. "It's symbolic, not cannibalistic."

Seeing the startled look on the detective's face, Hardesty calmed himself before continuing. "The bread of communion is representative of the spiritual sustenance offered through belief in Jesus Christ. That he who believes will never hunger, never thirst, and have everlasting life."

"You mean immortality?"

"Everlasting life in the spiritual sense, not the physical."

"Of course." Marles nodded. "Not cannibalism. But, you know, to a sick mind ... or a group of sick minds..."

"I see your point. They could also just be thrill kills."

"We've considered that too. There's a theory that a large number of certain violent crimes are committed by a surprisingly small number of people. Transients. Did I tell you that? They go into a town, commit some crimes, and move on before they're caught. If someone really doesn't want to be found, it's easier to stay hidden than people realize. Even when you've got fingerprints and names."

Blake didn't know what to say to that, so he said nothing. After a moment, Stan Marles turned away, facing the front of the sanctuary.

The two sat in silence. Shadows continued to creep into the room.

Sanctuary. Blake felt it almost as a solid thing, and he thought again about this building, this room, and the protection it offered, or should offer, from the violence of the outside world.

And he realized how much he needed this place; what a terrible thing it would be if he ever lost it.

The two rose together as if of one mind, then looked at each other. "I guess it's time to go," Stan said.

"I guess," the minister agreed.

"I don't know what's going to happen with this. Like I said, if they are transients, they could be gone already. We may never catch them. At least if they leave town, there'll be no more killings. While I'm on this case, though, do you think ... I could bounce some ideas off you...?"

Blake hesitated. Did he really want that? But he found he liked this man.

"Sure."

"It must be tough being a minister," Stan said suddenly.

"Why do you say that?"

"Well, it seems to me you're always dealing with other people's problems. Must be tough being, what, a spokesperson for God? Whom do you go to when you have a problem?"

"I can go to other ministers. And I pray."

"Does it really work?"

The minister hesitated only briefly. "It helps."

"It must be nice having God online like that."

Blake laughed.

"Hey, that sounded nice."

"What?"

"You laughing. That's the first time I've heard it. Sounds good."

"Feels good." He looked at the detective. "You've stopped shaking."

"What?"

"You were nervous when you came in here. You seem fine now."

A look of surprise appeared on Marles's face. "You're right." He patted the minister on the shoulder. "Must be the company."

Blake laughed again. Sanctuary, he thought.

On the way out, he flicked off the light switch and gave the church over to the shadows. And the two men, fast becoming friends, stepped out into the early evening.

CHAPTER NINE

The old man smelled of piss and booze. They'd found him lying on a heating grate and pulled him, whimpering like a dog, into the alley. Now he cowered against the metal trashcans, his eyes darting back and forth between them, looking for some hope of salvation.

Bluejay was lecturing again. "A person like this has little value to us. Certainly not as food. The part of him that is worthwhile..." He bent down and put his hand against the man's rough cheek. The old man stared into Bluejay's eyes, probably hoping he had found the salvation he was looking for. "Good boy," Bluejay whispered. "Good boy." The old man began to smile, nodding his head. Scott felt sick watching the display.

The man reached out his hand to touch Bluejay's face. Bluejay smiled.

Then flicked open his knife and slit the man's throat.

The man's eyes showed shock before they began to glaze over. Their leader placed his lips against the newly formed mouth and drank. Jimbo and Bobby whooped and hollered until he pulled away, wiping red from his lips. "If nowhere else, my disciples, there is always the blood."

With a sweep of his hand, he gestured magnanimously to the others, and Bobby and Jimbo ran to the body, fighting over what was left, lapping up what had spilled out.

Scott kept his expression neutral as Bluejay sauntered over. "I swear, sometimes I think they're retarded."

Scott said nothing.

"Aren't you going to imbibe?"

Draven shook his head.

"I wish I knew what was going on inside that head of yours, Scott."

"Why do we stay in hiding so much?"

"We're night creatures."

"You're afraid the cops are going to find us, you mean."

Bluejay said nothing, staring.

"I'm going for a walk."

"Don't go too far," Bluejay called out to his retreating form.

"Fuck you," Draven muttered under his breath as he turned the corner.

The center of town had turned quiet. Early Sunday evening, and only a few people walked the streets. Stores were closed. Only one out of every three streetlights worked.

Bluejay was a man too much in love with his own voice. Too caught up in hisvision of himself as a self-proclaimed messiah. He spoke of power, but he was really a coward, too dependent on the presence of those weaker than himself for his prophetic crap to have any meaning. Anyone could terrorize. Like Draven's own father, with the back of his hand and the lighted end of a cigarette. Easy to take one's fear out on a scared boy. And, later, on women, with a gun to their heads and terror in their eyes. False power. Now the old man was in prison, probably getting his ass ripped open on a regular basis. Where the hell was his power now?

Nowhere. Because it had never existed. Just as the power Bluejay preached about came from the intimidation he practiced, nothing more. It might have been enough for the likes of Jimbo and Bobby, but it wasn't enough for Scott Draven. If he believed that was all he was ever going to learn from hanging around with these guys, he'd have left by now.

But something was happening to Scott. Something he hadn't expected.

He was changing. Growing. Satisfying the physical cravings of his body with human flesh was no longer enough. He wanted more. Not just the food. He wanted the knowledge that came with each new feeding. The very essence of each victim coursing through him, forming, reforming, turning Scott into something that was a combination of him and the ones he dined on. A new being. This was true power, made even stronger with each victim. As if each sacrifice brought him closer to God. What would happen if he were more selective with his victims? What more could he learn? Would eating his own father help him to understand the frustrations that had driven his old man's life, the self-hatred that made him abuse the ones he loved?

Scott's hunger was no longer for the thrill. It was a hunger for knowledge. For the first time in his life, he felt connected with something greater than himself. God, the greatest cannibal of all, the eater of souls. Making all humankind one.

The thought sent sweet chills through his body. A feeling akin to one felt by lovers at the beginning of a new relationship. Only love for Scott Draven was represented by the taste of flesh and blood.

One thing he knew for sure, as he walked along this quiet street with the darkness of night slowly moving in, was that if he wanted to continue on his journey for knowledge, he could not hang around with Bluejay and his tiny band of pseudo-vampires much longer. Soon, he would have to strike out on his own.

He found a secluded spot. Then took off his clothes and waited.

There were not many people out tonight, but soon a young man came walking by. Moving casually. His eyes dilated, probably just finished making a big score. A poor sacrifice. But pickings were sparse.

And Scott was hungry.

His dad had been a scrawny, wiry pissant of a man, but his son had grown up huge, strong.

Silent.

It was a simple matter to wait in the shadows until the young man passed him, then reach out and pull him into the alley. The knife opened his neck before he could make a sound of protest, and he laid the young man out on the ground to let him bleed. In less than two minutes, the man was dead, and Draven stripped the body of clothing. A plastic bag filled with pills fell out, which he ignored.

He began by eating the flesh of the arms and legs, slicing it off in long strips. He gnawed on the fingers until they were bone and cut open the chest and stomach, eating the liver, spleen, kidneys, bladder. Heart.

He broke open the skull and ate the brain.

He dined quickly, working efficiently, cleaning the bones and tossing them aside. Finished, he felt the essence of his next incarnation forming even as he lay back with a sigh and closed his eyes. Memories of this man still alive in the sweetness of the flesh, the richness of the brain matter. Feelings that had long been buried under a blanket of drugs were now rising up to take their place in this new vessel. Mingling with the feelings of those Draven had feasted on these last few nights. Anguish, pain, joy, exhilaration. Offering him more than any drug could. Making him better.

If someone as weak as this could offer so much, what could be learned from one with more power? Would a college professor make him more intelligent, an athlete stronger, faster?

He rested, sated. This was enough for now. There would be other nights. Other offerings. More revelations. This was wonderful. Even Bluejay, with his incessant preaching, would not be able to spoil how good he felt.

He needed to get back. The others would be missing him.

Draven rose, and finding a plastic bottle filled almost to the top with water in a trashcan, he used it to bathe himself, then got dressed. On a whim, he checked the victim's pockets and found fifty dollars, which he pocketed, and half a pack of Peppermint Life Savers. He popped two in his mouth.

This was beautiful. Special. His own private worship.

The night air felt good. He walked with a new bounce in his step. His vision seemed sharper, his hearing more acute.

Picking up his pace, he moved swiftly along the empty streets.

"Where the hell have you been?" Bluejay asked upon his return. Behind him, Jimbo and Bobby were taunting a stray dog. The animal fought back valiantly, barking, snapping.

"I told you, I went for a walk."

"You were gone a long time." Bluejay stared at him. "What happened? You seem different."

Scott suppressed a smile. "Nothing. I just walked."

"Yeah, well. We've been waiting." Bluejay seemed not to know how to react, and, for just a moment, Scott saw himself ripping the bastard's head off and sucking his worthless brain out through the eye sockets.

"Come on. We gotta find a new hideout." He turned to the others. "Hey, assholes, leave that dog alone and let's go."

Reluctantly, Jimbo and Bobby backed off, and the dog ran away.

As the four of them walked, Draven felt the hunger growing inside him yet again, but he pushed it down. He would have to let his earlier meal suffice. At least until tomorrow night when they would find their next family of victims, and he could embark on the real work at hand. Blood work. Whatever they did in the meantime, the insignificant acts of intimidation, would be a waste of energy. But let the others have their fun.

He could wait.

CHAPTER TEN

The darkness surrounding the building seemed a real, tangible thing, ready to engulf him at any moment.

But it's only a building, Hardesty told himself. The state hospital. Eerie, yes, making the night seem more foreboding than it was. He could not suppress a shudder.

Nevertheless, the troubled people residing here were God's children too. In need of his love as much as anyone, probably more so.

Earlier, after waving goodbye to Stan Marles as the detective drove off, he'd started the short walk home. He'd hoped to find Bethany still up when he got there, and planned, finally, to sit with her and talk.

That had been his intention.

But before getting to the front door his cell phone rang.

Detective Frank Torrance was on the line. Calling from the state hospital. Margaret Haas wanted to see him. Tonight. Had to see him, right away. He wouldn't have bothered the minister, but she seemed so insistent. Though it went against the detective's better judgment, he'd decided he'd let the reverend make up his own mind.

Of course, he had agreed to come. How could he not? A troubled soul from his congregation was calling to him. Walking into his house, Blake found Bethany wasn't home yet. He'd have a talk with her after he got back.

The trip up the long driveway to the parking lot had seemed to last forever. He hated driving and did not like using the beat-up old Dodge the church gave him to use. As he'd gotten out of the car, the air seemed deathly still. Unnatural.

The air inside the building seemed even worse. Stale.

Manufactured. What an awful place. How could they expect people to be healed here?

The halls were quiet, patients already in their rooms or in bed. Torrance walked at his side, having met him in the main foyer, and now led him to Margaret's room on the fifth floor where the most violent residents were kept.

"Her shoulder wound is much better," the detective said as they walked. "She's tried to escape several times and actually got away once or twice, hiding here in the building until they found her. Sometimes she hurts herself on purpose. One time she tried gnawing at her own wrists. She's been severely restrained. She's quiet now. Has been for several hours. Like she's waiting for someone." He glanced at Hardesty. "You, I guess."

They reached the door to her room. "You don't have to go in there if you don't want to." Torrance placed a hand on Blake's shoulder. "But if you do, I'll be in there with you, just in case, or I can also get one of the attendants—"

"I want to be alone with her," Blake said.

"I can't allow that."

"You said she's restrained."

"Yes, but—"

"If you want, you can stand right outside the door. If I need you, I'll call for you. I'm her pastor, Frank. She's asking for my help. I have to talk to her alone."

"Why did I know you'd say that?" Torrance studied the minister for a moment then acquiesced. "All right. But I'm giving you fifteen minutes. Then I'm checking on you whether you call me in or not."

Blake nodded, then opened the door and entered the room.

He regretted his request for privacy as soon as the door closed behind him. But he had questions to ask that he didn't want the detective to hear.

The room was lit by a single small lamp. Bland music played quietly from a speaker somewhere. Margaret lay on her back, four thick straps around her body binding her to the bed. Her arms were pressed into her sides, her legs pressed together. Only her head was able to move.

Her eyes were closed. Had she fallen asleep while waiting

for him? He hesitated, cleared his throat. Spoke quietly. "Margaret?"

She opened her eyes. Looked at him and smiled. "I was praying. I see my prayer was answered."

"I understand you wanted to see me."

"He still talks to me, you know," she said. "My Kenny. He's been staying close by, making sure I'm all right. I tell him, I'll be fine. He loves me so much. He's seen what heaven looks like. He says it's beautiful beyond humans' ability to describe it. And there's already a place..." and with this she gave a quiet sob before continuing "...already a place for me there when my work here is finished."

The warmth in the woman's voice surprised Blake. This was contentment he was hearing. A person at peace with herself.

He took a step toward her. "Margaret..."

"I suppose you have a lot of questions."

"Yes." He rubbed his hands together.

"I was wrong, Reverend," she said before he had a chance to start asking them. "I'm sorry. I thought the Satanists were the ones who made him that way. I thought ... when Kenny was killed ... that maybe Satan had sent you to destroy my son. I didn't realize that you are as blessed as he is. But Kenny knew, just as he knew there was nothing more he could do on this Earth. He was always so strong in his other form. Free for a few hours to run in the moonlight. But it would frighten me. I didn't understand that God had chosen that for him." She paused. "Despite that, he knew his crippled body would ultimately betray him, so he waited for the time when someone came along who could replace him."

Her stare made Blake uneasy. "I don't understand," he said.

"Let me tell you a story. About my son. About the gift God gave him, and through him, gave me. So, you'll understand why you've been blessed."

She closed her eyes and remained that way for such a long time he thought she might have dozed off. It pained him to see her like this, tied to a bed, despite what she had done. Should he try to wake her or just leave? As heavily sedated as she must have been, it was probably best she sleep. He turned to exit the room.

"For a while, not too long ago, really," she said suddenly, making his heart leap, "my son was in this dreadful place because they thought I couldn't take care of him." He turned back to see the pain of the memory apparent on her face. "I had to prove myself, play their games. They let him come home eventually. But, for a while, they took care of him here, bathed him, fed his body. But not his soul. No, that was made barren by their lack of compassion. You see, even then, I knew my son was special. That God had plans for him. The days we were separated ... until I was allowed to bring him home ... were torture. As close to Hell as I ever want to get. They didn't know him ... the way I did ... the way he spoke to me...

"But one night, in this place, just before he was about to be returned to me, a man came to him. Kenny didn't talk to anybody here, of course. Yet this man understood. I've never met him. But I saw him in my son after he was returned to me. The way I see Kenny in you now. The passing of the mantle. A whole new understanding of the Lord and His work."

"This man," Blake asked, enthralled by her words in spite of himself, "did he do something to Kenny?"

As soon as he asked the question, a great space seemed to open in his mind—erupted suddenly, even violently, as if he was being admitted access to a world that co-existed in the same plane as the one he and everyone else lived in, but a world that no one else could see. He knew immediately that what he was seeing came from the past—Kenny's past—knew he was viewing it as if Blake was Kenny. Knew he was experiencing events the same way Kenny had.

He fell back a step, brought his hands up to his eyes.

"Don't try to block it out," he heard Margaret say. "Let it come. He's trying to help you."

He saw the man who had approached Kenny. A resident in the hospital like Kenny was. A stubble of gray beard on his face. Wildness in his eyes. Trapped here for whatever years of his life he had left. His hand went out to the wheelchair-bound man, stroking the thin arms, the angular, dispassionate face. "Yes," he whispered, "you will do nicely." Pulling close, his breath smelled of bloody meat and ravaged flesh. "The Lord needs a champion," the man whispered. "I can't do Him any good in here. I'm tired, and ready to move on. My reward is waiting. But you're young, strong. You see things others don't. You know things others don't want to know." He wiped his mouth, saliva coming away from his lips in thick strands.

And something began to happen. The older man's skin appeared to slide off, melt, as if something behind the man's skin was fighting to get out. He quickly shed his clothing. Then, naked, he raised his face in ecstasy, Blake experiencing what Kenny experienced that night as if the minister had been there to witness the change himself. Blake shuddered at the sight of hair sprouting, teeth growing, the thing that stood before him now no longer a man, though it stood on two legs, growing taller. Something between man and beast, but with the razor-sharp claws of an animal, laughing with utter joy at its release.

Hardesty screamed as the beast-man grabbed him and opened its jaws...

Then, suddenly, Hardesty found himself on the floor at the foot of Margaret's bed, his arms raised against nothing. He remained where he was, unable to move.

"Now you know what Kenny has chosen you for," he heard Margaret say. "The lycanthrope has existed in this world forever, Reverend. The least understood of God's creatures. Defined in the world of myth because humankind refuses to acknowledge the animal inherent in all humans. Shunned by us for centuries. Forced into hiding. The true nature of what they are disguised. Surely you are familiar with the legend of the werewolf.

"Wolf-men and women. Feared and hidden away. Stopped only by silver and fire. The most loved of God's creatures because, just as the angels represent His love for His children, the lycanthrope represent His anger and disappointment at the world He has created. They are as misunderstood as His son was. Made to suffer and die for human sins. The lycanthrope serve as His avengers. For the sins that the evil ones on this Earth continue to commit.

"Someone has to fight, Reverend. You know that yourself. Look at your own life. The injustice. The senseless tragedy. Your parents. What those men did to your wife. God feels their pain, and yours, because it is all His pain too. But now you can strike out against that. When you avenge them you avenge Him as well. People like you and my Kenny help bring balance. You are now God's rage made real in the world."

Her words seemed to come from all directions, filling the room. Of course, he had heard of such myths. From books, movies. Stories. Legend. But as something real? As much a part of God's world as any of the other living things He'd created? That was something beyond the minister's capacity for acceptance.

And yet, somewhere deep inside, in a part of his being that he was too frightened to acknowledge, he sensed there was truth in what she said. He understood God's reason for anger, as full of rage as his own.

He rose from where he lay at the foot of the bed, looked down on Margaret Haas in her prison bed. Now looking frail under the straps that kept her still. This woman was ill, he reminded himself. He felt pity for her and wondered if the stress he had been under lately had caused this strange, hypnotic episode. Surely it had nothing to do with Kenny's attack.

And then he remembered what it was about the beast-man who had attacked Kenny that stood out the most.

The eyes.

The charcoal eyes.

"Remember, silver is your enemy," he heard from the woman in the bed. "And fire. And, though it is true you will be at your strongest on the nights of the full moon, you may will the change at any time. Accept it as part of you. As the gift God intended for you.

Blake took a deep breath. "Margaret—"

"You don't believe me."

"I—"

"Look at your hands."

He hesitated.

"Look at them!"

He felt the pain before he saw it. The mark in the center of each palm. Beginning to bleed. The agony from the nails biting the flesh as real as if they were being driven through his skin at that very moment.

He stared helplessly. The blood running out onto the floor. The pain not only from the nails but also from the sins of all humankind.

He groaned with the sheer immensity of it and fell to his knees.

Something began shifting inside him. Turning. Power coursing through his body. Feeling as if he was about to explode, his hands curled into something claw-like.

"No!" he tried to shout, only it came out a hoarse whisper. He turned to the woman in the bed watching him from eyes filled with a terrible knowledge.

God doesn't work this way, he told himself.

And, with that thought, he felt whatever it was leave him. Or was it merely retreating to some, heretofore unknown, part of his soul, from where it would rise up another day?

He fought to stand, his weak legs almost giving way. Finally, he managed to steady himself. The damage to his hands was gone. There was no sign of blood.

"I don't expect you to understand it all now," Margaret Haas said. "But soon you will. And then you'll realize the gift you've been given."

He backed away from the bed. Her eyes were closed now; whether she was praying or had fallen asleep, he couldn't tell.

He opened the door and found Detective Torrance waiting for him, giving no sign he had heard anything. Hadn't he cried out, Blake thought, or had that been his imagination? All of it just a grand illusion created by a tired mind.

"Everything all right?" the detective asked.

"Yes, thank you." He rubbed his arms, though he didn't feel cold.

"Did she say anything?"

"What someone talks about with their minister is private," Blake said.

"Sure, I wasn't trying to... Some shrinks are coming to see her tomorrow. To evaluate her." Hardesty looked at him. "Psychiatrists, I mean."

The night seemed very still as they left the hospital. Too still. "I wouldn't want to be living in this place," Torrance said, looking back at the state hospital building. Blake did not respond other than to wish the officer a good night before he got into his car and drove away.

Vampires, they called themselves. Yet here it was, the night still young, and Bobby, Jimbo, and Bluejay had already fallen asleep. All they'd accomplished was finding a new place to hole up in. Another basement of another building. Another shithole. Conserving their energy for tomorrow's fun, Bluejay claimed.

But Scott Draven couldn't sleep, so, after the others' snores had developed a steady rhythm, he rose from the floor and headed out.

For where, he didn't know. He'd be back; he knew that. He had no plans to leave yet. But sleep was out of the question. He had too much energy from his earlier kill. Too much thinking to do.

The night air lay still, heavy. He'd walk for a while. See if the night held any promise.

The new him felt good, powerful. He could sense the uneasiness of people he passed, too stupid to recognize the change he'd undergone. Bluejay might if he wasn't so busy playing messiah. But Scott felt it. The soul of his recent victim offering up his gifts to him, creating this new being that was now Scott Draven.

He had never known before that there were such things in the world, such knowledge to be gained. The world had become a different place in a matter of a few days, with incredible possibilities. And as he turned right down a long street, he sensed there was something new to be learned tonight.

He kept walking, anxious to find out what.

Blake parked the car in the driveway of the parsonage, but decided he wasn't ready to go in for the night. He needed to walk, and it looked like Bethany wasn't home yet, so he decided he'd go once around the block. He needed to work off this nervous energy he was carrying around.

In the first block, he tried thinking of nothing. In the second block, he couldn't help thinking back to what had happened at the state hospital.

The werewolf as God's champion. Ridiculous. God's world was not like that. The Almighty did not need to concern Himself with petty revenge.

Yet didn't God have a right to be pissed off?

Enough, Blake told himself. He had more important things to think about. The cancer inside him gave him little time to waste. He needed to talk to his daughter. Reconnect with her. Rounding into the third block of the square, he was anxious now to get home. Maybe she'd shown up while he was walking.

He heard something then. A scuffle. Someone in trouble?

"Ow! He bit me! Son of a—"

In the shadows between two buildings, he saw two teenage boys holding a third boy against a wall. The two of them obviously stronger than the scrawny-looking third teen. The one who must have been bitten was bent over in pain, holding his hand. The other had one hand around the skinny kid's throat, who clearly couldn't breathe. In the other hand he held a knife. "We were just gonna mess you up a little," the knife wielder said. "But now I'm gonna—"

Something terrible rose inside Blake, so quickly it would have scared him if he'd had time to think. Unaware of what he was becoming, he growled from deep inside his belly, and all three of the boys turned in horror at the thing that advanced on them. A razor-like claw slashed the teenager holding the knife, ripping the shirt he wore to tatters and leaving deep scratches on his chest.

All three fled, even the one who'd been held against the wall, sheer terror etched on all their faces.

He growled again, then a third time, before Blake, or whatever Blake had become, suddenly stopped, something inside changing, shifting back...

When Scott first heard the animal-like growl, he was unable to tell where it had come from. Hearing it again, he pinpointed the direction and turned.

The two teenagers almost bowled him over running out

from between two buildings, their faces bright with terror, one wearing a shirt ripped to shreds, scratch marks on his chest. Hesitating, Draven moved slowly into the dark passage, curious as to what had frightened the boys so much.

He gasped at what he saw. Something huge. An animal but on two legs. Claws extending from its long fingers. Growling once more before beginning to change. Into human form.

A man, naked but for the tatters of clothing hanging on him, seemed exhausted as he leaned against one of the buildings. Scott could not see his face and was about to move in carefully for a better look when the man suddenly straightened and ran the other way. The movement caught him by surprise, and he hesitated before running himself, between the houses and out. He saw nothing at first, then saw a figure in the distance running down the street. He tried to follow, but it turned the next corner, and by the time he reached the same spot, there was no one in sight.

He pondered what he had just seen. A man. But what kind of man? How had the night stolen him away so quickly? Because he must live around here, Draven realized, in one of these very houses. Draven studied the neighborhood around him with new interest. Which house? He could only guess.

So, what had he just witnessed? A man who was also a beast? What kind of being was that? Draven did not question the possibility of such a creature existing. In the context of the cruel, hard world he believed in, it did not seem impossible at all. He only wondered why such a man existed. What was his purpose in life? With his new thirst for knowledge, he ached to know.

He hadn't seen the man clearly enough to make a search of these buildings worthwhile. But he could return to his compatriots now, confident that he had discovered what he had been meant to find tonight.

A man who was also a beast. Somewhere close by. Just waiting for Scott to find him again.

So close he could almost taste him.

CHAPTER ELEVEN

Blake had come home, changed out of his tattered clothing into a fresh pair of pants and a shirt, and now sat in the darkness of his living room, waiting for Bethany to come home. Trying to take things one step a time. One hour at a time.

First, make sure his daughter was home safe. After that, he could start dealing with what had happened to him out on the street. Try to make sense of it. What had the attack by Kenny Haas done to him? What was he becoming? Or was it possible the cancer in his brain was making him hallucinate? The doctor had told him he'd be fine for a while. But if the disease growing inside him did not cause these hallucinations, then maybe he should seek psychiatric help, even if the time he had remaining was precious.

At the sound of a key unlocking the front door, he sat up and watched his daughter enter the room, her form silhouetted against the light of the moon until she closed the door and began groping for the banister by the stairs.

He turned the table lamp on next to him, and, with a gasp, she looked back over her shoulder.

"Dad, what are you doing still up?"

He didn't answer right away, mesmerized by what he saw. So much of Barbara in her, in her posture, the lilt in her voice, even the defiant way she held her head. Why did she have to grow up looking so much like her mother? Why hadn't he noticed it before his wife's death?

"I couldn't sleep. I was hoping..." He tried to swallow; the inside of his mouth felt as dry as sand. "I was hoping we could talk."

"I'm tired, Dad, I'm really tired." He heard the pleading in her voice, but there was something more. Fear, maybe? Was she frightened of him?

In the dim light, the way she was turned, he couldn't make out most of her face. "Please, Bethany, let's go into the kitchen. Have some hot chocolate like we used to when you were little. We need to talk. I ... need to talk."

"The kitchen?" she said, a tremor in her voice, her hand clutched to the banister. "What do you want to talk about?"

"About what happened this morning. And what happened before you left with your friends. About ... a lot of things. Do we need an agenda? It seems we fight so much. I know ... I haven't been a very good father lately." She seemed to flinch, and he felt himself wanting to cry. "Maybe you could help me..."

"Dad..." She pulled her hand from the banister.

He put his head down. Sudden emotion made it difficult to talk. "I just ... miss her so much, Bethany."

"I miss her too, Dad."

He looked back up as she moved into the light. Her hand shooting up, but not fast enough for him to miss the ugly bruise below her left eye. Dark, puffy, and red. Her apparent attempt at covering it up with makeup had not done enough to hide it.

"My God, Bethany, what happened? Who did that to you?"

"No one. It was an accident. I tripped."

"That wasn't from a fall. Someone hit you. Who did it?"

"Dad, I told you—"

"One of those boys you were with. It was one of them, wasn't it?"

"Dad—"

"What have you gotten yourself into?"

"Nothing you would care about!"

"What do you mean, of course I care. I'm your father!"

"No, you're not! You were never my father!"

"What—?"

"Just because you put the sperm inside my mother doesn't mean you've been a father to me. You're no one! I hate you!"

He staggered back as if physically struck. "Bethany—"

"You're not here for me now any more than you were when

she was alive. She was the only family I had. All I had! And you killed her!"

"How dare you—?"

"She was always so lonely, but you never knew it! Never cared! You were always too busy! Doing things for others, but never here when we needed you!"

Blake struggled for words. "I'm a pastor. I have responsibilities. Your mother understood that."

"You just don't listen, Dad," his daughter said, "You don't see things. She loved you. But I found her in your room, crying. Alone. She didn't want you to..."

"Didn't want me to what?"

"If only you had done something. You never do anything! Maybe if you'd been different, stronger, maybe Mom would be alive today!"

"No, you ... you take that back!" Blake's head seemed to be spinning. "You hear me? What do you know about your mother and me? You take that back—"

"What do you care what I say, anyway? I'm just an ungrateful bitch! Remember?" And then she was running up the stairs, and he was trying to call out his daughter's name. But he couldn't because his mouth was as dry as a desert, and his mind swirled, and suddenly he thought back to that day. The day his wife died.

They had planned to go to a restaurant that night. A small place, out of the way. Barbara's idea. Their first night out together in months, just the two of them.

He insisted on paying with cash, always did, and Barbara ended up going to the bank to withdraw the money they'd need because he'd forgotten to go get it earlier. As usual, he'd been involved in something for the church and forgot.

He remembered the surprise on her face as he'd walked in, because he was home much earlier than he said he'd be, which hardly ever happened. She told him she'd go withdraw the money. No problem.

He hadn't even said goodbye because the phone started ringing. Blackburn, the board chairman, bitching in his ear again about some such thing as he'd watched his wife go out the door.

At the bank, all she would have had to do was withdraw the cash from the money machine.

But she didn't use the machine because it was shut down for its daily run on the computer. So, she went inside the bank.

Less than a minute later, the two robbers showed up.

He had been so tired by the time he got off the phone he fell asleep in the chair only to be awakened later by the cop knocking at the door. Telling him there had been a bank robbery, shots were fired, and Barbara Hardesty was one of the victims, so sorry for the loss.

He learned the robbery happened at a little after one o'clock. But Barbara had left the house at noon, and the bank was only a few minutes away. Why had it taken her so long to get there? He remembered then that she'd been holding her coat when he'd gotten home. Had she already been planning to go out and stopped somewhere else before showing up at the bank just ahead of the robbery? It still bothered him that he didn't know. That he would never know.

"Barbara!" he called out. "Please come down here. I just want to talk. I..." He stopped when he realized what name he was using for his daughter.

"Oh Lord," he whispered as he felt pain in his hands and looked down to see the fresh bleeding wounds. "What's happening to me!" He fell to his knees, moaning. Praying. His eyes closed.

He felt something touch his shoulder. Something with sharp claws and the smell of raw flesh on its harsh breath. "Blaaaakkke," it hissed.

"No!" he yelled. Without looking back, he stood up. Ran. Up the stairs. Past his daughter's closed door. Into his own room where he slammed the door behind him. Too scared to care about anything but keeping out the beast of his nightmares, the creature with the charcoal eyes.

He knelt by his bed. Brought his hands up to pray. Waited for a sharp-clawed hand on his shoulder.

What came instead was a smooth caress. Gentle, soothing.

"I'm here," she said by his ear. Her voice husky.

She helped him rise. He let her turn him. When she began

unbuttoning his shirt, he opened his eyes.

There she was. The angel from his dreams. My God. She looked like Barbara. No, she was Barbara. Dressed in white. Her hair golden. Eyes clear.

She removed his shirt. "How...?" he started, but she shushed him, smiled, and helped him shed his clothes. Then she shed her white gown and his angel wife stood nude before him, her hips smooth, slim, her breasts round and full, her skin creamy white. The fine down of the hair below her soft belly as golden as the long hair that framed her face.

She pressed him back onto the sheets then lay down next to him. "Please," he said, and she gestured him to silence. Took his erect penis in her hand and began working it smoothly up and down, making him gasp. Next, she leaned over and surrounded the head with her lips, her nipples brushing his stomach as she worked him until he thought he was going to explode. But she pulled back and repositioned herself above him.

"Where have you been?" he asked. "I've missed you so much."

"No questions," she said. "Just look at me. What do you see?"

He stared into her face. Wiped tears from his eyes.

It was Barbara he saw. So beautiful, her eyes so filled with love. For him. And now she was back. He cried tears of joy as she put him inside her and began to move.

He came almost immediately, giving a soundless cry as she reared her head back, holding him inside her for as long as possible before lifting herself off and lying down next to him.

"Now sleep," she whispered into his ear.

And sleep, he did.

Bethany lay awake in bed for a long time looking at the pills she held in her right hand. If she was five, she might think they were candy and would be taking them for a very different reason than the one she was considering now.

This wasn't the first time she'd imagined herself swallowing the pills then waiting for her mother to come and take her to the place where she now resided.

But Bethany was smart enough to know what it was she was really considering. And what if the thing she sometimes told her father in rebellion was true?

What if there was no God?

Slowly, she put the pills back in their bottle, then wrapped the bottle in an old T-shirt and hid it in the far back left corner of the night-table drawer before closing it. Sighing deeply, she placed her head on the pillow. Bethany deeply regretted what had happened downstairs. She knew on some level that hiding the bruise from her father would be impossible, even if she had succeeded in going to bed tonight without her seeing him, then sneaking out early the next morning as she'd planned.

Now things were worse. Unable to control herself, she'd said cruel things. In her anger and fear, she'd wanted to hurt him, and she'd succeeded.

Her sense of despair was so deep the idea of taking enough pills to send her into oblivion was more than tempting. But what if there was nothing better on the other side? What if it was worse? That, more than anything, kept her from opening the drawer again. Made her determined to talk to her father. Make him listen. Find the right time before...

Before what? He went completely off the deep end? She worried about him, saw how depressed he was. Heard him talking to himself downstairs after she'd run up the stairs and slammed the door. She didn't know what a nervous breakdown was like exactly, but she suspected her father was on the verge of having one. If it hadn't started already.

What if she was the one to take the first step and ask for forgiveness? Hadn't her mother always told her to be herself? Her mother was dead, but Bethany hadn't forgotten what she'd promised her. To be self-reliant and never afraid to express her true feelings. Now she felt ashamed for not having done so.

Remembering her mother made her feel sad, but she fought back the tears. Because the idea of approaching her father and asking for his forgiveness while granting him hers had a sudden, liberating effect on her. Made her feel differently about herself.

She had a sense of hope that she hadn't felt in a long time.

What if she actually tried taking responsibility for her feelings, her pain, and talked with him about it? What would happen? The idea both frightened and exhilarated her.

She heard sounds from the hall. Her father going into his room. But hadn't she heard the door being slammed shut earlier? Next came the sound of him getting into bed. He must have gone downstairs for a while without her hearing and was only now returning. Was he unable to sleep, like her? Her newfound sense of direction made her want to act now and show her father she was growing up, maybe a little. At least it would be a start.

She pushed back the covers and got out of bed. She hadn't bothered to change and was still wearing the clothes she'd worn that day. She'd go quietly into the hall in case he was asleep. Walk by his room. If the door was open, and she thought he was awake, she'd go in. Tell him she wanted to talk. Why wait until morning? Why put it off any longer?

As silently as she could, she opened her door.

And headed toward his room.

Again, he dreamed.

He was with Barbara. Her warm body wrapped around him like a comfortable blanket. Her flesh pulsing against his. Her heartbeat...

All at once, he found himself outside, walking the last block toward the church. For some reason, to his left there was a dog walking next to him. There was also someone to his right. He turned and saw the beast. Even this close the face was in shadow, the charcoal eyes burning. It didn't look at him as it matched him step for step.

They reached the front of the church. He'd locked it before leaving, of course, and now Blake watched, mesmerized, as the thing walked up to the door, rattled it then turned back. "Open it," it said in a low, gravelly voice.

"I can't," Hardesty responded.

"I SAID OPEN IT!" It swung a massive paw against the door, causing a loud, booming sound upon impact, the building rattling from its very foundation.

"I can't let you in there," Blake pleaded.

"Yes, you can. Open it!"

Blake looked around for help. But there was no one, not even the angel. Somehow, he knew she would not come this time.

This was his battle. Alone.

"Open it!" Again, the beast pounded on the door.

"I—"

To his horror, the beast lashed out against the dog, catching it with its claws and sending it flying. The dog hit the side of the church where it slid, broken, to the floor.

"Open it! Or else."

Abruptly, a figure appeared on the steps between him and the beast. Bethany, six years old, an age when she'd still worshiped him.

"Ride me, Daddy, ride me!"

Bouncing on his knee. So excited, so precious. Daddy, her hero.

"Ride me, Daddy! Ride me!"

The creature picked her up, but she didn't react, even as it raised her above its head. She still smiled. R"ide me, Daddy! Ride me!"

"No! Don't—"

"Let me in," the beast roared.

"Please…" He took a step, hesitated.

The beast held her straight out above its head, and, as easily as a thin branch, snapped his daughter in half, the sound of her back breaking as sharp as a gunshot.

"Nooooo!" he screamed.

The thing tossed the broken shell away then grabbed him and forced his hand to the handle.

"Open it!"

The handle turned.

"Do it!"

And he thought he heard a voice from the other side. Barbara's voice. Was that his name she was shouting? No, it was someone else's. But whose?

The beast laughed. "You're only going to learn the truth if you open that door."

The door opened.

And there was Barbara, her head thrown back, her naked breasts bathed in sweat, a look of shock, even horror in her eyes as she saw him...

Blake bolted upright from the dream and found himself in his bedroom. The space next to him in bed empty.

"Barbara?"

Someone walked into the room.

"Barbara?" He rose and moved quickly. The figure hesitated.

"Barbara." After all this time, she'd come back to him. "My darling..."

In two steps he had her in his arms, caressing her. They still had hours left until morning. Hours to spend making up for lost time.

"No!" he heard. "What are you doing!"

"Barbara," he whispered.

"Stop..."

"My darling..."

"Please stop!"

Why was she fighting him? "Barbara, what's wrong?"

"I'm not—"

All at once, something rose up inside of him. The voice of the beast again. Shouting. "Just kill the bitch! Kill her!"

"No! What are you...? I wouldn't do that. I love her. I love you, Barbara!"

"Kill her!"

He heard Barbara shout, "No! Daddy..."

He stopped. Pulled back. "What...?"

Again, he heard the small, frightened voice. "Daddy..."

"Bethany?" His daughter stood in front of him now, not his wife. She looked disheveled. Shock was in her eyes. "My God, Bethany."

"Daddy, please stop."

For the first time, he realized he was naked and searched for something to cover himself with. "Bethany, I don't know what's going on. I'm sorry..."

And then she was gone, running out of the room, and he thought maybe this was just another hallucination. He prayed that that's all it had been, a horrible nightmare. Please, God, let it be so.

Until he heard the front door slam downstairs.

Outside, the sky, which had threatened rain for the last several hours, let loose with a crack of thunder. He stood very still, unable to move or make sense out of what had just happened, waiting for the nightmare to end.

And then he heard the skies open outside, and the night turned to violence.

CHAPTER TWELVE

Scott woke from two hours of sleep to morning drizzle, the last of the night's storm petering out. The other three snored loudly. The case of beer they had stolen sat nearby, almost empty. Scott lay back, thinking about what his next step should be.

His main priority? Find the man-beast he'd seen last night. He'd heard of such creatures. From movies, television. Legend. But the idea that such things really existed? Delicious.

Each victim so far, each sacrifice, brought him one step closer to God. Life had taken on new meaning. He had a purpose now. A religion of his own. It was beautiful, this thing he was becoming. As beautiful as the thing he'd seen last night. Tall, mighty. If only he could find him. Touch him. He felt a kinship with the creature, though he had barely seen him.

He had to learn more about him. Had to find him.

Scott listened to the others snoring. Bobby mumbled something in his sleep, shifted position, and farted.

They wouldn't be waking up for a while.

Again, he went for a walk, the day newly born and growing.

"Let's see if I have it all now, Reverend. She's wearing blue jeans…"

"I … I think so…"

"And a light-blue blouse."

"Yes."

"Anything else? A jacket or sweater?"

"She left without her jacket."

"What about a cell phone."

"She left that here too, I'm afraid."

"Uh huh." More writing. Scritch scratch. Every line digging deeper into Blake's psyche.

"You say she ran off between one and two AM?"

"Yes."

"It's seven-thirty in the morning. How come you waited so long to report it?"

"I thought she might ... come back."

"Bitch of a storm last night. Was it raining when she left?"

"I think so."

"You two had a fight? She must have been pretty mad to run out into a rainstorm without a jacket."

"Actually, I think it started just after she left."

"Uh huh." Scritch scratch. "What'd you fight about?"

The uniformed cop stared at him. Arrogant, cocky. Most cops showed a little deference to a minister, some respect. But not this guy; he stared at Hardesty as if he thought there was more here than meets the eye. "She came home late," Blake said. "We had a disagreement about it."

"You sure it isn't something else?"

"What do you mean?" Blake tried not to sound defensive.

"I don't know. The things you see in this job... You're the minister at the church on Seventh and Livingston, right?"

"Right."

"It could be in a better neighborhood, you know." He shrugged. "Anything else about her? Any distinguishing marks?"

"No," Blake answered and thanked the younger man.

"Don't worry, she'll probably turn up some time in the next twenty-four hours," the officer said. "That's the way these things usually turn out." The officer nodded goodbye, and Hardesty closed the door, leaned against it.

What the hell to do now? Wait for Bethany to return? If she returned. No, he mustn't think that way.

How could he have made such a horrible mistake? Thought his daughter was Barbara. It all seemed so confusing now. Like so much of his life was lately.

He'd been dreaming. About standing outside the church, while the thing tried to enter. Before that, Barbara had come to him. Made love to him. But that must have been a dream, too. Of course. Barbara was dead. Killed by a couple of thugs inside the bank because the money machine had been shut down. Because she hadn't gotten there earlier. But she should have. It only takes five minutes to get to that branch. Where the hell had she been between the time she'd left home and the time she'd arrived at the back of that bank line, the first to get shot?

Back to the dream. Standing outside the church. The door opening. The creature laughing. And on the other side of the door, his wife, sweaty, turning toward him with a look of surprise and shock on her face.

He moved to a nearby chair and sat. It was becoming too difficult to distinguish between reality and dream. It had felt good chasing those cruel teenage boys in his new form. Filled with so much power and righteous fury. But that had that been a dream too, right? Or a hallucination.

What the hell was happening to him? He went through it again. His daughter entering his bedroom, in the dark. Blake confusing Bethany for his dead wife because he'd been dreaming about her. He'd woken up confused. Thinking it had all been real. Weren't dreams like that sometimes? When he'd realized his mistake, he'd wanted to explain to his daughter what had happened.

But then the voice had come again, had risen from inside him. Just like in the church that morning. Making him say things he didn't want to say. Horrible things.

When next he saw Bethany, he would explain. Then he'd get help for himself. Professional help. He'd even accept hospitalization if necessary. Could the brain cancer be causing his breaks from reality? He would tell Bethany about his diagnosis. About the time he had left. She deserved to know. To have time to prepare. She hadn't had time to prepare for Barbara's death. Whatever it took to make the time they had left meaningful he would do it. Bethany was more important than anything. He couldn't bear the thought of hurting her further, and he swore not to. Even if it meant spending the rest of the time he had left locked away in an institution and never seeing his daughter again, he would do it. So, she would be safe.

Blake took a deep breath. At least now he'd made a decision. And he ached to see Bethany again, to give himself the hope of a second chance.

The phone rang. He jumped from the chair. Maybe it was Bethany calling for him to come get her.

"Hello?"

"Blake." He recognized the coarse voice of Louise Calabrese. "I'm at the church."

Something in her tone. "What is it, Louise? What's the matter?"

"You've got to get over here. Now. I've already called the police."

"The police? Why...?" Suddenly there was a banging at his door. "Come in," he called out without thinking. The door opened, revealing the same young cop from before standing in the doorway.

"I just got a call to come get you, Reverend."

A sick feeling filled his stomach. "Is it my daughter? Did they find her?"

Louise still at his ear. "The sanctuary, Blake." He heard her sobbing. "Somebody trashed it. Destroyed it."

"What...?"

"Apparently there's been some vandalism at your church," the cop said. "I'll take you over there."

Louise was crying openly now. Into the phone, he said, "I'll be right there." Then hung up.

And followed the cop out the door.

For the second time in twenty-four hours, Blake found Stan Marles blocking his entrance into Hell. "When I heard about it, I came right over," he babbled. "I promise you, Blake, whoever did this..."

The minister brushed the detective aside and entered the church.

The first thing he noticed was the carcass of a dog hanging from the cross over the communion table, held in place by several knives. Its limbs were stretched out, the head pulled back, the eyes open and glazed, its tongue protruding.

The animal's throat had been cut and blood had dripped onto the silver communion tray on the communion table below. Next to it was a large mound of feces.

Somebody had drawn lewd pictures of nude men and women, men and men, women and women committing various sexual acts on the front of the altar behind which he stood every Sunday. The carpet had been ripped down the center aisle. Urine stained the rug and several of the pews that had not been broken.

Various stains of God knew what, blood, even semen, were on the walls.

Blake took it all in. Frozen in the moment. This special place, holy, offering peace, sanctuary, protection. Now defiled. Sullied. Destroyed. He could envision God lying broken and bleeding in front of him. His home ruined. His work wasted. The Almighty in tears.

As Hardesty should be, though he wasn't. Louise sat in the last row, looking at him. Alone, in shock. He knew he should go to her, offer comfort.

Instead, he turned away from the scene before him, numb. Unable to feel anything.

Just another dream, he decided. That's all. Just like everything else in his life recently. Dream blending with reality.

He turned to Stan Marles. "My office?" he asked, his voice dead.

"Intact. So's the rest of the building. They only trashed the sanctuary."

"I'll be in my office." He turned away, feeling everyone's eyes on him, hearing Louise's sobs, and was that Paul Blackburn's voice somewhere, ranting?

He entered his office and sat behind his desk. The room was untouched but felt just as violated as the sanctuary. He knew he should feel something. Sadness. Devastation. Anger. Something. But, still, he felt only numb. Everything from the past year had deadened his nerves, making him incapable of feeling anything any longer.

But he could still act. He needed to be available to his members. Once they got the news, they'd want support. Even counseling.

But he couldn't do it here. He'd set up something at home.

"Blake?" Louise stood in the doorway, her trembling hand working to bring a cigarette to her mouth. "Can I come in?"

He nodded, and she approached his desk, but didn't sit. Continuing to smoke, she reached into the pocket of her corduroy jeans for another one to light off the end of the one she had.

"Blake, who ... who would do such a thing? Bastard ... fucking bastards..."

"Louise..."

"The scum of the earth, that's who. People who don't deserve God's love. Who deserve to die a painful death, then sent to Hell. If I could kill them slowly, with my bare hands..."

He rose and crossed around his desk. "Louise..."

"You don't understand, Blake. I've seen things in my life— cruel things. My husband ... he didn't just beat me ... he raped me ... I never told you that. The church... It's my place away from all that. Those awful memories. I thought I was safe here. Now it's ruined. I want ... God help me, I want to kill someone..."

It felt so natural to put his arms around her, one human comforting another. What he didn't expect was how good she felt in his arms, how soft she looked in her vulnerability, this woman who was usually so gruff and hard-edged. It suddenly felt easy, and the right thing to do, to lower his face to where her expectant mouth awaited his.

"Excuse me." Stan Marles stood in the doorway. Looking flushed, uncomfortable. "I didn't mean to intrude—"

"You're not intruding," Hardesty said abruptly, pulling away.

"What happened here... It's horrible, horrible..."

"Yes, I..." Louise was already heading out the door, passing Detective Marles. Blake tried to read the expression on her face, but she was gone before he could.

"She works here?" Marles asked as he entered the office.

"She's the church sexton. And my assistant, kind of. What happened here has affected her very deeply." He looked at Marles. "I'm surprised to see you here."

"Surprised? As soon as I heard—"

"I mean you must feel... Would you rather we talked outside?"

"No. I do feel nervous. But ... since our talk last night, I think I'll be all right."

Blake nodded. Waited.

"I want you to know how sorry I am," Marles said. "I'm going... We're going to do everything we can to find out who did this. For now, we're going to have to treat the sanctuary as a crime scene. Can't let anybody in for a while. Until we're finished compiling evidence."

"Why are you on this case?"

"I'm not, but I came over when I heard it was your church. I can't help but wonder if there might be some connection ... you know ... with the other case I'm working on. Both have religious overtones. That poor dog on the cross. It's a gruesome thing, gruesome. To be honest, it reminds me of what was done to Mrs. Holder."

"You think the same drifters you're looking for might have done this?"

"It's possible, isn't it? If I need to talk to you about anything, I can find you...?"

"At home. I want to make myself available for anyone from the church who might need me."

"Of course. There might be reporters, you know. Coming here."

The two stood in silence. "I'd better go," Marles said. And with that, he was gone, hurrying out like a kid who'd just admitted to masturbation in the confessional.

What now, Blake thought. Go home, yes. Make some phone calls. He had to do something.

"Blake." Paul Blackburn stood in his doorway. Hardesty's office was a revolving door now. The chairman of the church board could barely contain himself. His face flushed. His large hands clenched tightly at his sides. He was a tall man, the kind who got what he wanted, mostly through intimidation, before claiming it in the name of the church.

There was no love lost between these two men. But, out of a sense of duty, and really because he didn't have much of a choice, Hardesty did his best to get along with him.

"What are we going to do about this?" Blackburn said through clenched teeth.

"For now, let the police do their work. Then—"

Blackburn cut Blake off. "There are going to be reporters. They'll want to talk to you. Let me handle them."

"I appreciate that, Paul. It'll make it easier for me to be available to church members. I was thinking about making some phone calls, putting together a support group, have them meet at my house."

"Damn, you get organized fast. Something like this... Don't you feel like killing somebody?" The larger man moved across the room until he'd reached the far wall, then turned. "Still, maybe this is a blessing in disguise."

"A blessing...?"

"Maybe it's even for the best."

"What are you talking about?"

Blackburn looked at him, resolute. "At our meeting last night—"

"What meeting?"

"At my house. I told you about it. I asked you to come."

He'd forgotten. Damn it.

"When you didn't show up... Well, the whole board was there. First time we had every member attend a meeting in I don't know how long. We talked about what happened to you yesterday morning. We know you've been under a lot of pressure, even now, almost a year after ... Barbara's death. After what happened to you at Margaret Haas's house ... anybody might snap. I made a motion that we have you removed as pastor. You know how I feel about you, Blake, how we feel about each other, there's no use beating around the bush. I'm being truthful here. Some more time off ... significant time off, a year or more, maybe. Let's face it, you haven't been much of a minister lately. Understandably so, don't get me wrong. I miss Barbara too, you know."

Blake only stared.

"But last night," Blackburn continued, "the more we talked about the situation here, membership dwindling, no new members in over two years, facing the very real possibility that we won't be able to meet our bills, much less keep up with our outreach obligations..."

"What are you saying, Paul?"

"I'm saying... We're saying ... it's time to close this church. We're very small. It wouldn't be hard to do. We'll bring it to a vote at a congregational meeting, but I don't think it'll be a close vote. I've talked to some of the membership."

"You've talked...?" Hardesty suddenly became aware of something behind him. Was that something touching his shoulder?

"Now, we have enough to give you a good severance pay. You don't have to worry about that. And the regional office can even help you find a new church. If you want one. Maybe a good assistant pastor position somewhere."

Something rough, sharp. Accompanied by the odor of raw flesh and blood.

"You can use this time to rest. I think you've earned it."

Whatever it was began stroking his shoulders and back.

"It's for your own good."

Seemed to reach inside him.

"Blake, are you listening to me?"

And then his hands began to bleed.

"Do you hear me? What's—?"

"You stupid, sanctimonious motherfucker!"

Blackburn's face turned pale as he took a step backward.

Blake knew the voice was the same as the one that had spoken yesterday morning in front of the congregation, but this time he didn't try to stop it. "You think I never noticed the way you watched Barbara when she was alive? Always eyeing her, staring at her legs, her ass. Hoping to get her into your bed, another one of your conquests? Didn't you think I knew you wanted to fuck her?"

"What...?" Blackburn blurted out. "What are you saying?"

"You flirted with her more than once. Brushed up against her. Came on to her. Did you think I was blind? Too busy to notice? I know you were planning to proposition my wife before she was killed. You wanted to shove your cock in her mouth—"

"That's enough, Hardesty."

"Just like when you had an affair with Alba Reynolds right after her husband died. I'm the minister here, remember? Some people tell me things in confidence. Hell, you couldn't even wait for the body to get cold before you had to get your slimy dick into poor Alba—"

Blackburn swung at him, and Hardesty, anticipating it, ducked, his body tingling, seeming to shift, wanting to change into...

Galvanized by what he felt, Blake grabbed the chairman by the lapels of his jacket and lifted him off the floor. Then shoved him hard against the wall with a force that knocked the wind out of him.

Blake let go and Blackburn crumpled to his knees, gasping for air. Suddenly aware of what he was doing, Hardesty stared at his hands as they began to curl into something like claws.

My God, he thought. My God.

"How dare...?" Blackburn gasped. "How dare you...?"

"Paul, let me help you." Blake moved toward him, the hand he extended no longer curled.

"Stay the hell away from me!" Blackburn tried to stand, pushing his back against the wall. "Who the hell do you think you are?"

"Paul, I—"

"You're finished around here, do you hear me? Even if we were to survive as a church, I would do everything in my power ... everything..."

He knew he should apologize, but all Blake did was stare at Blackburn with disdain. Remembering clearly the look in the other's eyes just before he'd taken a swing at him, confirming Hardesty's accusations. A poor, pitiful, disgusting man living off the weakness and vulnerability of others.

Blake didn't move as Blackburn backed out of the office, struggling for a shred of dignity, but failing. Once he was gone, the minister smiled. He couldn't help himself. He felt good. Great, in fact. Powerful. How many other women besides poor, helpless Alba Reynolds had there been? How long before he would have made a move on Barbara, had she lived? He would have enjoyed hearing from her how she snubbed him, the two of them laughing about it afterward.

He suddenly felt very tired and almost didn't make it to the desk chair before sitting down. Too much had happened in the past forty-eight hours. Too much for any man. He still had his daughter to worry about. He wondered if she could have come home—could be there right now. Waiting for him. A chance for reconciliation.

He rose, unsteady.

"You should go home." He looked up. Louise stood in the doorway again, her arms folded. "The reporters are here. Blackburn's talking to them. What did you say to him? He looks..." She hesitated then shrugged. "Why don't you go out the back?"

"I think I will." She appeared to be back to her old self. "What if the reporters try to talk to you?"

She waved the idea away. "I'm only the church sexton. They won't want to talk to me." She pulled herself up. "And if they do, I'll tell them to fuck off." She said it with the defiant and straightforward vulgarity he'd come to depend upon from her.

"I'll be home if anybody needs me." He moved from behind his desk. Headed toward the rear exit.

"I'll stop by later," he heard her say. Was there a slight tremor in her voice?

"If you want." He kept his back to her as he responded.

Exiting the building, he took a back way home to avoid the crowd that had formed out front. The air fresh from last night's storm made him feel rejuvenated, and he picked up his pace at the prospect of Bethany waiting for him at home.

The sweet smell of the air misled him, giving no hint of the darkness that was soon to descend upon them.

CHAPTER THIRTEEN

Scott hadn't been in a library since dropping out of high school, back in the days when he'd enjoyed reading the likes of Ray Bradbury, John Steinbeck, and William Golding. It felt strange to return. Foreign. Yet how quickly he adapted.

The woman at the main desk seemed the matronly type at first. A bit severe. But that soon melted away in his presence. A new part of his personality. The ability to charm another person by merely listening, smiling, and giving back what he thought the other wanted to hear while, in the process, studying and learning what the points of vulnerability were. Not feeling anything about the woman, of course. She was simply someone whose knowledge he needed.

After it was over, he didn't even remember her name.

"You're talking about werewolves," she said. "Legend, of course." Smiling a secret smile. "You'll want to look in our occult section."

"You mean you really have books on that subject here?" he'd said, feigning astonishment.

"Well, of course. We have many books dealing with myths and legends." She smiled. "We may be a moderately-sized library, but we're not hicks."

"I didn't mean to imply you were," he responded, smiling back. Disarming her. "Myths and legends, did you say?"

"Occult. Only..." She hesitated.

"Yes?"

"I know you may not think so to look at me. But I have an interest in such things myself."

"Really?"

"Well, yes. Does that surprise you?"

"No. You seem like a … smart, complex woman."

"Thank you."

"And attractive."

She blushed. "Well, I'm smart enough to know that humans place limits on their understanding of things. What did you say your name is?"

"I didn't." He smiled again. "It's Scott."

"What if I was to tell you, Scott, that I believe there might be some truth to the legend of werewolves?"

"I'd say that's amazing. You know a lot about them?"

"Yes. If I had time, I'd tell you more. But…" She looked around the room. "Maybe after I've finished my shift here, you could meet me outside. We could go somewhere. Talk. In the meantime, I'll show you some books you could check out."

She showed him four books, which he took with him after she issued him a library card, looking the other way when he didn't have the proper identification.

Once outside, he threw them in the first trashcan he could find. Then waited for her to finish her shift.

"There you are," she said later. "You didn't finish those books already, did you?"

"I looked at them a little. Left them at my apartment."

"Is your apartment close by?"

"Very."

"Why don't we go there? We can … talk some more."

Was she coming on to him? He couldn't be sure. He wasn't used to such behavior.

"So, you know a lot about werewolves."

"I guess you could say it's my hobby," she said. "Anything to do with the supernatural. But I especially like werewolves. All that rage smoldering inside. A human's uncontrollable passion."

"And you believe in them?"

"Why not? All legends are based on some level of truth. Why couldn't such creatures exist? Hiding behind human guises?"

"And you know a lot about them," he said again. "How to stop them, control them, that sort of thing."

She laughed. "Why? Do you have a werewolf you need to catch?"

He motioned for a change in direction. "This way."

"Down this alley? Do you live in one of those alley apartments?"

"Yes. It's not that far now."

They entered the passage, Draven allowing her to walk a few steps in front of him. "You know," she said, not quite looking back, "you may not think so to look at me, Scott, but I'm a woman who could make you feel good. Very good." She turned toward him, her hand resting lightly on his chest. "If you'd let me."

He leaned forward and broke the woman's neck before she knew what had happened. She collapsed like a puppet whose strings had been cut, and Draven brought her down gently to the alley floor.

Where he took off his clothes, then hers. And ate her.

When he was done, he leaned back with a sigh and closed his eyes, already feeling the change take place within him. The rush of knowledge.

This woman's past. Memories. Desires. Liaisons with men. Most important, her knowledge of the occult. Especially werewolves.

His ability to charm this woman had surprised him. He'd had sex with very few women, and the times he did had been rushed, violent affairs. But the changes he'd undergone in recent days obviously had had a profound affect. The knowledge he was gaining from his victims was making him capable of doing many new things.

He remembered the first meal, with Bluejay and the others. The first family. The man had been what, a teacher? Something like that. He hadn't cared at the time. Had not been aware of the possibilities such a victim offered.

But now that he understood what was happening to him, he could recognize each giant step he took, each new opportunity as it arose.

The librarian having knowledge of the supernatural had been an unexpected benefit of his trip to the library, and now he lay back, feeling the rush of two beings becoming one. A marriage most perfect.

After a while, Draven stood. He needed to get back. A lot of time had passed. Bluejay would be pissed.

"Where the fuck you been?" Bluejay growled at him when he returned to their latest hideout.

Scott merely walked past him, noticing Jimbo and Bobby as they nervously kept watch on the battle of wills.

"I'm talking to you." Draven turned, resisting the urge to kill him. It would be easy, as easy as the woman in the alley.

"I had things to do," he said, recognizing the look of the endangered animal in Bluejay, the weak leader afraid of having his authority usurped.

"What things?"

"I can't stay cooped up here all the time. It's a waste."

"We're preparing. Conserving our energy for tonight. Besides, what if people saw you and wondered who you were?"

Scott almost retorted, then backed off. It wasn't time to rebel yet. After all, it was Bluejay who had introduced him to this new way of looking at life, even if the guy didn't understand the power he was playing with. Tonight would be their last night in this city. One more family of victims. And then they were moving on. Leaving town. After that, Scott could strike out on his own. And if any of these three stood in his way...

I should kill Bluejay, Scott thought. And, right then, Scott decided he would. After tonight.

But, for now, he needed him. "I'm sorry," Scott heard himself say. It was easy to apologize, even easier to make Bluejay think he meant it. "I really did just need to get out for a while."

Bluejay hesitated, then put his arm around Draven. All smiles again now that he was back on top. "It's all right," he said. "I understand. Soon, Scott, you'll understand too. We need these times for meditation. Preparation. Because we're a special breed."

Scott felt another sermon coming on and tuned him out. Found it easy to listen with a small part of his brain while he nurtured his own thoughts.

The communion with the librarian had been wonderful. But there was something far greater. The man-beast was out there. Waiting for him.

Early evening. The bell at the Catholic Church eight blocks away tolled eight times.

There had been no calls. None. Well, one. Louise, calling to see how he was doing. Telling him again she might stop by.

Nobody else from his church. Not Bethany, or the police telling him they'd found her. Not even Stan Marles to give him an update on the investigation. On the radio he'd heard a report about the attack on his church. Too hideous even for the radio to go into detail. The sanctuary forever soiled. As if God himself had been raped. Maybe Blackburn was right. Maybe it was best to close the church. Who would feel comfortable worshiping there now, worship run by a minister whose own life had been tainted by disaster and violence and whose misfortune had rubbed off on his congregation?

He felt something smoldering in the pit of his stomach. Burning. Maybe once Bethany returned, and they'd had a chance to talk, for him to explain what had happened last night, they could move away somewhere, start fresh, make the most of the time he had left with her. Get to know each other again as father and daughter. Surely, she'd at least give him a chance to explain, wouldn't she? Or maybe after she was home, he'd discover that last night had only been a dream as well, like so much of his life seemed to be these days.

A nightmare.

If they did go away and start over, he wouldn't have to be a minister. He could find something else. Work in a convenience store if he had to, a fast-food restaurant, for God's sake.

For God's sake. That's what his life had been about. Doing for Him, and for others. But what had it brought him? For that matter, what good did it do God? Trying to help others who didn't want to be helped. Why did He love them so? Hadn't they disappointed him, constantly? Crucified His only son? Sacrificed Jesus rather than face their own sins?

Surprised by his sudden rush of anger, Blake knelt, bowed his head, and closed his eyes.

But what good did prayer do? Why would God even bother to listen?

He felt something touch him. The angel who had appeared to him before? Maybe he could talk to her. God's liaison.

But it wasn't the angel. For it had a rough, hard, sharp touch, and its breathing was hot in his ears. And it whispered things, made promises...

He opened his eyes. Rose. Looked.

Nothing there. He was going crazy. He knelt again. Closed his eyes. And still the anxiety grew, born of anger. The unfairness of life, the damn fickleness of fate. So easy to let himself cross over to anger. Embrace it.

When the change occurred, it happened suddenly. Burst upon him. Rushing up from inside, uncontrolled. His body itching, growing, changing.

Like it had the previous night when he'd been walking home. Had seen those two boys terrorizing a third. His senses suddenly sharpening, tingling. More aware of things around him. The presence of things that normal human senses could not pick up. Somewhere he heard a baby crying and realized it was several houses away. He smelled the odor of hamburgers sizzling on a grill. The hamburger joint several streets over?

And, for just that moment, he understood everything. Had a clear view of the direction he must go. The future spread out vividly in front of him.

He had to see for himself. See what physical beauty this change in him had wrought.

The mirror beckoned. He went to it.

And saw the beast from his dream looking back at him from charcoal eyes. His own face behind those eyes.

The sight of it made him scream, the sound an animal howl.

He stopped abruptly at the sound of someone coming. At the door... No. He realized the person was still several blocks away, though he could hear footsteps on the sidewalk as clearly as if she was just approaching the front door. Louise Calabrese. With his heightened senses, he could smell her, hear her breathing, a little shallow, a combination of nerves and the cigarettes she was constantly pumping into her system. He could even hear her heart beating.

And he knew that it was the pulse of her blood pumping

through her veins and the sweet odor of flesh even years of a hard life could not mask that made him salivate.

She was getting closer. He couldn't let her see him like this.

And with that single thought, his body shifted once more, swiftly, until he was back to being only a man again, everything about him as unchanged as before, normal human senses, the smell of blood no longer pervading his nostrils.

The length of time he'd been in beast form had been short enough that he could almost convince himself it had been another dream. If not for the realization he was naked. His clothes piled near his feet. Where, somehow, he'd had the wherewithal to remove them before the change. Quickly, he put them back on. Finished as he heard the knock at the door.

For a brief moment, he hoped he'd been wrong, and he'd find his daughter standing on the other side.

But there was Louise instead, as he'd known she would be.

"May I come in?" she asked.

"Of course." Stepping back, he motioned her to enter.

Soon they were sitting in the living room, each holding a wine glass, the smoke circling her head beginning to permeate the room.

"They're bastards," she whispered. "All of them. They don't deserve you."

"Don't, Louise."

"It's true. Why do you work so hard to always see the good in people? Don't you realize that most people are pricks?"

"It doesn't matter anymore." Hearing those words come out of his own mouth surprised him. "The church is going to be closed. People will move on. Things will change. It really doesn't matter." He looked at her. "But what will you do?"

She smirked as she ground her third cigarette in the last fifteen minutes into the ashtray he'd given her. "I'll be fine. Don't worry. I've got some money put away. From my husband's life insurance policy. Investments." But there was something. He could hear it in her voice, see it in her eyes. Something she wanted to say. "Where's Bethany?" she asked. Changing the subject.

He told her the same thing he'd told the police officer. He

still clung to the hope that, once he talked to Bethany, he'd discover that what had happened last night had only been a dream. Something else had driven her out into the night and the rain. He told Louise he blamed himself for the argument. She was still a child, and he hadn't been much of a father, even when Barbara had been alive. He'd made his wife do too much of the parenting alone. She'd died, and they'd both been left floundering. Unable to reach out to one another.

Now Bethany had run off, but he'd promised himself that when the police found her, things would be different. He would force himself to listen. And he would try to tell her how he was feeling and how unfair he thought he had been to her. He would ask her for a second chance and get whatever help they needed, a family counselor if necessary.

Once he was finished, Blake and Louise sat in silence. Drank some more. Soon the bottle was empty.

Watching her, he'd become aware of her every move, the way she averted her eyes, then brought them back to gaze on him. The way her body curved as she moved. The softness, the vulnerability he saw behind her rough exterior. Had he been blind before or always aware, just afraid to act upon it? There was beauty in this woman. More than just her beauty of soul. It was her physical beauty he saw now, shining through despite years of hard living.

The silence became too heavy. They both moved. "Maybe I should get another bottle..." he said.

"How come you don't keep her picture around here?" Louise asked suddenly.

Knowing whom she meant, he asked anyway. "Whose?"

"Barbara's."

He looked around the room, but Blake already knew she was right. Except for the one in Bethany's room, they had all been put away.

Louise stood suddenly. "I have to go."

He rose too. "What, you have things to do?"

"Yeah." Not looking at him. "Lots." Fiddling with something on her blouse. She hadn't worn a coat.

She turned to leave.

"Please don't go." It was out of his mouth before he could stop it.

They didn't move for what seemed a long time. Her back to him.

"I've done things I'm sorry for, Blake."

"What do you mean?"

She turned to face him. Were those tears in her eyes? "After my husband died... I was glad he died. I used to think God killed him to give me a second chance. Maybe I still think that. Does that make me evil? I thought finding this church was God's way of bringing me back to Him. Of saying He forgives me. To have it taken away now... I don't understand anymore what He has in mind for me."

She looked so beautiful standing there. A lost soul. Or maybe not lost, just struggling, like so many of His children.

"Maybe God..." Has another plan, he was about to say. But did he really believe that anymore?

"I love you," she whispered, her voice whiskey soft. "I always have. From the first day I saw you."

Blake didn't move, didn't breathe. The world pulling away, leaving only him and this woman. Nothing between them. No more barrier to keep him from feeling anything else but the pain, sadness, despair, and grief that had defined his life for the past year.

He went to her, intending to offer comfort. Only comfort. Perhaps she misunderstood, lifting her face up to kiss him. Perhaps he meant to explain his intentions, but for her mouth meeting his, his senses expanding in the touch of her surprisingly soft lips, their sweet tobacco taste. Then he was pulling her closer, kissing her deeply, losing himself in the intimacy offered by another human being. Then leading her upstairs. Into his bedroom, where he watched her undress.

As she stood naked before him, he sensed her defiance, offering no apology for the body she displayed. Tired and worn, creased and scarred. The reminder of an old wound below her right breast, a scar inside her left thigh. Damage done by her ex-husband? Breasts that hung with the weight of difficult years but for the way she held herself, proud, not defeated. Aching for someone's touch that was not rough.

She unbuttoned his shirt, undid his pants, ran the flat of her palms down his chest, to the bulge in his underwear, pulling them down all the way to the floor. Then taking hold of him.

Everything about the way she touched him intensified his sharpened senses even more. They lay on the bed, and he caressed her, felt every nook and cranny and fold and bend. Touched her body lovingly, until not a single part of her had been missed by either fingers or mouth. She did the same for him, her hands greedy, her eyes caring. When he had held off long enough and went to enter her, she stopped him with a hand to his chest, pushed him back gently, then rolled over onto her stomach, rising up on hands and knees so he could enter her from behind.

He felt his control slipping, passion driving him to a frenzy, rubbing her between the mounds of her buttocks with his penis, her body undulating as she moaned, his hands on her dangling breasts, his body ready to burst its boundaries of flesh and bone.

He felt something familiar rush up inside him, part of him wanting to stop it, the other willing it to happen, and he felt his body change, enlarge. Turn rough. His hands curling.

And then he entered her, through soft flesh into warm wetness. She cried out, almost looked back, but he held the back of her head with one clawed hand and pumped, back and forth, keeping her head from turning and seeing the mirror on the inside part of the door where he viewed himself and the beast, now one creature, one being, surely not a hallucination this time. This was his true self breaking through, what he feared had been inside him all his life, since the death of his parents and the nightmares of his childhood. The beast. But he didn't want Louise to see, so he held her in place, making love much more violently than he thought he was capable, working inside her, back and forth, resisting the urge to cry out in an animal howl.

As she cried out in her orgasm, she pulled away unintentionally and his own orgasm sprayed forth, splashing her buttocks and back. He collapsed almost on top of her, then into her arms, where, before falling asleep, he saw in the mirror that, just as quickly as it had appeared, the beast was gone.

But Blake knew the truth now, and he did not question it. The beast, brought to life initially by Kenny Haas's attack, was the reality, and everything in his life before it was the illusion. The dream.

It would only be later, when he thought back to this night and the sound of her crying softly as they fell asleep, that he would wonder why she had not fought harder to look back at him while he held her in place, had never questioned the rough turn their lovemaking had taken, his violent handling of her. And he would come to realize that, in him, she had been looking for love that was gentle and giving but, instead, only confirmed the truth she'd known all along and had lived with all her life.

About the beast that lived in all men.

"Stan, you up for some dinner?"

Marles looked up to see Frank Torrance standing at his desk. "Thanks, but..." He indicated the work spread out in front of him.

"I could bring you back a sandwich."

He thought about it. "No. I don't think I could eat anything anyway."

Tonight, the entire force was on call. Days off cancelled. Every available cop called in. Extra patrols ready to head out. The ones who killed the Rheman family had skipped a night before invading the Holder family's home. Last night nothing happened. So, the theory was, tonight the four men would strike again. Tonight might be the best chance to get them.

If they hadn't already left town.

Earlier, as the detective in charge of the case, Stan had worked with Captain Guthrie on coordinating patrols, telling them what to look for, what to expect. Now he sat in the special office he'd been given, studying the evidence yet again, looking for anything he might have missed. Later, he would go out himself. He was not comfortable just sitting around waiting.

"Are you worried we're going to miss them?"

"Hmm?" Stan looked up. Torrance was still standing there. "Sorry. Got a lot on my mind."

"Of course. Sure you don't want something to eat?"

Marles reconsidered. "Well, I probably wouldn't turn down a ham sandwich if you brought one back."

Torrance smiled. "Anything on it?"

"Just mustard."

"You got it." Torrance turned to go.

"Frank? You're a member of the church that was vandalized last night, aren't you?"

Torrance turned back. "It's been a while since Martha and the kids and I attended. We're going somewhere else now. You're not working that case too, are you?"

"No. I was just looking for a connection."

"Did you find one?"

"Not really." He paused. "Why'd you leave there, Frank?"

Torrance shrugged, looking uncomfortable. "My wife and I were looking for something else."

"That's all? It didn't have anything to do with the minister?"

Frank thought he caught something in his co-worker's eyes. "I like Reverend Hardesty," he said. "He's a good man. Martha... just wanted..." He hesitated. "He certainly didn't deserve..."

"What?" Marles asked quietly.

"The things that have happened to him."

"Did you know his wife?"

"Barbara? I knew her pretty well." Frank smiled. "Everybody in the congregation loved Barbara. She had a kind word for everybody. She was a good minister's spouse, a good partner for him. It was terrible what happened to her."

Marles said nothing.

"I was with him when he identified her," Torrance continued after a moment. "They thought it might help, me being a member of his church and all. It was the worst thing I've ever had to do. The look on his face... If I ever had to identify Martha like that..." He hesitated, dropping his gaze to the floor. "I considered leaving the police force after that."

"You left his church instead."

Torrance looked up sharply. "What do you mean by that? It wasn't because..." Again, he hesitated.

"I'm sorry," Marles said. "I shouldn't have said that." He

meant it. Stan liked Frank Torrance. He thought he was a decent man who worked hard to hold on to his decency in a profession where that was hard to do. "He's been helping me with this case," Marles continued. "His church isn't far from where the first victims lived, and I thought the opinion of a minister might give me some perspective. After I started talking to him, though, this thing happened to his church. I thought maybe there was... Actually, I'm not sure what I thought."

Torrance sat on the edge of Marles' desk. "I don't consider myself the superstitious type, Stan, but ... do you know what a jonah is?"

"Somebody who seems to bring trouble on himself," Stan responded, "and by association, on others close to him. I've known a couple cops who've gotten that reputation. They have a tough time getting anyone to partner with them."

"Did you know Blake's parents died in a fire when he was a kid? An aunt raised him. Then his wife gets killed in that bank job last year. Then there's what happened to Margaret Haas and her son while he was serving her church. Now with what's happened to the church sanctuary itself... You've got to admit, it's spooky—"

"That's not fair, Frank," Stan interrupted, sharper than he intended.

"I didn't say it was," Torrance muttered. "It's an observation, that's all." He took a deep breath. "Look, if it was up to me, I wouldn't have left. Martha insisted..." He stopped again.

The two men sat with an uncomfortable silence between them while outside the office the station hummed with activity, extra uniformed officers on their way out to patrol.

"I'd better get going," Torrance finally said, "before it's time for me to be back." He rose. "I can't say I envy you this case, Stan. But anything I can do..." He let the offer dangle as he turned and left the room.

Marles returned to the information laid out in front of him. His case reduced to lurid photographs and police reports.

As ugly as the destruction of two families had been, the two crimes had a kind of symmetry to them, made a kind of sense. He'd always been a fast reader, so he'd perused a few books on cannibalism, some of the theories behind the practice, looking for cases of it in recent history. Not that these guys were into it for anything other than the thrill of the violence.

And yet he wondered.

His gaze found the photograph of Clara Holder impaled crucifixion-style on the wall of the living room. Her body cruelly mutilated. Was the religious symbolism meant to portray a message?

Why had he thought there might be a connection between the vandalism at Blake Hardesty's church and these crimes? Maybe if they'd found the same fingerprints as were found at the second household. But such had not been the case.

There were fingerprints, of course. In a public place such as a church there were plenty. But the fingerprints found on the handles of the knives used to impale the corpse of the dog onto the cross were those of Reverend Blake Hardesty, who'd had himself printed over twelve years ago along with his wife and child as part of the creation of a national database used for missing children.

The knives had come from the church kitchen, though, so it made perfect sense his prints could be on them. But the placement of the prints, a thumbprint in particular, suggested a possible stabbing motion. One could certainly leave prints like that when impaling a dead dog's carcass to a cross.

But, really, the placement of the prints was not conclusive.

There was the semen, of course. DNA tests could reveal something, but it would take a while to get the results and would only be effective if the person was in a database somewhere. Fleetingly, Stan wondered what the chances were that Blake Hardesty's DNA was in a database. Then, feeling guilty, he pushed the thought away.

There had been one more thing found at the scene in the church, something admittedly strange. Animal hair throughout the sanctuary. Some of it could be from the dead dog. But some of it—most of it—had come from a different, larger animal.

Stan liked Blake Hardesty. Thought he was someone he could become friends with.

But Stan was a police detective who had to do his job, follow the evidence. So, quietly, he'd looked more deeply into the minister's past. Had already found the tragic history Frank had talked about. It was a lot for anybody to handle.

Marles had also found the recent report on the missing Bethany Hardesty, the man's daughter. They'd had an argument and she'd run off. So, he was having difficulty with her. That meant nothing. What parent didn't have problems with their teenage children? It came with the territory. The fact she'd lost her mother just a year ago in a particularly tragic way made things even more difficult. Still, she'd probably show up on her father's doorstep tonight, not interested in another evening out on the street.

And yet he kept wondering what the pressure of so many tragic events over the years might do to a man. Who was it in the Bible? Job, who had so many terrible things happen to him and his family. And yet he had continued to love God, to have faith in him. In reality, could a normal man—a minister even— continue to have such faith without finally striking back?

Detective Marles sighed. He should be bringing this to Captain Guthrie's attention. But he didn't want to, not yet. Besides, finding the murderers of two families had a much higher priority than the vandalism of a church, even vandalism as grotesque as this had been. Especially tonight, with every police officer on the lookout for those murderers.

So, he had time. Time to talk to Blake first. He hoped he'd get the chance tonight, even with everything that was going on. Maybe later, while he was out patrolling the streets, he'd get a chance to stop by the minister's house. Just for a chat.

CHAPTER FOURTEEN

Scott daydreamed of fresh, hot blood running down the sides of a protruding snout bearing massive, powerful jaws that ripped and tore. His body tall, strong, and bristling. His senses acute, aware. One step closer to God, the Father of the Burning Cigarette.

He was the man-beast. The misunderstood child.

He had learned much from the librarian, the woman housing many secrets and smoldering passions beneath her brittle cage of meat and bone. Her knowledge about the werewolf, also known as the lycanthrope. The perfect marriage of man and beast. Its only weakness, silver and fire. So much of the truth hidden in legend and myth. These once great creatures emasculated. Relegated to fiction in books and movies, and in stories told to scare children. Humankind's arrogance never so apparent as when they declared themselves the only beings created in God's image. The librarian, who was now as much a part of him as his other victims, had done extensive research and believed that these beautiful beings had once roamed the earth freely. Back when human and animal co-existed in a symbiotic relationship. When humankind had understood its role in nature. When the eating of animal flesh had been something holy and nothing had been wasted. The werewolf was natural, accepted. Lycanthropy was not a disease, but something special. Part of a species born with the unique ability to live the life of both animal and human.

But humankind changed. It gradually lost touch with the part of nature that had spawned these beings. And placed God outside of nature instead of keeping Him within, where He lived in all creatures, human and animal.

And werewolf.

Over time, humans began to see their animal side as evil. The killing of animals was no longer considered holy. And no being suffered more than the lycanthrope. They became symbols of ultimate evil. Hell's spawn. Humankind's enemy. Making it easier to persecute them and slaughter them. Those that escaped hid, spawned, and fought to keep the race going. Future generations learned to live among humans, letting their animal sides out only when the moon was full and the desire for release was at its strongest and could not be denied. Still, many were found and killed.

But, though smaller in number, the lycanthrope still lived. And Scott had seen one of them, he was sure of it. As sure as he was of the accuracy of this new information gained from the librarian. He had to find him. He had no choice; he would not be satisfied until he had located the man-beast and learned from him.

Become one with him.

He came out of his trance hungry, with Bluejay preaching. "We are stronger than they are," he was saying, Bobby and Jimbo giving him their rapt attention. "Remember, it is all out there for the taking. It's our final night here, let's make it a good one."

"Enough talk, let's go," Draven said, the hunger inside driving him as he moved. Past his leader and the other two, to the exit leading out to the alley and the street where night waited. He turned back in the doorway when the others didn't follow and saw Bluejay watching him with hooded eyes while the other two stared, eyes darting back and forth, very much aware of the tension that had been building between these two the last couple of days.

"We go when I say we go," Bluejay said slowly, deliberately. Mouth curled. Features distorted. Draven saw himself reaching out, cutting the flesh just above the bastard's eyes, then ripping the skin down, peeling that ugly face off the bone like the skin off an orange. He took a step forward. The hunger and desire inside him so great he almost trembled.

But he shouldn't do it. Not yet. Not ... yet. He needed these three for one more night. Just one more night. He could wait that long.

Scott backed down, nodded, keeping his expression nondescript.

Don't let them see what's going on inside.

"We stay together," Bluejay said. "No more going off alone." That last directed at Scott. Re-establishing authority.

"How are we going to know when we've found the right place?" Bobby said, scratching his balls, anxious for the tension to end.

"We'll know." Bluejay kept staring at Scott. "Any problems?"

"No," Draven said. Allowing himself a slight smile. "I'm just hungry."

"Good." Bluejay seemed satisfied. "Let's go. We have work to do. Blood work."

Bluejay made a show of leading them out into the darkness. Head up. Grooving on the power rush.

Stupid fucking asshole, Scott thought. But he said nothing, only listened for the sounds of heartbeats pumping blood through cages of flesh that drew Scott ever deeper into the darkness.

Blake dreamed he was running. The beast of his nightmare, its face still in shadow, ran by his side, the angel riding its back, shrieking into the air. His senses were alive and tingling. Muscles working. He was aware of a world full of tastes and smells. Of hearts pumping through fragile armors of flesh and bone. Easy to break, pleasant to feel the meat grinding between razor teeth. God's brutal power working through him, His righteous rage pulsating inside his body. Driving him. *Father, into Your hands, I commend my spirit.*

He awoke suddenly, bathed in sweat. Thinking he heard the phone ringing, he picked up the receiver, only to hear the dull sound of the dial tone.

Returning the phone to its cradle, he lay back and heard the clock ticking from across the room. Oh, Lord, he prayed, please help me to hang on. Until my daughter gets back. Then I'll place myself into Your arms. I'll do whatever You ask of me. With whatever time I have left.

The telltale odors of stale cigarettes, sweat and lovemaking made him sit up. Had Louise left? How many hours ago? Was

she ashamed? Or was she downstairs, making coffee, perhaps?
What time was it? He looked at the clock. It was late evening.

He rose, threw on a bathrobe. Went downstairs. The first
sound he heard as he entered the living room was the ticking
of another clock. Reminding him. Precious time wasting away.
Where was his daughter? Why had he let so many opportunities
pass him by? Did he dare ask God for a second chance? Checking
the entire downstairs, he confirmed that Louise was gone.

What was she thinking now? Dare he call her?

The phone rang.

"Hello?"

This time there was a response at the other end. "Reverend
Blake Hardesty?" the gruff voice said. "Officer Navarro at the
Latham police station. We have your daughter here."

"Thank God. Is she—?"

"She showed up at the 4th Street Shelter. One of the workers
there recognized her from our APB. You wanna come pick her
up?"

Not a hint of anything in his voice. Oh, and by the way,
Reverend, she had something very interesting to tell me.

"Reverend? You there?"

"Yes. I'm coming right now."

He replaced the receiver and hurried outside without even
bothering to lock the door. The darkness seemed to engulf him
as he got into his car and drove off.

The silent house seemed empty, though a couple of lights were
on. The four men crouched in silence across the street, facing
the back door, Bobby and Jimbo watching Bluejay for a sign.
Waiting for a signal for the fun to begin.

But first they needed to make sure the house was truly
empty. It was best to break in while the family was out and
surprise them when they returned. Welcome to hell, fuckers.

Not that Scott gave a rat's ass about theatrics. For all he
cared, they could bust down the door and kill them right off; he
saw no need to draw it out. Not when there was a feast waiting
to be had.

Finally, Bluejay rose. "Let's go."

The other two stood, but Scott hesitated, not knowing why. His senses were buzzing. Trying to tell him something.

"What is it?" Bluejay asked, obviously annoyed.

"I don't know. Something." Or maybe nothing. A premonition, perhaps, but of upcoming events good or bad he couldn't say.

"Well, you coming or not?" He heard fear behind the anger in Bluejay's voice. Fear of losing control.

Draven finally nodded. There was no satisfactory way he could explain what he was feeling. To them or to himself.

"Then come on."

They moved across the street and into the back yard.

The low chatter of the police radio kept Stan Marles company as he drove through the neighborhood. Few cars passed him. The city had closed up for the night. Shored up its walls against possible invaders.

Marles hoped the four men they were after had already left town. That they'd shot their wads here and decided to find excitement in some other city.

He passed Blake Hardesty's house. Empty. The car gone. He knew why. He had asked each of the police stations in the area to notify him if one of them ended up with the man's daughter in custody and the Latham station had done so just before he hit the road. After Blake returned, Marles hoped to be able to talk to him. He didn't want to wait until morning if he could help it. With what was going on tonight, Captain Guthrie wouldn't have had time to take a look at the evidence the detectives on the church vandalism case had collected so far. But by morning, things could be different.

He liked Blake Hardesty a lot. But it was clear to Stan that the man's suffering ran deep. He hated the suspicions he was having and wanted to grant the man the dignity of a one-on-one with the detective before doing anything else.

Perhaps he would hear something from the minister that would waylay his suspicions. Maybe he could come back in an hour, talk to him then. Especially if nothing was happening.

As if on cue, the radio came to life.

"Stan, it's Guthrie. Come in."

He brought the microphone to his mouth. "Yes, Captain."

"A woman just called the station. Says she saw what looked like some men running through the back lawn of one of her neighbors."

The detective's heart started to race. "Where?"

Guthrie gave him the address.

"That's only three blocks from the Rheman house."

"She thinks she saw three or four of them."

"This could be it, Captain."

"Then get your ass over there. The call's already going out."

He had already started a U-turn as the sound of his siren blaring sliced through the night.

No police had arrived on the scene yet. The night was quiet, with no indication of anything going on inside the house.

Then a gunshot shattered the silence.

Turning the corner two minutes later, Marles saw the flashing lights of the police cruisers arriving just ahead of him.

"We missed them. Damn it, we just missed them."

The captain was so pissed Marles thought he might take the gun confiscated from the man who'd used it and shove it up his ass.

A body lay on the floor, a bullet having obliterated the face. "We'll get the rest of them," a uniformed cop said. "They can't have gotten far."

"Let hope they haven't," Guthrie said. "I want every cop we've got pounding this neighborhood. The rest of the city can go to shit tonight for all I care. I want these bastards. I want them! And I want the permit checked on that jerkoff's gun," he said. "If there's anything, anything wrong with it, I want the guy who used it ripped a new asshole. Damn it, we missed them by two minutes. Two minutes!"

"It wasn't them," Stan said quietly, and Guthrie stopped his ranting to look at him.

"How the fuck do you know that?"

"The guy said he saw two of them. We know there are four."

"The woman who called it in said she saw three or four."

"She miscounted or counted shadows. It's dark."

"Maybe the other two decided to take the night off. Maybe the homeowner was too busy playing Lone Ranger to notice the other three running out the door!"

"It doesn't fit," Stan said. "The guys we want are sloppy in a lot of ways, but in other ways they're careful. Too careful to be caught with their pants down like this." He pointed at the dead body. "This guy was just a burglar. He's not one of them."

"How the hell can you be so sure? The body doesn't even have a face."

"He's not one of them, Captain. It's all I can say."

"Well, go say it somewhere else!"

Stan moved away from him, lost in thought. After a moment, Frank Torrance came up behind him. "I just got here. What happened?"

"The homeowner comes home with his wife and is told by a neighbor before going in the house that she saw some men running through his back yard, that they might be inside. The homeowner decides not to wait for the police and marches in firing. Had the piece right on him. And a carry permit. You can see the results." He indicated the faceless corpse.

"From such occurrences are heroes made," Torrance said.

Marles gave him a sour expression. "I don't think it was them. The neighbor said she saw three or four men, but it looks like there were only two, the other one ran off. The one he shot was looking in jars like he was searching for money. There were drawers and cabinets opened. One thing about the other two attacks, no money was stolen from either house. That was not what they were interested in. So why would they start looking now?"

"You said they may be about to leave town. Maybe they need money."

"Maybe. But it doesn't feel right."

Stan crossed to the window. The darkness was lit up as bright as day. The other guy probably was far away by now. Or guys. Maybe he was wrong. Maybe it had been them, and now,

after what had happened here, the other three would just get
out of town.

"What are you going to do?" Frank asked.

"I'm going to drive around the neighborhood. See what I
can see."

"You want company?"

"No thanks."

Torrance started to say something else but seemed to think
better of it and closed his mouth.

Blake had chosen the long way home from the Latham Police
Department, avoiding Route 22, sticking to the back roads.
Giving him and Bethany extra time to talk. But he'd been
unable to find the words to break through the silence between
them. His daughter sat on the passenger side, pressed against
the door, arms crossed. Brow furrowed. Staring through the
passenger window, not acknowledging his sideways glances.
Wearing a jacket one of the officers at the station had given
her. The bruise Blake had seen on her face when she'd gotten
home last night was still very apparent, and he still didn't know
where it had come from.

He'd kept expecting one of the policemen to say something.
Before we let you take her, Reverend, your daughter told us
a very disturbing story. Or, at least, comment on the bruise.
But apparently, she had said nothing. Perhaps the beefed-up
patrols because of the recent murders in Allenside had left
them short-handed at the station, which was why they'd been
so perfunctory with him. A female officer, who had talked
briefly with Bethany before he'd arrived, gave him a card and
said, "Have you thought about counseling for your daughter,
Reverend? This place specializes in runaways." He'd thanked
her and took the card. "Give her a good spanking" one of
the male cops had whispered in his ear as they were leaving.
"They're never too old for it."

Bethany, the entire time, said nothing.

Now they had covered three-quarters of the distance home
and still he had said nothing to her. What the hell was he scared
of? That if he explained what he was feeling, she'd think he was

going mad? Maybe he was, in which case she had the right to know the reason he was putting himself away. To protect her. Could he even begin to explain what was happening to him?

"Bethany..." he said and was surprised at how quickly she looked at him. Eyes moist from tears, how had he not noticed she'd been crying? Barbara's eyes... No, he mustn't think that. This was his daughter. This was Bethany. Why did we cheapen our children's lives by looking so hard for signs of ourselves in them, while blind to the things that make them unique? Made in God's image, but also made in an image distinctly their own.

It was his responsibility to accept the truth. His wife was dead. But his daughter was alive and needed him.

Once she had worshiped him, had ridden up and down on his knee.

Ride me, Daddy, ride me!

But those days were gone.

He suddenly pulled the car over to the curb, only a block away from their home. He didn't notice the police lights off in the distance, several blocks away.

He turned to her. Saw her looking at him now with, what, fear in her eyes? Oh, no, please, God, don't let her be afraid of me.

"I'm ... sorry," he started painfully, haltingly. "For being ... such a bad father. For not understanding your pain was as great as mine. For letting my rage and sorrow get to the point where ... last night ... happened. There is no excuse for what I did. You've done nothing ... absolutely nothing wrong.

"It's my fault. There's something wrong with me, Bethany, and I don't know what it is. You saw what happened to me in church this past Sunday. Ever since I was in the hospital it seems... But I'm beginning to think maybe it goes back even further. But whenever it started, I want you to know that it stops now. Right here. I haven't got time..." And he almost told her right then about the cancer, about the ticking of the clock reminding him whenever he entered a room. But how could he tell her, so soon after her mother's death? And yet, she deserved to know.

But not now. Not at this moment, with so much to make up for.

"Life is too short, too important," he continued. "You are too important. And I want you to know I will do anything … anything … to make things better. I'm going to get myself help. Even if it means going away for a while … having myself put away so I can't hurt you … until I can understand why … until I stop—"

The sound of his daughter's cry stopped him cold. "No!" she shouted, fumbling for the car door handle and yanking the door open. "Nonono!" she continued, as she fell out, regained her footing, her father so shocked he didn't move right away, as she shouted yet again, "No!" as if begging the night to intervene.

Finally, he acted, sliding across the seat to exit on Bethany's side, standing and facing her now as he pleaded, "What? What is it?"

"Why do you have to leave?" Tears streaked her face. "Why does everyone leave me?"

"Oh, Bethany…" He went to her.

"No," she said, backing away. "Don't touch me. I don't want be touched."

"All right." He retreated a step, his heart heavy and full of recrimination. "Let's go inside the house. Come on. We'll leave the car here. It's close enough."

"I'm scared, Dad. Why did Mom leave me?"

Now he was crying too. "She didn't leave you, Bethany. It was a … she just shouldn't have been in there."

"Why did those men kill her?"

"I don't know, I don't know."

"Why does God allow it? Why does He hate me so much?"

Her words stopped him, and he could only stare at this child crying in front of him, a part of himself and Barbara joined together out of love to create this unique and beautiful individual. Beautiful even in her pain. Crying out for guidance as she tried to define her place in the world.

While he had spent the majority of her young life ignoring her out of his own insecurity and inability to show how much he truly loved her.

"God doesn't hate you," he whispered. "It's me He hates. Not you. Me." The truth of what he was saying suddenly made sense. What had he done to anger Him so? He'd spent his whole life feeling like he had to make up for something he'd done while never knowing what it was. Too afraid to go deep inside himself, where the beast resided. Afraid to risk and lose the ones he loved.

And yet he had lost them anyway. Barbara for sure. And now, maybe, his daughter.

If ever he was going to do something about it, it had to be now. This minute.

"Let's go inside the house," he said again. "We can talk some more." He began to walk, then turned when she didn't come with him.

"Dad, I miss her," she said quietly, her voice ragged. "I miss her so much."

"Oh, Bethany," he cried, the tears blurring his vision. "I miss her too. I miss her too."

"Don't you think I know that?" she replied, moving toward him. "Don't you think I see the pain you're in? Holding it all back for my sake? I don't need you to hold it in, don't you see? I need you, Dad. I need you! Please don't leave me!" And then, suddenly, she was in his arms, both of them crying. And it was all right, this was all right, father and daughter sharing their pain, coming together in the way they should. Arm in arm now as they turned and walked toward the house. "I will never leave you," he said. "I'm going to be the father I should have been. I promise. This is our chance to start over. You and me." He told her this while resolving to himself that he would somehow beat the cancer. He would take the chemo and look for other ways—prayer, love, anything—to give him more time.

Now that he had something to live for.

He thought he saw her nod in response to what he'd said, and, silently, he thanked God for this second chance and promised Him that he would never make the same mistakes again.

Later, he would wonder if his words of thanks had given the Old Guy a good laugh.

He noticed the police lights off in the distance for the first time but decided not to comment. Leaning her head against his shoulder, Bethany didn't see them. He could always find out what was going on tomorrow. Maybe give Stan Marles a call.

Once inside, the first thing he noticed was not that the lights were off, though he had left some of them on when he ran out earlier, but the lack of sound. No telltale ticking of the clock, which he found lying smashed and broken on the floor. He also noticed what seemed like other things broken and scattered around the living room. He felt Bethany raise her head, and as he reached for a wall switch, a single light from a lamp came on across the room, revealing a figure with long black hair and a rough-hewn face standing in the soft glow. "Well, well," the figure said, smiling. "Look at what we have here."

More movement caused him to turn, not in time to stop the front door from being closed and blocked by two men, one with a gut hanging below his belt, the other skinny, lanky, bearing a pockmarked face as he giggled, showing broken teeth.

A fourth man, huge, stood by the fireplace, silent, staring at them from tiny eyes in a face with no expression, scaring him more than the other three combined.

"What...?" He faltered. "What do you want?" Noticing the way they were staring at his daughter.

"We've been waiting for you." The man who seemed to be the group's leader nodded, and someone clubbed Blake from behind, sending him to his knees. He did not pass out right away, aware of Bethany's cry and someone shouting, "Shut up!"

Then she began screaming, and he could do nothing as he fought against the encroaching darkness moving in around him. Helpless. Always so damn helpless.

The last thing he heard was the long-haired man's declaration, "Get her ready," and then even his daughter's screaming was not enough to keep him from passing out. The darkness, his friend before, was now his enemy, as it took him away once again.

CHAPTER FIFTEEN

Draven ignored his companions while they prepared the girl. Ignored the sounds of male laughter, taunts, furniture being moved, clothes ripping, muffled pleas ignored. She was too young; her life lacked the experience and knowledge he needed. She had nothing to contribute to his metamorphosis. Let them do with her what they wanted.

The man on the floor, though—the girl's father—was a different matter.

As Bobby and Jimbo held the girl, he and Bluejay had stripped the unconscious man to his underwear then tied him up with his hands tight behind his back. He was still unconscious as Scott watched him, holding the book he'd discovered earlier when checking the place out.

A Bible.

With the owner's name printed inside. Reverend Blake Hardesty.

This man. A confirmed man of God.

The thought excited him, though he showed nothing on the outside.

If communing on a college professor could make Scott smarter, on an athlete make him stronger, faster, then could a minister bring him into direct communion with the Almighty?

Draven ached to know. For that was what this was: a communion. Whether the other three assholes understood it or not.

It would be so easy to take the preacher now. While the other three were busy. But he could not afford to piss Bluejay off. Not yet.

So, he waited. But when the time came for him to partake of his own special communion, he knew from whom would come his bread and wine.

And nobody, especially his companions, had better stand in his way.

Still ignoring what was going on in the other part of the room, Scott knelt and stroked the man's chest, stomach, and legs, imagining he could feel with his fingers what waited for him beneath this cage of flesh and bone.

Scott felt the body start to move. "He's waking up," he said, rising to his feet.

"Great. She's ready," he heard Bluejay say, and the four men waited for the minister to open his eyes, the evening's events about to begin.

Driving for nearly an hour, Marles had not seen any further signs of trouble. No telltale light in a house that seemed out of place. No strange shadows. Nothing to indicate that violence was about to occur. The two nights the Rheman and Holder families had met their fates not a single neighbor or passerby claimed to have heard anything. The thought that people could insulate themselves so completely disturbed the detective.

Barring knocking on every door he passed, he didn't know what else he could do. He still wanted to stop by Reverend Hardesty's place and confront him with his findings. Hoped that a conversation with the man would quell the detective's growing suspicions. But as late as it was now, perhaps it would be best to put it off until tomorrow.

Or would it? Blake Hardesty did not seem the type of man to chase somebody away no matter what the hour if that person was in need.

Even if the questions were: Why does the placement of the fingerprints on the knife suggest you might have been the one who stabbed the carcass to the cross at your church? or: Why did one of the cops at the Latham police station tell me there was a bruise on your daughter's face when you picked her up, even though his associates chose not to address it?

But he couldn't give up the search just yet. He'd do one more run through the area, then he would see what time it was and make his decision whether or not to see Blake Hardesty.

For the third time in the past forty-eight hours, Blake found himself in Hell. And he knew in that moment of pure terror, unable to move from the ropes holding him in place as he sat on the floor, that God had truly abandoned him.

One of the men, with long, greasy hair and a death's-head grin, moved to the side, extending his arm like an emcee introducing the guest for the evening. Revealing his daughter Bethany.

Oh God, Blake's mind screamed. Oh God!

Wearing only her underwear, Bethany was tied to a table that the men had leaned against the far wall, so she was three-quarters upright and able to see her father. Her eyes were wide with panic, her breathing coming in short quick bursts. Her gaze pleading. Do something, Daddy. Do something!

"Bethany..." he breathed. She seemed unable to speak, as frightened as she was. The long-haired man, who was obviously their leader, crossed to her, producing a knife from his jeans. Hardesty fought against his bonds as he brought the knife toward her, but then the man stopped and turned to face Blake.

The skinny one was standing on the other side of his daughter, giggling. Nearby, the heavier one was rubbing his crotch, his face slack-jawed.

The largest of the four, the huge man with tiny eyes, remained next to Blake and watched the scene without expression.

My God, the minister thought. Why hast Thou forgotten me?

Their long-haired leader, holding the blade upright, stepped forward and opened his mouth, about to speak. "Stop this," Blake pleaded.

The man's eyes blazed at the interruption, the knife coming up. Then he hesitated and closed his eyes, taking in deep breaths. When he opened his eyes again, he faced Blake and told him in a subdued voice, "Don't interrupt me again."

It wasn't enough to silence Blake. "The police are only a few blocks away, I saw them. If you leave now, you'll be able to get away. Whoever you are, in God's name, please—"

The leader crossed the room quickly and struck Hardesty across the face. Lights flashed in front of Blake's eyes as his attacker knelt down and said, "My name is Bluejay, and I asked you nicely before. Now I'm telling you: shut the fuck up! We're in charge! We do what we want; we take what we want. Maybe I'll change my mind and we'll do you first and let your dear little girl watch. How about that, little man?"

"Do whatever you want to me," Blake pleaded, "but spare her."

Bluejay sneered. "Ain't that noble. But no. That's not the plan."

Leaning closer so that his mouth was at Blake's ear, he whispered, "There's nothing you can do about this, Daddy. So, you might as well watch."

Returning to where his daughter lay strung out like a carcass, Bluejay, again, turned around to face Blake, the knife point, again, raised. He seemed more subdued this time as he said, "We are vampires, and it is time to feed. But we take more than blood. We take everything the victim has to offer. Their power becomes our power.

"But your daughter has been chosen for a special meal. It's easy to eat the flesh after the person is dead. But what about while the person still lives? Ingesting the meat when it is most powerful? Keeping her alive until the last morsel is taken. Two nights ago, we tried and failed. We allowed ourselves to lose control. To cut too deep too soon. The victim died before we could finish. But we learned from that experience. And, tonight, we will do better. Tonight, we will not fail."

My God, he's insane! Blake watched Bluejay and the other two move into position around Bethany, who was still staring at her father, her eyes pleading for him to do something, as if he had the power to stop this. The other two had pulled out knives of their own, and Bluejay told them, "The spot we picked to start cutting last time hastened the girl's death before we were ready. So, this time, we'll start with the limbs. The arms, the legs. And don't cut too deep. Slice. Carefully. We want this meal to last."

Bluejay paused, and for an insane moment, it seemed as if he was praying.

But then they began, Blake terrifyingly aware that there was nothing he could do to stop this. No prayer of his own, no call to God to come strike these animals dead. No hope that this might only be a nightmare, fantasy once again meshing with reality.

All he could do was plead with madmen, then scream, matching his daughter's own, as the big man held him in place and forced him to watch.

Scott waited impatiently for the others to finish. The three of them savoring each piece of flesh they placed in their mouth, chewing and swallowing, before cutting again, moving up her body, drawing it out as Bluejay had told them to do. Her screams were annoying, but he showed nothing. He just waited. After a while, thankfully, the girl's cries began to diminish.

Long before that, Scott had stuck a rag in the reverend's mouth to stifle the man's own cries. So that had helped some. But as the meal continued, Scott became bored and turned to watch his prize. Before the minister and his daughter had arrived, he had made it clear to Bluejay that he wasn't interested in the girl. Only the minister, whose heart he felt beating hard in his chest as he held him in place, blood pumping through the man's veins. This man who might be Scott Draven's bridge to God.

He wanted to cut him now. But his job for the moment was to hold the girl's father in place while the others feasted. So, he waited, anticipating the moment when the others would finish, and it would he his turn to feast on his chosen meal.

But it was taking longer than he'd anticipated, and he was getting itchy. The minister had finally passed out, in danger of missing the conclusion Scott knew Bluejay would want the girl's father to witness. He'd considered waking him up but decided if Bluejay wanted him alive to see the end, he could wake the guy himself. Scott certainly didn't care if the minister was awake or unconscious when it was his turn to eat.

More time passed, the girl no longer looking all that human anymore. Was she still breathing? Maybe Bluejay was going to pull this off after all.

By now, Bobby and Jimbo had given up, sitting on the floor looking sweaty and ridiculous as they tried to catch their breath. Only Bluejay remained standing, the bloody knife still in his hand, looking for some place on the carcass he might have missed.

But then he stepped away. "We've done it, gentlemen," Bluejay proclaimed. "She still breathes. Time to end this now. Time to take the last of her power."

Bobby and Jimbo looked like taking one more bite was the last thing they wanted to do. But like two guys who had eaten too much at Thanksgiving dinner, they got up reluctantly from the floor and moved toward what was left of Bethany Hardesty. Bluejay looked at Scott. "Why isn't he awake?" he growled. "I told you to keep him awake."

Draven didn't like the way Bluejay was looking at his prisoner. "He passed out."

Striving forward, Bluejay demanded, "I want him the fuck awake!" and slapped the minister. When nothing happened, he did it again.

Scott was ready to rip the long-haired prick's head off when Scott thought he felt a slight movement, a subtle change in the man's breathing. Bluejay knelt down and said to the minister in a singsong voice, "Wakey, wakey. We're not done yet."

The minister was stirring, and Scott took a firmer hold of him because there was no telling how the man would react when he saw what was left of his daughter. And, though his huge form didn't show it, Scott Draven felt his own heart pound against his chest as the moment he anticipated, the partaking of his own communion, was, finally, close at hand.

Stan Marles had done all he could. Maybe Captain Guthrie was right. Or maybe the four men they were looking for had grown tired of the game and not come out at all.

He felt tired, aching for bed and a few good hours of sleep. He'd stop by the station on the way home. Go see Blake Hardesty first thing tomorrow morning.

No, wait. He was only a few blocks from Blake's house. Why not stop by now? If there were no lights on, if it didn't look like the reverend was awake, he'd return in the morning.

Satisfied with his decision, Detective Stan Marles turned the car and headed in the direction of his new friend's house.

Blake woke to the sight of shadows dancing around him. Forms flitting by. He chose to ignore them. They were dreams, nothing more. He was still seven years old and lying in bed, and Aunt Ruth had just come in to comfort him after his latest nightmare. He felt her behind him, holding him. Soothing him. Closing his eyes, he lay back in her arms. Her gentle, loving touch would wash away the monsters. And, if not, then the angel she had taught him to conjure would protect him.

"Blake?" he heard. "Blake. Look at me." He looked. Saw Barbara standing close by. "Blake, there's something I need to tell you. Something I should have told you. I was planning to the day I died. The reason it took so long for me to get to the bank that day—"

"No, darling, you don't have to explain. I love you."

"There was something I had to do. Something I had to take care of."

"No, Barbara, please, you don't have to say anything. I didn't tell you enough how much I love you. I should've—"

"Listen to me. The reason it took me so long to get to the bank—"

"No! Please don't—"

"I had to tell him it was over."

"I don't want to hear—!"

Ride me, Daddy! Ride me!

All at once, Bethany ran up to him, smiling, and climbed up on his knee. He started moving it up and down. Faster, faster!

"I love you, Bethany. I never should have—"

Don't you dare go out looking like that, you ungrateful bitch!

"I'm sorry, Bethany. I didn't mean it. I didn't—"

Ride me, Daddy! Ride me!

His knee began moving faster, up, down, up, down. Unable to stop. Bethany now gasping, eyes wide, mouth open. Blood pouring from her eyes, her mouth.

"*Bethany!*"

Another voice. Rough. Mocking him. *Bethany...*
Bethany's body spraying blood.

"What the fuck's wrong with him?" Jimbo asked. Draven eyed his three companions warily.

"He's not making a sound," said Bobby. "What, has he gone off the deep end?"

"I'll make him talk," Jimbo said, rearing back to hit Blake. But Scott stopped his arm.

"It doesn't matter," Bluejay said. "He's no good to us now. I thought he would be stronger. We've accomplished what we said we would do. We might as well kill him. Unless..." Bluejay looked at Scott. Draven noted disgust in the bastard's eyes. "...you really want him. Isn't that what you told me? Go ahead, take him. I don't care. This town's starting to bore me. Time to move on."

Wearily, Bluejay turned to Bobby and Jimbo and pointed to what was left of the girl. "Cut her loose. We'll finish her in a minute."

"Sure thing, Bluejay," Bobby said.

Scott missed the look Bluejay gave the two men. His focus was all on the minister. The man's eyes staring straight ahead now. Staring at what? God, perhaps? Draven took out his knife. Wondering where to start. He felt himself trembling as he made the first cut.

The first thing Marles noticed was the reverend's car parked on the street two houses down from his home. Why would he be parked there? A single light seemed to be on in the house. He approached the front door. Stopped. A tired voice in his head said, *Come back tomorrow. Do this in the morning.*

He was about to turn away when he heard a voice from the other side. "Cut her loose. We'll finish her in a minute."

Another voice responded, "Sure thing, Bluejay."

Bluejay. The nickname of one Kenneth Beltmore.

His hand went for his gun, but he hesitated. God knew what was going on in there. If he went charging in blind, he might make things worse. But waiting too long could make it worse, too.

If he wasn't too late already.

He ran back to the car. Radioed for reinforcements. How long before they got here? No more than a few minutes, surely. Maybe he should wait until they arrived.

Scott started with the right arm, slicing one good-sized piece of flesh. The minister grimaced but said nothing. It tasted sweet. Like no other flesh Scott had eaten before. His mouth tingled. The knife did its work again. He took another bite.

"Enjoying yourself?" He had not heard Bluejay move up behind him. Growing ravenous, he swallowed two more pieces then reached with the knife again.

"Hey, don't hog it all. Save some for the rest of us." Annoyed, Scott turned to see Bluejay with his own knife out. Bobby and Jimbo, having cut the girl loose, stood a couple steps behind him. "You said this was mine," Draven said, flinching at the whining he heard in his voice.

"Maybe we should say something first. I saw the Bible. This is a pastor we got here, right? Maybe we should say a prayer." Bluejay's eyes were twinkling. "What do you say, Scotty?"

Draven hesitated, confused for the moment. His senses heady with the taste of the meat. His tongue felt thick as he spoke. "You said ... I could have him..."

He didn't see it coming. Bluejay's hand attacking with the knife, slicing Scott's left cheek. He fell and immediately tried to get back up. But a lamp held anew in the long-haired man's hands came crashing down on Draven's head, and his vision exploded. He fell forward, fighting off the blackness that threatened to engulf him.

"What do you think I am, stupid?" Bluejay hissed into his ear. "You bastard! You never planned to leave with us. Maybe you thought you'd kill me and take over." Scott tried to stand, but couldn't, his senses groggy. "You think you're better than the rest of us? Well, guess what? Tonight, we're gonna have a third sacrifice. Bobby, Jimbo, hold this fucker down!" Scott heard the sound of scuffling, hurrying feet. Felt the pressure of being held to the floor.

Bluejay again. "Time to end this, boys."

Stan Marles found a window with the curtain not quite closed all the way. Able to see only part of the room, he still recognized Kenneth Beltmore—alias Bluejay—from his mug shot, talking into the ear of some big guy who lay on the floor while two others held him down. He recognized those two from their mug shots as well: Robert Henneman and James Gresham. Bluejay rose and crossed to another figure: Blake Hardesty, almost naked, on the floor, tied up and wounded.

Where the hell were the sirens? It couldn't be long now. But then he saw the knife in Bluejay's hand and knew he had no more time. He tried the window. It was unlocked. He inched it up slowly until it stopped; he could only open it partway. The three men didn't react, as focused as they were on Blake. Should he shout a warning? No. Beltmore was poised above Blake, ready to stab him.

In his years of police work, Stan Marles had never shot his gun except at the practice range, and he felt clumsy, the gun unwieldy, as he brought it out and took aim through the partial opening.

His finger wrapped itself around the trigger. "God help me," the atheist out of necessity whispered.

"Mom?"

"Here, my darling." When Bethany looked, she saw her mother above her, reaching down and pulling her up and out of the ruined shell of her body in which she had lost all feeling, her mind shutting down from the pain, the terror. Now free. Now rising up as she peered down at her ruined self on the floor.

"You're safe now," her mother said. "You're safe."

She looked at her father. "Is Dad coming with us?"

"No, not yet."

Bethany knew she should go, but, still, she hesitated. Taking a moment for one last look.

The shadows moved in on Blake Hardesty, and he felt something sharp, cutting, but ignored it as he searched for his daughter who he suddenly couldn't find. "Bethany?"

"Goodbye, Dad." He looked up and saw her peering down at him. Barbara at her side, both looking so beautiful. "Goodbye."

"No, Bethany. Barbara... Please—"

"Goodbye."

"Barbara—!"

And then he couldn't see them. His daughter and wife were gone. Making him feel totally alone. He looked around the room, becoming suddenly aware of his surroundings. The shadows taking shape. Becoming whole. Three men. Two holding him down. The third holding a knife. Ready to use it on Hardesty.

And beyond him … oh my God, was that Bethany? Her body lay raw and red and bloody on the floor.

Bethany. BETHANY!

And all at once, he felt the rough touch of the beast again. The creature with charcoal eyes.

Followed by the pain in his hands. From nails being driven through the flesh. Wet blood pooling there.

And Blake screamed. No, it was more like a roar. He felt something tingling, moving inside him. Itching the skin. Pushing out against the flesh.

Muscles shifting.

Stan Marles stayed his trigger finger because something was happening to Blake Hardesty.

And when the police detective saw what it was, he couldn't help it.

He screamed.

Something had made Bluejay stop talking, had made Bobby and Jimbo let go of him. Although Scott's head still pounded, and his cheek burned, he tried to rise.

At the sound of Fat Jimbo's pitiful cry, Draven sat up and saw the change overtaking the minister.

With a great lifting of his spirit and a desire to cry hallelujah, Scott Draven realized that fate had brought him to the right place.

He'd found what he was looking for.

The change overtook Blake as quickly as it had the two times before. Skin bristling, hair sprouting, muscles thickening, skin falling away. The beast of his nightmare bursting forth, shedding its mask of human flesh. The werewolf, with its legacy of persecution and disdain, came fully alive in him.

Roaring, he lashed out and dug his claws into the large-gutted man's arm, tearing the limb loose; the man's scream cut off as he went into shock, his gaping shoulder jettisoning blood. When Blake saw the behemoth of a man who'd held him prisoner coming toward him, he swung the arm and hit him with it, knocking him backward. Turning, he saw the skinny guy running toward the door and caught him easily, ripping his head off and flinging it against the wall. The body remained on its feet for a moment before toppling to the ground.

His rage spun him around to face the only one remaining.

Bluejay was crouched down behind his daughter's ruined body. With a knife held at her neck.

"You come any closer and I'll cut her fucking throat," Bluejay hissed.

Silence lay heavily between them. The change still feeling clumsy to Blake.

"She's still alive," Bluejay said. "I planned it that way. The tiniest spark maybe, but still there. Can you take the chance? I don't think you're fast enough to stop my hand,"

Blake remained where he was. Unsure. Holding back the full wrath of the beast as hard as he could.

"Change back," Bluejay ordered. "Now. Change back and I won't cut her throat. I'll walk away. You'll never see me again."

"Let me go back, Mom. I can—"

"No, my darling. It's too late. You can't help him."

Silence. He didn't know if he could change back just by willing it, but then, immediately, he felt his body shift, his muscles contract, the hair shrinking back through their follicles, until he was nothing but a man again, panting, sweating, helpless once again before the sight of the knife at his daughter's throat.

The two men held each other's gaze.

Then Bluejay smiled. "Damn fool," he said and plunged the point of the knife straight into her throat.

"NNNOOOO!" Blake screamed as Bluejay pushed her into Hardesty's outstretched arms.

Next came a loud crack. A gunshot. Bluejay turned as Draven ran past him and out the door.

At the sound of approaching police sirens, Bluejay ran from the house as well. From outside came the sound of Marles shouting, "Stop! Police!"

Blake held his daughter.

Police burst in. Eventually, Stan Marles appeared and tried, gently, to pull the minister away. But when he refused to let go, the detective left him alone to hold what was left of his only child, rocking her back and forth and whispering her name again and again.

PART TWO

CHAPTER SIXTEEN

Where was he? All Hardesty saw were shadows. Dancing above and around him. And heard voices talking, though he couldn't make out what they were saying. Then the shadows and voices went away. Leaving only darkness for a while, after which the darkness dissipated, revealing images he recognized. Margaret Haas, with the razor blade in hand, coming toward him. Blood flying from the bullet wound in her back. The same color as the blood pouring out of Barbara on the bank floor. Her body twitching. Life measured in scarlet seconds. The same color as the blood dripping from the mutilated breasts of Mrs. Holder nailed to the wall in a bastardization of crucifixion.

The same color as the blood shed by his daughter for the sins of her father, as he lay bound and helpless.

The images reformed, and from out of the blood stepped the beast of his nightmares, carrying its sacrifice in its massive arms, laying the body down, then kneeling before it.

Only now he saw the body bore the face of his daughter, Bethany. Eyes wide and glazed. The horrors of her death forever emblazoned on her features. Her body raw and ugly. Then her features transformed until he saw the faces of his parents as they would have looked after the fire, nothing but charred and bloody meat. Then Barbara's face, frightened and lonely as she lay dying on a dirty bank floor.

He stared at the face of the beast. Hidden in shadow before, but not now. Now, the beast's face was revealed, and it was his own face. The truth exposed. No compassionate God offered him a light of hope. No benevolent Lord offered him guidance and unconditional love. There was only the beast that had lived inside him all his life. Kevin Haas's bite had awakened it. Now it waited for Blake to release it once again.

Gently, he reached out and touched the creature's ravaged face. Amazed that he had missed the pain there. So much suffering. His suffering. His pain. Why had he not seen it before? Why had he not recognized it for what it was? A child of God. Put here by the Father for His own purposes. Something to be embraced. As he did now, feeling its strength become his until Blake Hardesty, the beast, and the angel were all one. Now it was only a question of what to do next.

The shadows returned, moving above him.

He waited.

"Blake," Louise called out softly through the pane of glass. Then again, "Blake," as if just calling his name would draw him out of his comatose state.

He lay bandaged and still in the hospital bed, with his eyes half-open. His soul, perhaps, trapped somewhere between living and dying. She had already decided she would stay with him, even if he remained this way a long time. She'd remain with him and care for his daily needs. She wished she could take him away from here now to a place where she could shelter him, and with nothing but simple love, bring him back to the world of the living.

Louise had received the call after midnight, just as she was getting into bed. She'd run the few blocks from her apartment to Allenside Hospital, not caring about the hour or her safety. She had made love to this man mere hours earlier, yet found him silent and unmoving when she arrived. And nothing much had changed since then. Man reduced to still form.

Lost in a world of horror only he could see.

Why hadn't she waited for Blake to wake up, instead of letting fear and recrimination send her away while he still slept? She'd had sex with many men and women following her husband's death, and she'd remained next to them in the morning, even though they'd offered nothing more than the heat of a warm body.

But she'd woken up next to Blake aware, all at once, that her deepest fantasy had been granted. He was hers if she wanted.

The love she had always sought, had always told herself could never be. All she had to do was give herself over to it. Not just bare her body but lay bare her soul for someone else to see, to judge. To say, Yes, I love you just the way you are.

But, instead, she'd run. Like a coward. Leaving him to wake up alone. After telling him she loved him. As much a selfish bastard as any of the men she'd known.

Now she couldn't help but wonder if her staying would have broken the chain of events leading up to what happened tonight, giving fate the chance to take a different turn.

At the sound of footsteps, she turned and saw the cop who'd called her walking up to the window. Marles, that was his name. Stan Marles. He walked over to her and asked in a quiet voice, "Anything?"

"No," she answered. "He's still the same." They continued to stare through the window. "Thank you for calling me."

"I didn't know who else to call."

Silence. Then, Louise asked, "The men who did this…?"

"Two of them are dead. The other two got away."

"Did … Blake kill them?"

She sensed him hesitating. "I'm not sure."

"I thought you were there—"

"I got there late. Too late. We have APBs out. Unfortunately, we still don't have a name for one of them, but at least we have a description. Every cop in the area is looking."

"Do you think you'll catch them?"

When he didn't answer, she didn't question. They were only words anyway, something to pass the time while they waited.

"How can one man, one good man, bear so much tragedy?" she heard Marles say.

Surprised, she turned and saw the pain in his eyes. And knew right away this was more than just a case to him. When had these two men become friends?

After a moment, Louise asked, "Are you familiar with the Bible, Detective?"

Stan cleared his throat. "I used to be."

"Do you know the story of Job?"

"Yes."

"God allowed him to face one tragedy after another. His faith was severely tested. And yet, Job continued to profess his love for the Almighty. Does that make him a great man or a fool?" She paused. "Do you think God likes to play with us like that? See how much we can take before we crack?"

Marles didn't respond, nor did she expect him to. They both turned as the young intern on duty came shambling up to them, looking tired, rushed, and overworked.

"You the wife?" he asked Louise.

The harried doctor pushed on, cutting Louise off before she could answer. "We can't get in touch with his regular doctor, he's out of town. We ran some tests. As far as his physical injuries, he'll recover. But the cancer … it's spread with incredible speed. I'm surprised he wasn't in here earlier complaining about symptoms."

"Cancer…?"

"I've never seen anything like it. I checked the MRI from when he was here before. It was late stage, but even with him refusing the chemo, he had at least a few months before it should have gotten this bad. Chemo wouldn't help him now, I'm afraid. I'm sorry…" He finally stopped when he noticed Louise's expression. "You knew about this, didn't you? You said you were his wife, right?" He looked at Marles. "And you're Detective Torrance, right? You were with him when the doctor first told him?"

"How long does he have?" Stan asked, his voice tight.

"I'm not an oncologist. But the way the cancer is now? A couple of weeks."

Louise couldn't breathe. Her chest constricting.

Was that laughter she heard from somewhere up high? A voice saying, Still have faith in me now, chump?

"I'm sorry," the doctor said, trying to backpedal. "I thought you knew… You said you were his wife, didn't you?" He began backing away. "If there's anything I can do… We're still trying to contact his doctor…"

"I think you've done enough," Stan said in a low, dark monotone.

The doctor straightened, trying to salvage a shred of dignity.

Failing that, he shambled off the same way he had come.

Louise watched the unmoving body. "The son of a bitch kept it to himself," she said quietly.

"Why don't you go home, get some rest," the detective said. "I'll call you—"

"No. How can I leave him now?" Hearing the tears in her voice, but not caring. "I want to be here when he wakes up." If he wakes up, she told herself, then banished the thought.

In her mind, she told Blake, I'll stay. I'll stay and take care of you and feed you and clean you.

And, if necessary, when the time comes, I'll help you die.

The detective said something, which she didn't hear, then left her alone. Tears now streamed down her face, but she didn't try to wipe them away as she continued to stare through the window. Watching for a sign.

But Blake remained soundless and unmoving.

Shadows. Unintelligible voices.

He ignored them. Listening to the new voices growing inside of him.

A few hours later, with the dawn very near, Stan Marles sat drinking his sixth cup of coffee in one of the hospital's small staff rooms. Churches made him nervous, but hospitals made him ill. The smells of medicine, the odor of desperation and helplessness.

He should be at the station house. Captain Guthrie, and now the commissioner, wanted an accounting of what had happened in the Hardesty house. A fifteen-year-old girl had been tortured and murdered. Two of her attackers were also dead, and mutilated. Every police department in the area was on the lookout for Kenneth Beltmore, alias "Bluejay," and the other man of whom they had a description but no name. Marles had managed to hold Guthrie off by convincing him he should wait here at the hospital for Blake Hardesty to wake up so he could question him. But it wouldn't be long before the captain would be calling and screaming for Marles to get the hell back

to his office. Somebody was going to have to take the fall for
this.

Everything indicated that the four men who had invaded
the Hardesty home had intended to do the same thing as in
the previous two households: torture and eat their victims.
Had they forced Blake to watch? My God, how horrible. Had
they known they were breaking into the home of a minister
when they chose this house and started to perform their
unholy communion? He found himself thinking back to his
own experiences with the taking of communion, the look on
his mother's face next to him in church when, as a child, he'd
watched the priest place the Eucharist on her tongue. Then his
mother grasping his hand, holding him in place as the priest
placed the wafer, dry death, on his tongue. His throat closing
when he tried to swallow, while the leering face of his parent,
the judgmental face of the priest, and the all-knowing face of
Jesus in the picture that towered over them all, watched him.

Jesus' face following him wherever he went. Condemning
him.

But what Blake Hardesty had experienced tonight had
been true hell on Earth. In fact, he'd experienced more hell in
his lifetime than God had the right to ask of any man. It made
Stan's own insecurities carried over from childhood seem
stupid and insignificant. His father, a cop too, had been killed
in the line of duty before his son had a chance to know him.
His mother responded by taking all the passion she'd had for
her husband and giving it to the church. To another man, really,
who'd become a symbol after supposedly dying centuries ago
so the rest of us could be saved. Saved from what? What did it
mean? Hadn't his own father done the same?

Were these tears in his eyes now, after all these years? He
wiped them fiercely away, admonishing himself.

Fool. Damn, nervous fool.

He'd become a cop, like his dad. Never any question about
that. His mother crying, saying he'd only be killed too. Don't
do it, come to God. Come to Jesus. She went to God a few years
later. A stomach aneurysm. Her deity had let her die alone on
the floor of her apartment where her landlord discovered her

after her body had started to stink up the place. Her reward for all those years of service to Him. Better to think there was no God rather than accept the idea that He could be so cruel.

Better to believe there was no such thing as magic.

But then along came Blake Hardesty. A man—a minister no less—capable of shaking his convictions. A budding friendship, something he hadn't had in more years than he cared to count. Cut off before it had the chance to flourish. Their relationship reduced now to waiting for the man to die. Or wake up to become a vegetable. If he woke up at all.

Why would so much disaster befall one person? Could God be so cruel to a man who professed to love Him?

Or was it all coincidence? Arbitrary fate. His cop's mind had been trained to look for connections, to not accept coincidence so easily. There were actions and consequences to actions. A connecting chain of events that you could usually find if you looked for it. Blake's parents had been killed in a fire caused by faulty wiring, nothing else. And even if there had been something, Blake was only seven years old at the time and had been spending the night at a friend's house.

His wife had been an unfortunate victim. In the wrong place at the wrong time. Wicked fate at it again.

The incident in Margaret Haas's house had been an act of bravery on Blake's part. From all reports he'd read, the man had done all he could to avert disaster.

The vandalism in the church, coincidence again? More bad luck? Fate once again playing its ugly version of Russian roulette? What about Blake's fingerprints on the knife? Stan didn't want to consider that right now.

Or consider what the cop from the Latham station had said about the bruise on Bethany Hardesty's face. Had there been more to her running away than just teenage angst? Something more than an argument with her father? Perhaps, now, he would never know.

Marles understood that even if he had reacted more quickly, he would not have been able to save Bethany, who was already too far gone. But he'd hesitated. He'd had his gun out, and, still, he'd hesitated. Because something happened. Something that made him freeze for a full minute. And what he'd seen—well, better not to share that with anybody right now.

But that was the real reason he was here, wasn't it, why he was waiting for Blake to wake up? Because if he could talk to Blake, then maybe he could tell himself that what he thought he'd witnessed didn't really happen.

But, deep inside, he knew that wasn't going to work. He couldn't deny what he'd seen, not to himself. So, he took a deep breath, then began taking a good hard look at it in his mind's eye.

What he thought he'd seen was impossible. Because men do not suddenly change their shapes, not in the world Stan Marles lived in, believed in. If he hadn't seen it with his own eyes...

Ah, but that was the thing, he had seen it.

And what he had seen through that window was Reverend Blake Hardesty of Allenside's 7th Street Disciples Church change into a monster. Something between a man and beast. A creature that had torn the arm off one man and the head off another. A creature certainly strong enough to tear a church sanctuary apart.

So, he'd hesitated, not only because—be honest—the idea of using his gun had always frightened him. But, also, because the sight of Blake Hardesty's body changing into that thing had terrified him in a way he'd never been frightened before.

And now, here he was, still hanging out at the hospital, drinking shitty coffee when what he really felt like drinking was several good shots of whiskey. He needed to come to terms with what he'd seen, to find an explanation, rational or otherwise, that he could live with.

He finished off the coffee, feeling coffee grinds on his tongue, which he spit out into the cup.

He exited the room, heading down the hall to where he'd left Louise Calabrese earlier. The love she felt for Hardesty was clear in her actions and words. Stan liked the woman, recognizing an honest person when he saw one. He'd recognized the way they felt for each other when he'd walked in on the two of them in the reverend's office, though he could tell they hadn't acknowledged it to each other yet. Stan had only just met her, yet he sensed she'd be good for Blake.

If tonight's events had not ruined any chance of happiness for them.

He entered from the hall, finding Louise asleep on a chair while the nurse at the desk glanced at him before returning to her work. Blake was the only patient in this area at the moment, and Marles walked over to peer through the window at him again.

Wait a minute. Had Blake moved? It seemed as if his position had changed. Maybe a little. Wasn't that a good sign? Or maybe it was a product of Stan's tired imagination, and the man hadn't moved at all.

As crappy as the coffee was here, he decided to have another cup. He'd bring it back here to wait.

Choosing to turn away at that moment and head back down the hall, Stan Marles missed the sight of the body in the bed moving once again.

The shadows came closer. Pulling at him. The voices, old and new, battled for his soul. Demanded his attention.

Rage boiled up inside him. Images exploded. Barbara and Bethany on the cross. Crucified for his sins. But also crucified because of the sins of others. Our Father, who art in heaven, hallowed be Thy name. Thy kingdom come, Thy will be done...

Thy will.

The shadows ever closer. The cancer growing rapidly inside him. Eating his time away.

He understood it now. The beast served not only as a manifestation of his own pain and anger but of God's as well.

Time to serve Him.

He opened his eyes.

No longer Reverend Blake Hardesty.

Louise realized she was dreaming.

She was back in Blake's bedroom again, offering herself to him, naked and scarred. Again, she reveled in the sight of him as he bared himself for her, took her in his arms, lay her on the bed. Entered her from behind as she had requested, wanting to feel the complete fullness of him. Again, she sensed something, a change, but didn't understand what it was, his hand holding her in place as he thrust inside her, though she did glimpse something in the periphery of her vision before being carried away by the pure animal action of it. His cock swollen and ready to burst, her moving to meet his thrusts, until she felt him slip, pull out unintentionally, his semen spraying her back, her buttocks, her body collapsing.

This time, though, in her dream, she turned, anxious to wrap herself around him.

Was she still dreaming, or had she awakened? What she saw facing her was magnificent. Oh, blessed beast, oh glorious creature. Beautiful, unlike anything she had ever seen. A thing that was part man and part beast, part God, and part earthbound soul. Watching her with eyes she knew intimately. Tender eyes encased in a mask of animal madness. Filled with pain and love so intense she began stroking the thick fur surrounding the face. God, he was so beautiful, it hurt to gaze upon him.

How could I have not understood before? I'm so sorry. Please forgive me.

The scream that came next shattered the air around her, revealing stark hospital walls and a desk across the room.

Where a nurse, with her mouth wide open, her eyes radiating terror, screamed again at the huge beast turning from Louise Calabrese, poised and ready to leap.

The sound of screaming caused Stan Marles to drop his cup of coffee, the hot liquid spreading on the floor.

The scream came again, and Stan started to run, past hospital personnel who were talking excitedly, then turned to follow him.

He arrived to the sound of shattering glass and the sight of a huge form running through the smashed doors at the other end. By the time he reached the doors he saw nothing, but he heard more glass exploding in the distance.

He came back to where chaos reigned. Several people surrounded the panicked nurse whose scream had brought them here. Two security guards appeared a moment later.

Marles saw Louise Calabrese standing at the entrance to Blake's hospital room, her face unreadable, and he crossed to it, already knowing what he would find.

Blake's bed. Empty.

"It was him?" he asked.

"Yes," she responded. Then looked at him. "You knew?"

"I wasn't sure..." He stopped himself. "Yes. I knew."

"We have to find him," she said. "He's all alone."

"He watched his daughter die horribly. There's no telling what he might do."

"It's more than that. Everyone he's ever loved has died. Please help me find him."

"I will," Stan said. "I promise."

They moved back into the main area. One of the big, beefy security guards approached Stan. "We've called the police, but you're a cop, aren't you?"

"No," Stan called back over his shoulder as he guided Louise out into the hall. "I'm not."

Together, they hurried out of the building.

CHAPTER SEVENTEEN

Frank Torrance wasn't sure what kept bringing him back here. He could be in bed right now making slow love to Martha as the dawn came in through his bedroom window. Instead, here he stood in Margaret Haas's room at the state hospital, watching the attendant check the straps on her bed. Big and crude, a guy who probably worked here because he couldn't qualify for a job at Walmart. They had started allowing Margaret Haas certain privileges as a reward for the decrease in her "inappropriate behavior." Letting her feed herself at mealtimes, for example. Or giving her time for one walk a day and a visit to a regular bathroom instead of a bedpan all the time, such as the one the attendant had just finished emptying.

Torrance knew the thought of this woman lying here—even strapped down the way she was—instead of sitting in a jail cell pissed off his boss. The sorry son of a bitch. Who cared if Margaret Haas ever stood trial? If anyone was nuts, it was her.

Still, this was not the kind of place he'd want to spend the remaining days of his life, no matter how crazy he was. Stark, gray walls. Hospital smells that made his stomach churn. Food that looked like somebody crapped in it before running it through a food processor. Attendants that treated you like the lowest kind of creature.

Not that Margaret Haas seemed to care. In previous visits, he'd noticed her talking to herself. Heard her speak her dead son's name as if his ghost was standing in the room with her. Other times she seemed to be speaking aloud to God. And still other times she'd invoked the name of Blake Hardesty. The detective getting a chill whenever he heard the reverend's name. He'd considered trying to find out what she was saying about him. But he felt enough like a peeping tom as it was. His sense of guilt, however, did not stop him from coming back here periodically to check on her. Truth was, he felt compelled to do so, even if he couldn't say what it was that fascinated him so much about her.

Or what the hell it was he was hoping to find.

As soon as the attendant finished and left the room, Margaret began writhing under her blankets. Her eyes glazed, her mouth open as she moaned and mumbled to herself. Frank moved closer, trying to understand what she was saying.

"I love these religious nuts," he heard from behind him. "All that sexual shit going on inside them. I know what I'm talking about. I hear the doctors."

The big goon hadn't left after all. From the doorway, he winked conspiratorially. "What do you think she's imagining? I see you in here a lot, so I'll tell you if you don't tell nobody ... sometimes I don't tighten the straps so much. In case she wants to, you know, play with herself. I figure it's the only thing she's got going for herself, you know?"

"Why don't you shut the hell up!" Torrance hissed.

The attendant abruptly dropped his smile. "Hey, you know I was just kidding." When the detective didn't respond, he turned sullen and muttered, "Shit, you were watching too," before quickly leaving the room.

Leaving the detective to wonder whom the mentally defective really were in this place.

Her movements had stopped. To Torrance, they hadn't seemed sexual. Rather, a kind of intense prayer. Like someone speaking in tongues.

It was time for him to go. Taking a deep breath, he sighed. Rubbed his eyes.

And, therefore, didn't see the figure that suddenly appeared at the window behind him.

The shadows had become real again. One illusion replacing another. His mind was clear now. His first mission was to find the source of the familiar voice calling to him, using his new body with the strength and agility to climb up the side of the building, to the eighth floor. To the window through which he saw two figures he recognized. His glorious reflection superimposed upon them in the glass, peering back at him.

From charcoal eyes.

God's holy spirit had opened her up, allowing her to see a part of His world she had been unaware of until her son's cool, soothing instruction from the other side had shown her the way.

Another chance. Thank God. Praise God. Her work was not yet finished on this earth. The Lord was sending one of His special creatures to help her, and when she opened her eyes, she saw it appear on the other side of the window. God's animal child. Coming for her. Wanting her. Needing her.

Margaret's Haas's shout of hallelujah came mere seconds before the creature lunged.

And the world exploded.

At the sound of Margaret Haas shouting, Frank Torrance's heart leapt into his throat, and he stepped back. When he noticed her staring past him, he turned, and the window shattered, and he threw his arms up just in time to keep glass from hitting his face. From somewhere an alarm sounded.

A huge form sailed past him.

Torrance backed up, feeling glass crack under his shoes. One piece had gotten under his fingernail, the pain intense.

But not as intense as the terror he felt at the sight of the creature rising to its full height at the foot of Margaret Haas's bed.

It seemed more animal than human, yet it stood on two feet, staring at him with a look of human intelligence. Some sort of mutation, a combination of man and wolf. Its body covered with thick hair, its hands animal paws, but bearing extended fingers with the dexterity of a man's, and razor-like claws. It growled, snarled, and Frank knew in that moment that the world, as he had believed it to be, was a lie.

The creature studied him, then, apparently deciding he wasn't a threat, turned to the figure on the bed.

Torrance pulled his gun out of its holster, afraid this thing meant to hurt Margaret.

He pointed and fired.

The shot caught the monster in the back of the shoulder. It howled, turned, and ripped the gun out of Torrance's hand, flinging it through the broken window. Oblivious to the blood flowing from the fresh wound, it reared back and slashed at the detective, knocking him backward as the claws ripped his shirt. The wall at the opposite side of the room stopped Frank's stumbling motion, the back of his head hitting hard enough to make his vision flash white light. But not hard enough to make him black out as, stunned, he watched the creature easily rip the restraints off the bed and lift Margaret Haas in its arms. The look on her face was like a mother's love for her child, as she stroked the thing's face and whispered something Frank couldn't hear. The expression on the monster's face became almost gentle.

A human expression.

The sound of running feet from the hall outside preceded two men who rushed into the room. They almost fell over each other at the sight of their visitor. One of them, the perverse one who'd been there earlier, shouted, "Jesus fucking Christ!"

The wolf-beast howled, and, moving swiftly, shoved the one aide's head against the wall, knocking him out. The one who had spoken to Frank earlier blubbered in fear as the creature wrapped a huge, hairy arm around his head and twisted, the loud crack informing Torrance that the man wouldn't be getting his kicks making room for patients to masturbate anymore.

The thing did all this while still holding Margaret with one arm, and now, cradling her in both arms again, it strode to the window. And, though the room was eight floors up, it leaped through into the outside air.

Torrance closed his eyes against what he had seen as he heard other people shouting, approaching fast. Then somebody screaming.

But even with his eyes closed, he still saw the face of the beast as it had stared at him just a few minutes ago. The two of them peering into each other's eyes.

With Detective Frank Torrance, God help him, now knowing exactly who it was he'd seen residing there.

They ended up in the basement of the 7th Street Disciples Church, a room too damp for proper storage, gone so long without being used that few even remembered it existed. But it was good enough for Margaret Haas and the minister. A place to hide while her new son rested. His body shifting, turning back to its original form, until he lay naked in her arms, and she bathed him after sneaking upstairs to steal a few necessary supplies from the storage closet. After she was finished, she rocked him back and forth, caressing him, comforting him. Whispering her prayers.

Thank you, God, for this second chance. For bringing this lost child to me. In so many ways she had failed her own son, had thought him tainted with the touch of Satan when the beast seized him, allowing him to leave his wheelchair on the nights the werewolf took him over and allowed him to run.

She would not make the same mistake again. When Blake awoke, she would teach him, just as her son had taught her while she lay strapped in the bed at the hospital. She would help the reverend understand his new existence. The power of it. The magic. The wonder of what he could accomplish in the name of our Lord and Savior.

Already begun in the way he had dispatched of that evil, perverse man at the state hospital. Working there under the pretense of helping others, when what he really wanted was to take advantage of them in their moments of weakness.

Her son had done well in choosing this man of God, this individual who had known pain. Just like her son had known pain. Just like Jesus Himself, praise God.

For now, he would sleep in her arms and dream of God's splendor. Safe from those who would persecute him.

There would be time for him to strike back.

Tomorrow night was less than twenty-four hours away.

CHAPTER EIGHTEEN

"So, you got yourself a little werewolf problem, do ya?" the little old man who ran the occult store at the corner of Ninth and London had said, looking a bit like a werewolf himself with his shaggy beard, flashing eyes, and hooked teeth. "Silver and fire are the only things that can stop it. That is, if you're planning to kill it."

"You believe in werewolves?" the detective had asked, incredulous.

"Well, sure. Don't you? That's why you're here, right?"

Louise sat in her darkened apartment now, waiting for Marles to return, thinking back to their conversation in the bearded man's store, two people looking desperately for a place to start in their search for answers. Louise aching to find her lover, wondering where he was, what he was feeling. So much pain and despair in the face she'd seen peering at her as she had awoken from her dream at the hospital. His face hidden within the animal mask.

"I've been known to help a few people with such problems now and then," the old man had stated.

"Wait a minute. You've seen them?"

The man studied Stan a moment before responding. "Well, now, I'm not sure I should be answering that. Let's just say I've had some ... experiences in my life. Enough to know there are more mysteries in God's world than we humans are aware of." He squinted his eyes. "So, what exactly can I do you people for?"

Marles seemed suddenly struck dumb, so Louise stepped forward. "You said silver can hurt them?"

"Sure. Silver bullets, a silver knife, silver anything. Fire, too. Flame is universal. Nothing on God's green Earth is impervious to fire. Silver or fire can do it."

"According to legend, you mean," Stan interjected.

"What do you think legend is," the old man said, "if there isn't at least an ounce of truth to it? The idea of humans changing into some kind of creature appears in many different cultures. The shapeshifter. Lycanthrope. Werewolf. You must believe in it some or you wouldn't be here."

Stan looked away. He'd reluctantly agreed with Louise to start here, and now he seemed embarrassed by the idea. "Does someone ... choose to be a werewolf?" Louise asked.

"Sometimes," the old man nodded. "Sometimes they're just born that way. Wolf-men and wolf-women can have children, too. And sometimes they're forced into it."

"Forced?"

"Bitten by another werewolf. If a werewolf doesn't kill his victim, and the bite is deep enough, the saliva works its way into the bloodstream and turns the one who's been bitten into a creature just like it. Of course, there are others who believe..."

"Yes?"

"Some believe that the werewolf is inherent in all of us. It shows itself in one way or another. It just depends on the person. For some, it's the bite that lets it out. But only letting out what was already there."

"I don't understand how you can believe any of this," Marles said. "How you can stand there talking to us like it's true. It doesn't make any sense."

"Makes no sense to you, maybe. There's nothing that says you gotta believe. Just like some people believe in God and some people don't. It's your choice. Who's to say if you believing in Him makes Him real or not? Maybe He doesn't need your belief at all."

The old man studied Stan a moment. "You're angry. I understand that. The unknown makes most people angry. 'Cause it scares them. You want to believe the lycanthrope's a myth. Maybe it is. Maybe life's a myth. You think if a tree falls, and no one's there to hear it, there's sound?" He chuckled.

"Why do they exist?" Louise said softly. "They must be very lonely creatures."

"Might be," the man said softly. "There was a time when

there were many. Before humans decided they were above them
and started killing them off. That was a long time ago, but they
still do it today, one way or the other. Truth is, there aren't too
many of them anymore. The beast isn't always bad, you know. It
serves a purpose. It was made in God's image, too. If God made
the angels, then didn't He make the beasts? I think we all have
a bit of the beast and the angel in us. Maybe it just depends on
the person which one comes out."

"How do we bring him back?" Louise asked, hearing the
desperation in her voice. "How do we make him human again?"

"I guess that depends on whether he wants to be human
again."

As they left the old man's store, she glanced back into the
room and thought she noticed something. Brief enough to be
considered imagination, but for the glint in the store owner's
eyes. His body seeming to shift. His outer appearance melting
away, revealing ... something. For just an instant. Then returning
to normal. The man smiling at her. Chuckling.

The sound of the detective's knock on the door broke into
her thoughts, and she rose to let him in. He brushed past her,
crossing the room in that nervous way of his to sit in a chair at
the opposite end of the small efficiency.

"How did it go?" she asked Marles, closing the door.

"I'm off the case. The captain's pissed, so he has to blame
someone. At least I was able to get away."

"Are the police looking for Blake?"

"Only as a missing person. The hospital reported him gone
after things died down. I think Guthrie wants to connect him
with what happened there last night, but he doesn't know
how. Right now, officially, they're saying some wild animal got
into the hospital. I'm not privy anymore to what the police are
keeping quiet." He looked at her. "But I do know he showed
up at the state mental hospital last night. Killed one of the
employees."

"My God."

"He also took away one of the patients. Guess who? Margaret
Haas. Haven't heard how they're going to explain that one yet."
He paused, peering off somewhere. "You know, they're not

saying it was Blake. Maybe it's possible it wasn't ... neither one of us actually saw the change this time."

"It was Blake."

"How do you know that? You were asleep. You woke up, saw the thing for maybe a few seconds."

"I saw his eyes." Softly. "It was Blake. How could you think otherwise? After what you witnessed at his house?"

The detective seemed about to say something more, then hesitated, rose, and crossed to the unmade bed in the other half of the small apartment.

"The man at the occult store ... did you believe him?"

"Yes."

"It must have happened at Margaret Haas's house. Kenny Haas bit him. That meant her son was one. But he couldn't have been. He'd been in a wheelchair all his life."

"Why is it so hard for you to believe?"

He looked at her. "The first thing I did while at the hospital waiting for Blake to wake up was try and deny everything I'd seen. Come up with a rational explanation. It's hard enough to accept what those bastards did to his daughter. And then Blake changing into this ... thing ... well, I thought if I worked hard enough at it, I could make myself believe it never happened. I still haven't told Guthrie everything I saw at Blake's house."

"But why do you work so hard to deny it?"

"It goes against everything I've ever believed."

"Well then, change your beliefs," Louise said. "Trust your senses. Know now that there are things alive in this world that you chose not to accept before. Beasts inside all of us.

"You're a cop; you've seen the things people can do to each other. You saw what those men did to poor Bethany. What difference does it make on what side the beast shows itself? We know it exists."

Louise paused briefly. "I killed my husband. Oh, technically, it was his heart. I didn't raise a hand to him despite all the times he did it to me during our marriage. He was hitting me when it happened. He fell to the ground unable to breathe. Reached out to me. The first time he'd done that except when using me as a punching bag in a long time. If I had moved a little faster to make the phone call, the ambulance might have gotten there in time to save him. But I didn't. Instead, I watched him die. And despite the story I told the cops, that he was dead immediately; despite the fact I had almost convinced myself it was true, I know to this day that I understood exactly what I was doing.

"And you know what? The cops on the scene did too, and the paramedics. They suspected the truth, but they didn't say anything because they knew a bad man had died in that room."

Now she looked pointedly at Marles. "And when I'm by myself, when it's just me and God, I know He approves of what I did. Because God knows a bastard when He sees one. He was offering me a choice. I could save my husband and continue to live my life the coward's way, or I could let him die and take control of my life. And if that sounds cold-hearted, I don't fucking care, because I believe it was right. God doesn't have to be all sweetness and goodness. He can be pissed off sometimes."

She picked up a pack of cigarettes from a nearby table, but like earlier, when she'd been waiting for Marles to return, she was unable to light one. Had, in fact, gone without one for several hours now. Maybe when they found Blake, she'd allow herself one again. "But I paid a price for what I did, just the same," she continued, returning the pack to the table. "All that shit I put myself through before I found the 7th Street Disciples Church was penance for what I'd done. Because the world usually requires balance and for actions there are consequences.

"When I found the 7th Street Disciples Church and became its sexton, I knew God had led me there. He was telling me that everything was all right now. I was forgiven, and it was time for me to move on with my life. My life is two things now: that church, even if they do plan to take it away from me, and Blake Hardesty, the most decent man I have ever known."

She looked at Marles again. "So, believe me when I say, I have a vested interest in what we're planning to do. I do believe in magic because I have felt it in my own life. And whatever it is that has happened to Blake, I'm going to do my damnedest to find him and bring him back to himself. If that's what he wants. With or without your help, it doesn't matter. I owe him that much."

In the silence that followed, Louise wondered if she had lost an ally with that speech, and how would she feel if the man walked out the door right now, leaving her to face this alone.

"You love him, don't you?" Marles said.

"Yes," she answered without hesitation.

"I'm glad," he responded gently. Remaining where he was. "I care for him, too.

"I was raised Catholic," he continued. "I don't go to church anymore, though. My dad was a cop; he was killed on the job. I might have accepted it if my mother hadn't turned crazy after his death. She threw everything she had into her religion, into loving Jesus. It became easier for her to love a man killed over two thousand years ago than it was to love her son who was still alive.

"I grew up in guilt. God wasn't someone who loved you. He condemned you. And the priest never said or did anything to tell us different. Going to church every Sunday scared me to death. Every Sunday I had to see Jesus' picture looking down on me, reminding me what an unworthy son I was. How could I ever hope to match up with His son? Once I was older, of course, I understood it was my mother's paranoia and unresolved grief that had turned her into what she'd become. But I could never get past the idea of a God that sat up there, judging us. Allowing terrible things to happen to His children. I became a cop like my dad. And never went to church again. Any church. I convinced myself that I didn't believe in God. But the truth is, I've always believed in Him. It's just that He scares the hell out of me.

"Then I met Blake. Here's this nice guy, a minister, who's experienced so much tragedy and still has faith in God. And I ask myself, if God can put a good man like him through such hell and the man still has faith, then maybe I've missed something all these years. Maybe I should be listening to what this man says. Maybe he can help me and show me what I've been missing.

"Then all this happens. And I wonder if I was right all along."

There it was. Each now an open book to the other. Necessary, perhaps, if they were to embark on this search together, to find and bring back this man who was lover and friend. She responded to the urge to touch him, and did, gently, placing her fingers against his cheek. He nodded. A contract sealed; agreement reached. In the past, she might have taken him to her bed at this moment as she had so often with other men, too willing to ease their pain at the expense of her own.

But not this time.

As if understanding this, Stan Marles pulled her hand away from his face. Smiling for the first time since she'd known him.

"What now?" she asked.

"We plan a course of action. Decide how we're going to go about finding him."

"Why do you think he took Margaret Haas out of the state hospital?"

"Maybe he's confused. Hopes she can help him, explain what's happened to him. Since it was her son who did this to him."

"What if we find him, but bringing him out of it kills him? The progression of the cancer must have been accelerated by his change."

"I know. We'll have to cross that bridge when we come to it."

"I want to help him, Stan."

"I do, too. If there's a way, we'll find it."

The two sat down to plan.

With the darkness only hours away.

CHAPTER NINETEEN

Nighttime.

The old woman exited the grocery store at the Allen Street Shopping Center and headed home toward the senior citizen high-rise just a block away. Carrying a single grocery bag against her chest like a shield, she concentrated on the sidewalk in front of her, careful not to trip on the concrete's many cracks and crevices, hazardous going for someone with fragile legs and bones.

She wasn't aware of the large man, hiding close by, until he pulled her into a space behind the building and broke her neck.

Quickly, Scott fed on leathered flesh, working through it to the soft, wet organs beneath and the bones, sucking out the marrow.

Fifteen minutes later, he was hiding near one of the classroom buildings at the local community college, watching the man walk out the main door, briefcase in hand, toward the parking lot. A professor who had just finished teaching his evening class.

Draven caught up to him just as he was inserting his key in the driver's-side door. Grabbed the back of his head and smashed it face first through the window. Using one of the large shards of glass, he sliced the man's throat, cut deeper, and severed the head.

Dragging the body into some nearby bushes, he finished his repast in five minutes, but for the head, which he saved for last. Using a fist-sized rock to crack open the skull, he scooped the brain out, savored it on his tongue. Then popped out the eyeballs and sucked on them for good measure.

Sated, he did not allow himself to relax until he had reached the rooftop he'd chosen earlier as his lookout point. From here he could see a large part of the city. Alone. Silent. He savored the change he felt taking place inside of him, the metamorphosis. Close, he was getting close. But he wasn't there yet.

Earlier, when he'd been sleeping in preparation for tonight, in the back room of an empty building that had once been a Shop Rite grocery store, he'd had dreams that he knew were not his. Dreams containing the girl that Bluejay, Bobby, and Jimbo had killed the night before. And another woman, who he did not recognize, lying dead on a coroner's table.

He dreamed of a beast taunting him. These were the nightmares of the minister. The man from whom he had cut off and eaten several pieces of flesh. That same flesh now serving as a lifeline, a connection.

There must have been great power in the man for the small morsels he took from him to have affected Scott like this. He ached to meet him again. But when he tried to focus, to zero in on the long, thin, invisible line now traveling between them, he could not sense where the man was. The other's thoughts and feelings would just burst into his mind in fits and starts, like flashes of insight. Better to relax, lay back. Concentrate. Just let the images come to him. Then he could interpret their meaning and act accordingly.

He had felt the minister wake earlier, naked in the arms of some woman, her madness so intense as to pierce right through the other's skin in the places where she touched him. And, through him, to Scott.

Hearing her speak, he only caught some of her words, moving in and out like a radio broadcast that was not tuned in properly. Something about God, that much he could catch.

So much pain in this man. That, more than anything. Pain that scarred deep within the soul. Pain, and rage born of pain.

And deeper still, the beast crying to get out. Pushing at the walls of the human cage that encased it. Demanding its first taste of flesh for the night, its first drink of blood. So exquisite the pain, the sorrow. The anger. God's angry child. Draven shuddered with the sheer ecstasy of it.

Each one of his victims served as a holy sacrifice. Each one bringing him closer in his quest to find God. Bluejay had been right about one thing. Most people wasted their power, the piece of God that lay nestled inside each of them. It was better for someone like him to come and take it out. Use it.

When the change came, he reared back, letting out a cry of passion akin to sexual release. Feeling blood drip from the palms of the minister's hands as if they were his own hands bleeding. The pastor's muscles shifting, reforming, as if they were his own muscles expanding, exploding. Thinking, if it could feel so wonderful living the sensation vicariously as he was now, how amazing would the ecstasy be once he had achieved the ability to will the change within himself?

Oh, sweet Lord. The sharp aroma of flesh. The harsh odor of blood. Letting go now.

Father, into Your hands, I commend my spirit.

The change overtook Blake swiftly. The images from his nightmare driving him. Bethany's broken body. Barbara, lying lifeless in the morgue.

His muscles expanding, bones shifting. Body itching, hair pushing through the follicles, growing new fur, thick, rich. Pulling back flesh to reveal tough new skin. And with it, strength he had never known pumping blood mightily through his veins. Crouched, but standing on two legs, his mind shared the intellect of man and the cunning of wolf. Senses sharper. The world made of sight, sound, smell, taste. Of pulsing heartbeats, the tangy odor of blood rushing through veins, and the musky aroma of flesh.

Leaving Margaret Haas behind, he ran from the church into the night. Aware of something moving at his side, he turned and saw the spirit of Kenny Haas running with him. Unencumbered by the crippled body that had once been his. Free. Powerful. Smiling. Guiding him.

Running, he felt kinship with all the ones who had come before him, the victims of ignorance, the misunderstood. All of them, like his wife and daughter, dying because of the sins of others. With no one to answer for them.

Until now.

He heard the voice of Margaret Haas ringing in his ears, instructing him with the words she had repeated over and over while rocking him in her arms.

God needs a warrior. Do not think that our Lord sits idly by while some of His children suffer at the hands of others. The time for revenge has come. Be that warrior. Feel His righteous anger inside you. Serve Him. Avenge Him. Remember His son dying on the cross. Just as so many have died on their own crosses while evil declares triumph. Hunt them; destroy them. Avenge all those who have died before and will die after.

Blake ran now with the spirits of all his werewolf brothers and sisters. Into the street, the warm night air. Following the aromas of blood, sweat, shit, piss, vomit, hate, despair, fear, disdain. Calling to him. Beckoning.

For just a moment, he thought he sensed someone else watching him. Someone huge, but with small eyes. Peering deep inside him. But then the feeling was gone, and he ran, the beast alive in him.

And hungry.

Scott Draven took a sharp intake of breath. Ran his hands over his body as if it were his own form that had changed instead of the minister's.

Images came and went, clicking on and off like a television malfunctioning.

Then, just when the images had stopped and he thought they were gone, he found himself seeing through the minister's eyes again. The man had turned himself back into human form for the time being. Better to mingle with the masses this way. Looking. Waiting. He wore a long coat that he'd found in a garbage bin to cover his nakedness. Draven could feel the cheap material rubbing against bare skin. As if it chafed his own skin.

The minister was entering a convenience store. Looking at shelves of packaged food and other supplies. Refrigerator cases stocked with more food. Other shelves with paperback books, magazines. With no one at the counter right now to mind the place.

He heard the sounds from the room in the back. Went with

the pastor, watching through the holy man's eyes, as he moved toward the rear storage area. Heard sounds of a struggle. Someone fighting back. Crying out. Someone else cursing.

Two men backed out of the room into the store. Breathing heavily. One with a pistol in his hand. The butt end bloodied. Both turning.

They were men like Bluejay and his companions had been. Men who dealt with their own cowardice by traveling in packs and preying on others. Seeking power in all the wrong ways.

Scott watched these men approach through the vessel's eyes. "Who the fuck are you?" the one without the pistol said. He turned to the other man. "Blow him away."

"No. I like that coat. Don't wanna damage it."

"Shoot him in the head then."

"Still might get blood on it."

"Well, hurry up, for Christ's sake."

Pointing the pistol. "Take it off."

When the minister didn't move, the man stepped forward. Reached out, then hesitated. "Don't you fucking move."

Scott felt the coat pull against his bare skin as it was whipped off. "Jesus. The guy's naked."

"So, he's a flasher. Shoot him."

"You like to flash little boys, pervert?" the guy let the nose of the gun drop down to touch the man's genitals.

Moving quickly, the minister grabbed the wrist holding the gun, brought it up for the asshole to see.

His own hand now the great paw and razor-sharp nails of the beast. Changing that fast. Holding the man in place as he worked the rest of the change slower, giving him time to watch. To gape in horror. His skin shrinking back inside itself. The new skin sprouting fur. Exquisite pain for just a moment, then ecstasy. The werewolf revealed. Scott believing if he touched himself here on this rooftop, he would feel the rich fur coating his own body, the sharp teeth pushing themselves out bloody in his own mouth.

The punk screamed as the beast snapped his wrist, the loud crack of bone sounding as if the gun had gone off. Only the pistol was falling to the ground, and the man's scream was cut off as the creature pierced his throat and pulled out the carotid artery, the body jerking like a marionette at the end of a madman's strings. The spurting blood bathing the dying man's attacker.

He turned to the second one whose mouth was open in a soundless scream. Still making no noise even as the monster slammed his head against the wall once, twice, smashing it open, then reaching in and scooping out the brain matter, eating it, soft like rice pudding, letting the body fall to the floor.

A sound from the back made the creature look. Scott saw a man, probably the store's owner, standing there, staggered, bloody, a gun shaking in his hand. A look of horror and disbelief on his face.

Blake ran quickly out of the store. Scott going with him. No choice.

Then there was darkness. Scott sat back on the roof again, out of breath. Why didn't the creature stay and kill the owner too? That would have made it complete.

But he decided it was okay.

For now.

It was not enough. Blake tasted their fear, and it was not enough. More than the desire for revenge, as great as it was, he needed to understand this desire of the human consciousness to destroy. To waste another human life, to throw away another's potential. He could understand anger. He felt it in his own bones, driving him, moving him. The need to rip and tear. He needed to understand by striking out himself. Using the very violence that was such people's stock and trade against them.

Having tasted the fear, the despair that drove them, in the flesh, the brain matter, what did it do but make him want to know more? Did not the Savior offer His body as bread, His blood as wine for the sake of enlightenment? Was not communion the search for knowledge?

It had taken the sacrifice of the two he loved most in the world for him to open his eyes. Just as God's son had died. If there is a God. If He hadn't died long ago in grief over the misery His children caused Him.

But it didn't matter now. Nothing mattered but the rage inside him. And this new desire to understand. He needed more.

But men like the two in the convenience store were easy to find. They were the obvious ones. What about those who did their dirty work in secret? The child-abusers, wife-beaters, prejudiced and ignorant. Those who put on happy, normal faces in public, then took the masks off in private. The date-rapers and pushers. Users who preyed on human anguish. Those were the ones he needed to find if he were to truly understand the dark side of human nature.

If his wife's and daughter's deaths were to have any meaning.

Before things had started to turn bad in his life as a pastor, Blake had been entrusted with secrets, privy to the darker side of some people's lives as they sat in his office, confessing. Plenty of dark secrets even in a church the size of the one he'd served. There had been nothing he could do about it before, as frustrating and burdensome as it was to shoulder the grief of the victims who'd sought out his counseling, then swore him to secrecy.

What if he had said, The next time your husband beats you, kill him? The next time your boyfriend forces sex on you, cut off his penis?

Once he had been a minister and had known secrets. But that had been his old life. Now he was the beast. The werewolf. Secrets were fodder for action. And forgiveness was an option no longer on the table. The beast was real, tangible. God was a myth.

Or, maybe, what Margaret Haas had told Blake was true. God was acting through him. The werewolf was God's rage made real in the world.

But whatever the truth might be, the night was still young, and he had work to do.

Blood work.

Her husband was a brute of a man and had been abusing his wife for a long time, according to what the wife's sister had told Blake in the confines of his office. She'd been unwilling to do anything about it other than lay the burden at the minister's feet. Would deny that she had told him about it if Blake ever said anything. So, he had done nothing before but listen and counsel.

But things were different now.

He found the man, who faithfully attended church with his family every Sunday, about to enter his home, already drunk over losing half his paycheck down at the local bar to some pool hustler. Preparing to take his anger out on the one he had promised to love.

After he beat her, he told himself, he'd make sure to fuck her; man's got to satisfy his needs.

His last living thought.

Blake lifted the man off the ground before his hand had even touched the front door to open it and turned him so he could see what was holding him, so he could understand that the Devil had come for him at last, with gnashing teeth and slavering jaws. The man screamed as Blake carried him swiftly up to the roof where the beast savaged him, tasting genitals, scrotum, flesh, eyes, hair, intestines, liver, kidney, ligament, cartilage, brain.

Leaving the heart for last, its juice running out from the corners of his mouth, down his jaw, feeling it sluice down his throat, until, finally, he roared aloud, reduced to a consuming inner rage as the man's history contained in the flesh became his own. Understanding the world of violence this man had been raised in, lessons taught by his father through violation. But it didn't matter. His inability to remember those feelings of shame and terror he'd lived with as a boy, willing as he was to put his own wife through the same humiliation, was enough to condemn him in Blake's mind. To declare the man unworthy of even a deity's forgiveness. This man carrying on his father's legacy, but no more, never again.

And still it was not enough. Still, the beast thirsted for more. His Father, he envisioned, looking down at him. Urging him onward.

"This is never going to work," Louise said. "At this rate, he's always going to be two steps ahead of us."

Stan knew it was true. They had driven around the city, looking for something, anything. Some indication. They found it with the call that came in over the radio. An aborted convenience store robbery that had turned bloody.

"What are you doing here?" Stan heard. He turned to see Frank Torrance facing him. His eyes looking hollowed out, his features sunken.

"I could ask you the same question. I'd heard the captain gave you some time off."

Frank moved closer. "You know something about this, don't you?" he said. "Don't you?"

"Frank, calm down."

"Meet me for breakfast tomorrow. The diner at 4th and London. We need to talk."

Marles studied him a moment, then said, "All right." They set a time. Torrance walked away, looking left and right.

"Now what?" Louise said from behind Stan.

"There isn't much we can do here. Let's go back out. Keep looking."

"For what? Another attack like this one?"

"Somehow we've got to get ahead of him. Figure out his moves. Where he might be going next. Then get there before he does."

"How do you get inside the head of somene who's out of control?" Louise said Somewhere, another police siren sounded.

Scott suddenly felt the darkness lift. The lifeline reconnected. While waiting for something else to happen, he'd gotten only flashes. In and out. Frustrating him.

But now he was seeing through the minister's eyes again. Entering a crowded place, wearing the same long coat. Feeling things with the minister's senses. The taste of recently digested meat on his breath.

He smelled cigarette smoke, body sweat, unspent passion.

Mixing with the rich aroma of flesh and blood.

While the beast cried out to be released again.

The bar reeked of smoke and sweat. Bad breath. Beer. He heard laughter. Sensed desire. Sensations pouring over him, infecting him.

Blake watched the human sleaze pass through the front door as he nursed his watered-down beer, bought by an inebriated man who seemed to be buying beers for everyone. Shitty beer with too much head, leaving a foamy, gritty aftertaste in his mouth. He noticed married men with their rings in their pockets working hard to pick up younger women sitting in small groups, talking and giggling. Bloated, overdressed older women painted up in makeup thick as crayon eyed these interactions and glanced periodically at the clock, waiting for the evening to die down, when these gloating men would grow desperate and work their way over to them.

A few people had glanced his way as he'd entered, an odd sight, this man, wearing a long coat, with his hands in his pockets. But for the most part, he was ignored.

His hearing had grown even more acute, and voices, snatches of dialogue rose out of the crowd.

"... freaking nipples the size of cherries ..."

"It's really only good if they swallow..."

"Fucking Jew ripped me off. As if he ain't got enough money..."

"I'm telling you, put it in her butt, before she can say no, there's nothing better..."

Hearing all this disgusted him thoroughly, and it was all he could do to keep from jumping off his stool and letting the beast take over, allow it to tear into the soft flesh around him and rip out the shallow hearts contained within.

After a while, he noticed some men making their way to a back area of the bar. Never more than two at a time, but the exodus was steady. Soon, he rose himself, leaving his beer on the bar, and made his way back.

The sounds of laughter reached his attuned hearing before he reached the door. Male laughter, coarse, rough. Opening the door, he found a small room filled with men. Two young women, nude, each on a pool table. One on her back, while a large bear of a man thrust himself inside her. Nothing in her eyes, reminding Blake of the look he had seen in Bethany's eyes right before she died. The other girl was on her knees, working her mouth up and down the shaft of another man, while a third man positioned himself behind her upraised buttocks.

The other men in the room watched with glee, those who had not yet had their turns waiting in eager anticipation.

A few noticed Blake as he entered the room silently and shed his coat. Naked underneath.

"Who the fuck is he?" one man grumbled.

"Here to get a piece, I guess," said another, obviously drunk. "Who cares?"

"Put your clothes on till it's your turn, creep!"

Hardesty smiled and brought forth the monster, his skin receding even faster now. He grabbed the closest man, and, in a matter of seconds, peeled the skin right off his face. His screaming causing the others to turn, the man's features now nothing but muscle and blood. Blake's rage knowing no bounds as he swept through the room, tearing off limbs and flesh, breaking skulls and arms, feeding on organs.

He grabbed the man who'd been about to sodomize the one woman and stripped him of his remaining clothes, then, just as swiftly, stripped him of his skin. Then he lifted the man up and impaled him on a pool cue, hoisting his squirming body until the stick snapped off inside him. Flinging the body at the door then, smashing it open and sending the dying man into the bar where there were new screams. The two women cowered in fear, but he did not touch them, seeing his daughter on each of their faces. Crying now, he ran into the bar, the patrons moving away, screaming and shouting. A gunshot sounded, and he felt the bullet strike his side. But it did not stop him. The wound would heal itself, as had his other wounds, his body able to regenerate. In the distance, he heard an approaching siren.

He howled in anger and sorrow and, finally, exited the building in time to cross in front of a police cruiser. The car braking, but still hitting him, knocking him up over the car, where he bounced off the top then rolled onto his feet again. He ran away from the chaos, the screams, the sirens. His body aching, but that would heal too. His heart aching for home. There would be other nights. His rage spent, for now, but waiting not far under his skin for the next time.

When there would be more work to be done.

Back at the church, in the little-used basement, Blake collapsed into Margaret Haas's arms, crying, and she held him, rocked him, as she felt his body reshaping itself back into human form, the way Kenny's had when she thought she'd been pushing the Devil out of him. After the change was complete, she rocked him some more and wiped his hot, soaked brow. Offering up a silent prayer. *Thank you, Lord. Thank you for protecting him.*

She felt him shudder, and his body grew limp, weaker than she ever remembered her son being afterward, and she wondered, for just a moment, if there was something wrong with him. Something that went much deeper than the tiredness he felt after tonight's work.

He fell asleep with her holding him and singing a religious hymn in his ear. His skin warm to the touch. His breathing finally achieving a strong, steady rhythm.

She barely heard the screaming sirens in the distance.

While somewhere else, Scott Draven felt drained but exhilarated. The destruction at the bar had been glorious, and still he ached for more. The ability to will the change himself. It was not enough to experience it through the senses of another. He wanted it for himself. He understood now how he could get it, and, for that, he would have to bring the minister-beast to him.

He began to formulate a plan.

CHAPTER TWENTY

Smoke encircled Torrance's head, a cigarette hanging from his lips. Marles had never seen the police detective smoke, had heard he quit over two years ago. But he said nothing, though the sour-sweet smell made Marles a little sick to his stomach in the enclosed space. There were "No Smoking" signs around, but if the waitress wasn't going to say anything, then neither was Marles. Marles was functioning on three hours sleep, but he knew he looked better than this man did with his bloodshot eyes.

They sat inside the diner across from each other in a corner booth, both having ordered only coffee.

"You look like crap, Frank," Marles said.

"Just crap? I feel like shit."

"You want to talk about it?"

Frank stubbed out the cigarette, though it was only half-smoked, then, as if it were an afterthought, lit another one. He hesitated, seemed about to say something then hesitated again before finally taking a deep breath and looking at Stan. "Lot of weird shit happened last night. Lot of people dead. Did you hear what happened in that bar at 8th and Tilghman? Eight people killed. A whole lot more injured. I never liked that bar. I hear they bring prostitutes in there, set them up in the back room. Have real bad parties there, but the neighborhood cops look the other way." He drew more smoke into his lungs, held it in a little longer than the time before. Old habits returning easily. Then, "Did you hear Captain Guthrie might resign? I hope he does. The man's a dick." He stubbed out his cigarette, again only half-smoked. "I've never seen anything like last night." Staring at Marles again, pointedly. "I was thinking, though, maybe you know more about what's going on than most."

Marles signaled the waitress instead of responding, had her refill his cup as well as Frank's. Then they sat, not talking for a few minutes. The coffee bitter on Marles's tongue. God, when was the last time he'd had a good cup of coffee?

"Tell me what's happening, Stan."

"What do you think it is, Frank?"

The man's eyes were sunken, his face unshaven, his breath bad. A decent man, Stan thought. But his world had been shaken. His system of belief shattered by something life, as he'd lived it, had not prepared him for.

Marles understood the feeling.

"When I was a kid, I thought there were monsters," Frank said. "Hiding in my closet, under my bed. All that shit kids believe. Adults tell you there are no such things as monsters.

"But there are monsters, Stan. There are. I saw one. I saw it ... take Ms. Haas ... through an eight-story window."

"What did it look like?"

"A wolf, but ... not just a wolf ... a man, too ... and Ms. Haas ... acted like she knew him ... like she wanted to go with him."

"Him?" Stan said. Torrance pulled out a fresh cigarette. "What, Frank? What is it?"

The man's hand trembled as he tried to light it.

Stan stopped his hand. "Tell me, Frank."

"I recognized him. I wanted to pretend I didn't, but I did."

"Who did you think it was?"

"Reverend Blake Hardesty."

"Have you told anybody?"

"No. How could I?"

"Do me a favor. Don't."

Frank stared. "Christ, you do know what's going on. Have you seen him ... like that?"

Marles hesitated then finally nodded. The man deserved that much at least.

Torrance sighed. "So, I'm not crazy."

"No. You're not. Unless I am too."

The other man suddenly seemed much better.

"You won't say anything?" Marles said. "Especially not to Guthrie?"

"Fuck Captain Guthrie."

"Thank you, Frank. I mean it."

"You know, he could've killed me, Stan, but he didn't. That's the thing ... the only one he killed was this guy who worked there ... a real scumbag. Hell, what he said to me, I wanted to kill him myself."

"But you didn't."

"What?"

"Nothing. I've gotta go." Stan rose, fumbling for some bills, throwing them on the table.

"You're trying to find him, aren't you?"

Stan looked at him, confirming nothing.

"Let me help."

"If you hear something you think I should know, call me."

"Okay. Anything else I can do?"

"That's enough." He extended his hand. "Thanks, Frank. I mean it."

"I've been thinking lately ... I might quit the force. I'm not sure I ever wanted to be a cop in the first place."

"Can I do anything for you?"

"Nah." He reached for his rumpled pack. Saw he only had one cigarette left. "Damn."

Stan left him sitting at the table, hoping that the man would quit the force. Get out.

Before the job ate him up.

Though it still carried the scars of its violation, Louise returned to the 7th Street Disciples Church. This place was Blake's second home. He felt closer to God in this place than anywhere else. So maybe she'd find him here.

The sanctuary lay like a bleeding carcass left to die. Her heart leapt at the sight of a man in the center aisle. Blake? No, it was Paul Blackburn, down on his knees with a cleanser and rags, working on the spots the excrement and blood had left on the carpet between the aisles. He would scrub the carpet, then stop, stare straight ahead for a moment, then continue. She watched him do it three times before she spoke.

"Hello, Paul."

Blackburn looked up, surprised. His hair, normally perfect, showed signs of disarray. His glasses had slipped down his nose. This man, who normally had everything under control, had part of his shirttail out and one pants leg stuck in his sock. His eyes appeared glassy as he stared at her.

"Paul? Are you all right?"

"Oh, Louise, I ... I didn't hear you come in. The police told me they were done in here. I thought I could clean up some of this crap..." He hesitated, then looked around the room, as if seeing for the first time how massive the chore was. He dropped the rags into a nearby bucket, sighing. "Oh, what's the use? It's ruined. Not even a professional cleaner could get the stink out of this place. Even if we could afford to pay one."

"Let me help..."

"No, don't bother." He waved his hand. "Let it die with what little dignity it has left." He stood. "I had such dreams for this church."

The board chairman seemed unsteady on his feet, and she thought she caught a whiff of alcohol on his breath. "Well, we won't have to worry about mortgage payments anymore if we can sell the property quickly." He sighed again.

She didn't say anything. Better to listen.

Taking her silence for anger, perhaps, Blackburn said, "Did you think we were rolling in money? We haven't been able to meet our Outreach obligations for a year. The regional office has been very understanding. This church is going to be something, I'd tell them. Just give us time. That was bullshit. Nobody knew how bad it really was, least of all Mr. holier-than-thou Blake Hardesty."

The man was drunk, for sure. "Paul, you should go home, rest..."

"Oh, by the way, let me give you your official termination notice. We won't be needing your services anymore, sorry. Gotta have a church in order to have a church sexton." He laughed, a harsh, strange sound. "I'm not sure we can squeeze out more than a week's pay for severance, though. Maybe we can afford a little more if we raze the building and sell the land. This city needs another parking lot. And if you want to blame me for that, well, go ahead. Who cares what I tried to do, how I tried to help?"

"What do mean 'tried to help'?"

The man turned toward her, his gaze unfocused. "You'd like me to tell you, wouldn't you?"

"Tell me what?" When he didn't answer, she said, "I guess it doesn't matter now anyway." She started to turn away.

"You think I'm lying?" he said. Swaying. "You think I didn't do enough? What the hell difference does it make now anyway? Might as well tell you. Confess my sins." Confessing his sins in the confessional booth of alcohol, Louise thought.

"It was going to be a one-time thing," Blackburn said. "Once and done. I wouldn't even have to see the merchandise, only the money. Just take my little piece off the top for putting the deal together. I deserved that, after all, and the rest would go back into the church coffers. Fifty times the amount that had been there before. After that, my part of the deal—our part—would have been over, and I'd never have to see them again. A one-time thing. I'd just tell everyone it was an anonymous donor. Praise the Lord. But the two men they brought in got drunk the day before I was supposed to meet them and decided to pull a bank robbery. Just for kicks. Thought it'd be easy. Only they got themselves killed. The deal was totally botched. What I was able to get back was only a fraction of what the profit was supposed to be, hardly worth all the work I'd done. And Barbara … poor Barbara…"

"What are you…?" A light went off in Louise's head. "You're saying … you used church money to buy … what?"

Blackburn looked at her. "Drugs. Cocaine, to be exact. We supplied the capital to buy the stuff, the guy I dealt with got the drugs wholesale, the two guys he brought in from out of town were supposed to handle cutting the merchandise and selling it back out to the different buyers, then give us our investment back plus profit. Instead, they fucked up royally. And killed my Barbara…" He almost fell, knocking against the pew.

"Blake knew about this?"

"What?" He seemed confused.

"Blake knew?"

"About Barbara and me? Of course, he didn't know. He didn't know anything, not how lonely she was, how much she needed someone to pay attention to her, to make her feel like she was something more than just a minister's spouse, an extension of him. No, he didn't know about us. How did you know?"

"I didn't," she said quietly. "I was asking if Blake knew about the drug deal."

The two stared at each other for a long, silent moment. Not a sound in the room but Blackburn's labored breathing. Blackburn looking like he just now realized what he'd said, what he'd confessed to her in his drunken state. Looking for a moment like he might try to deny it, chalk it up to the booze, but then realizing the gig was up. What more could he possibly lose by telling her the rest of the story?

"No, he didn't know about that either. The way he was after Barbara's death... By the time he was able to function again, I'd had time to doctor the books, disguise the deal so nobody knew. But I'd already paid for what I'd done. God made sure of that, when he made Barbara walk into that bank just before those two men I was responsible for bringing here came in shooting.

"The ironic thing about it was, before she went to the bank, she'd come to see me that day to tell me she was calling it off. She'd come to realize she truly loved her husband and decided she was going to talk to him, commit herself to trying to save their marriage. She loved him despite the way he'd been treating her. Despite how closed off he was. She was going to tell him everything. And then hope that they could start all over again. Blake didn't know what a good woman he had, the bastard. She walked out, and I was scared shitless. I'd had affairs break up before, but I was the one who always ended them. But she was different. I was worried about being found out, sure. But what scared me the most was the thought of being without her. And I prayed. I prayed, that something would happen so she wouldn't tell him. I only meant that something would make her change her mind, keep our secret, make her come back to me.

"I guess He misunderstood."

"My God, Paul," Louise whispered, fighting a wave of vertigo. "What have you done?"

He looked at her, eyes wide, swaying. "What have I done? I tried to save this church, tried to keep us from going under. Did you think some miracle was going to come along and save it? Did you think we were going to have this sudden influx of new members come rushing in, looking for Jesus in this dump? Do you think anyone wanted to worship with a minister who's a jonah? If anyone brought bad luck to this church, it was him. The only good thing he brought here was Barbara. My beautiful Barbara. The only good thing—"

She hit him. Not a slap, but a punch, her hand squeezed into a fist and delivered with all the strength she could muster into the man's soft stomach. He doubled over in surprise and pain, looking up at her before she pushed him, sending him stumbling backward, his already shaky equilibrium causing him to smash into a pew, then onto his back on the floor. He barely had time to react before she had the gun out Stan Marles insisted she carry. Pointed now at Blackburn, his gaze riveted to the pistol's short barrel, only inches from his eyes.

"I ought to kill you," she whispered fiercely, remembering her words to Stan Marles only yesterday. God knows a bastard when He sees one. "You worthless son of a bitch."

The room called to her then. Sanctuary. Everything about that word Blake had believed about this room. She saw her entire life laid out before her, God laying it out as He had done once before, giving her a choice. Guiding her to this place, saving her life. Her resolve wavered, and she released her hold on the trigger. Stepping back, she let the gun hang at her side.

"Get the hell out of here," she said to this poor excuse for a man. "If you ever set foot in this place again, I promise I will kill you."

He seemed about to say something, then changed his mind and started to leave.

"Besides," she said then, a smile slowly forming on her face, "Blake is going to find out. One way or the other. And when he does..." She let the sentence dangle as Blackburn half-walked, half-ran out of the room. The outside door closed seconds later.

She stood in the silence, crying without a sound. Reached for a cigarette, then realized she hadn't brought any with her.

Where was her lover? Soon, she would have to go and meet with Stan Marles at the prearranged location.

Was this the last time she would stand in this place? Had Blake abandoned his second home?

Taking one more look around, she sighed and headed for the exit. Wondering where she could look next.

It would be a while before she remembered the rarely used basement downstairs that even she, as the church sexton, had all but forgotten about.

Where the man she looked for slept naked in the arms of Margaret Haas, who pulled him closer now that she knew the two people upstairs were gone and closed her eyes once more.

If Scott was going to bring the minister to him, he had to entice him with something the pastor would want.

In his earlier life, Draven had spent a lot of time at a particular pool hall. He liked the beer, liked the price, liked watching the guys playing pool get into fights. Scott would buy himself one or two beers, then drink free the rest of the night from the rounds bought for him by others getting drunk.

It was where he had met Bluejay. Had first listened to him talk his shit.

He doubted Bluejay would come back here. If he were smart, he'd get out of town.

Or maybe he'd start looking right away for new followers to take with him.

Scott had a couple of beers, waiting. Was about to leave when he saw a kid, no more than eighteen, but getting served anyway, sitting in a shadowy corner of the room, listening intently to someone sporting long black greasy hair, and with a voice like a holy roller's. A familiar voice.

"We're vampires," the speaker was saying. "We can take their power. They'll be glad to give it to us."

The kid nodded. Stupid.

Scott, thanking his luck, but understanding that fate had been on his side for a while now, waited until the two rose to leave. Bluejay with his arm around the kid. Still talking.

Draven followed them outside to an alley along the side of the pool hall. The two not even aware of him as he approached. Bluejay saying to the convert, "Hey, you think you could lend me—?"

Draven yanked the kid backward by his hair, turned him around and said, "Get out of here." One look at the monster of a man and the kid took off down the alley.

"Hey," Bluejay objected, his reactions slow. Too slow. Scott slammed him against a wall, pressing his arm against the other's neck.

"Hello again," Scott hissed, making sure his victim saw the cut still on his face.

Bluejay's eyes grew wide. "S... Scott. Hey, I've been looking for you."

"Shut up," Draven said. Bluejay looked scared now. Scott reached into his pocket. "Just shut up."

The knife did its work, Scott knowing where to cut so the man wouldn't die. Not yet.

The man's screams telling Draven that, yes, vampires hurt too.

CHAPTER TWENTY-ONE

Blake dreamed of the church, only now *he* was pounding at the door, demanding entrance. And when the door opened, he saw his wife, Barbara, naked, her head thrown back, eyes wide, face and body glistening with sweat. A look of horror on her face as she saw him. The figure on top of her was hidden in shadow, moving in and out. Something familiar about him as his features became clearer.

He woke in the arms of Margaret Haas, a fire burning inside him. The beast crying to get out.

"Son?" Margaret said. Something seemed wrong this time. He seemed weaker. In pain. His breathing shallow. "What's the matter?" His face a pasty color. "God help him," she whispered as he rose, unsteady, and struggled to his feet. It shouldn't be like this. Having rested, he should be stronger. "Tell me what's wrong," she pleaded. "Please..." Even in obvious pain, he was beautiful. He mumbled something. "What?" she asked, moving toward him. He spoke again, and this time she heard, "Barbara."

Blake almost fell.

What's wrong with him!

When the change came, it seemed like God's answer to her cry, telling her not to worry.

As if God himself was appearing before her now in all His brutal power, through the vessel Blake Hardesty.

Hair itching skin, pushing its way through flesh. Bones pushing flesh that molded, remolded. Muscles expanding, exploding. Nails elongating into claws, sharpening on hands and fingers that became rough. Teeth lengthening in a widening mouth, cutting through gums, filling mouth with blood.

Senses expanding beyond the immediate sounds and smells. To the smell of blood being pumped through veins in cages of bone and flesh. The sounds of hearts beating, ripe for plucking. Sweet juices flowing. Meat warm and ready.

He left the room. Ran. Oblivious to everything except his desire. His need.

Calling to him.

As she watched him go, Margaret felt an immense sense of relief. Seeing him so weak had scared her.

But now she could tell herself it had been her imagination. God's way of testing her. How dare you doubt Me! I have power over all.

Continuing to watch long after he was out of sight, she took a moment to enjoy the fresh night air before heading back down into the basement to wait for him.

Margaret did not see the large man creeping silently up behind her until it was too late.

Stan and Louise sat in his car, listening to the police radio band. "If he's out there again tonight, we'll hear the reports," Marles said. "Maybe he won't come out at all."

"He will," Louise uttered. "The question is what do we do when we find him?"

He hadn't told her yet about the special silver bullets he had made today. The werewolf's weakness, the man in the occult store had told them. Silver wounded the lycanthrope. Through the heart or brain, it killed him. He thought about the night before last. His hesitation. And now he wondered, if the moment came again where he'd have to shoot, would he be able to? Or would he freeze again?

"I guess we'll have to play it by ear," he said.

Somewhere in the distance, a siren howled.

Officer Timothy Austin had jumped at the chance to pull an extra shift tonight at time and a half, what with his wife pregnant with their first child.

Now he wondered if he was going to get the chance to see his child born. Laying on his back here on a dirty alley floor, with Diamond, the city's most renowned pimp, looking down at him, the cop's own gun in his hand and pointing at Austin. Held in place by Diamond's bodyguard, or, to be more accurate, by the large man's foot planted on his chest. The girl he'd stopped for prostitution, no more than sixteen, stood at the pimp's side, wide-eyed, probably wishing she hadn't agreed to be the bait for Diamond's trap. Not that she had any choice. Why she had picked him out … well, guess it was not his lucky night.

Austin tried to remember if he'd kissed his wife goodbye this morning.

"It's nothing personal, you understand," Diamond was saying. His eyes glassy. Austin wondering what kind of shit the guy was on to try a dumb stunt like this. "I just gotta set an example. Too many of my girls have been arrested lately for all the protection money I pay you guys. It's hurting business. I gotta get the message across. So, somebody's gotta be an example." The gun pointing at his head now. "You understand."

Looking down the barrel, Austin saw his wife at the door, the two uniformed men bringing her the news. I'm so sorry, Jill. Tim closed his eyes. Never a praying man, he figured now was as good a time as any to start. Dear God, save me, and I promise I'll start going to church.

God works in mysterious ways.

"What the fuck was that?" No gunshot. He opened his eyes. The gun was still pointing at him, but the pimp was looking down the alley. He chanced a glance behind him. Saw only darkness.

"Go check it out," Diamond said to the bodyguard. "If someone's there, kill him." The big man nodded and moved off down the alley. "Don't get your hopes up," the pimp said to Austin. "Just a momentary delay." Giving him a smile. Austin would never get a better chance. If he tried knocking the gun hand away…

He heard something. A sound hard to describe. Soft, then sharp. Diamond, Austin, and the girl all peering into the alley now. Diamond shouting, "Did you get him?"

Something came flying out of the darkness. The girl uttered a shriek as something thumped against the pimp's chest, knocking him back as it rolled on the ground. Came to a stop. Looked at them with the bodyguard's shocked face. Except that the eye sockets were empty. And the nose was gone.

Diamond's scream was higher pitched than the girl's. The pimp shot at the head wildly, giving Austin his chance, and he moved.

But not faster than the form that suddenly shot past Austin, then lifted Diamond up in the air and, without ceremony, ripped the man in half. Spraying all of them with blood and guts, while the young woman screamed, and Timothy Austin wondered if his fear of never seeing his wife again might still become a reality.

This ... thing ... threw one half of the body away, then tore savagely at the other half, reminding Tim of the way he liked to attack a good set of barbecued ribs after a few beers at the annual police department summer picnic. Then it threw what was left away and turned to the girl. Her screams reduced to whimpering now as she pressed herself against the wall. Nowhere else to go. The thing reaching for her.

But what had been an animal's paw was suddenly a human hand touching her cheek gently. The face changing, becoming ... almost human. Gazing at this teenager with a look of infinite sadness.

And then it turned away from her and stared at Timothy Austin for a moment, showing him something in those eyes: pain—human pain that he hoped no one would ever see in his own eyes. Evoking something deep and profound in the policeman. Something that was going to stay with him for the rest of his life.

Which now looked like was going to last longer after all as the creature ran off, leaving Officer Austin to breathe a deep sigh of relief and to wonder how the hell he was going to explain this.

"The thing is," Austin said later to Detective Stan Marles, who listened with Louise Calabrese at his side, "I don't think it ever intended to hurt me. It just appeared out of nowhere and saved my life. Helped the girl, too." He'd told Marles how the hand had become human, touching the young prostitute's face, the detective the only one he'd told that part of the story to. "It was awful, but it saved my life."

"How old was the girl?" Louise asked.

"Young. Fifteen, sixteen."

"Thanks, officer," Stan said, his mind racing so that when Austin asked his question Stan had to ask him to repeat it.

"I said do you know any churches around here?"

Walking away, Louise said, "You know what he's doing, don't you?"

"Playing vigilante?"

"Trying to help."

"I'm not sure the people in charge of this city are looking at it that way."

"Did you notice how close in age the prostitute was to Bethany?"

He nodded. "I don't think he's got any great plans. He's just royally pissed off and has a lot of guilt driving him. He might be looking for the other two responsible for his daughter's death."

"You think if he does, he might stop?"

"Maybe." He hesitated. "If he isn't already too far gone."

They reached the car. "What do we do now?" Louise asked.

"I don't know. What we're doing doesn't seem to be accomplishing much. We're still one step behind him. If only there was something we knew, something, maybe, he doesn't know yet. Something we could use to get ahead of him."

They both thought about it. Then Stan said, "Frank told me Blake took Margaret Haas from the hospital. Where would they be staying during the day? Not Margaret Haas's house."

It only took Louise a second to respond. "The church."

"But you checked there."

"Maybe not enough. I got distracted."

Stan looked at her. "Distracted by what?"

He noticed something in Louise's gaze. "What?" he asked

"It's like you said … something Blake doesn't know. But we do."

"I don't know what it is. Tell me."

He saw the conflict in her eyes. "I'm not sure how we can use it," she said. "I'm not sure I want to."

"Do we have any other choice?"

"No." Convincing herself as much as him.

"Tell me in the car."

Inside, he turned down the police radio long enough to hear her story. When she was finished, they talked some more, and soon a plan was formulated.

Only Timothy Austin noticed their car as it drove off. He offered them both a prayer.

Scott watched the woman as she lay unconscious, her breathing shallow. He'd already decided not to partake of her. The religious fervor he sensed in her through his connection with the minister intrigued him, but not enough to want to partake of her. He had already decided from whom he wanted his next meal, his next holy communion. He didn't want anything getting in the way of that. But it still might be best to keep her alive, at least until the man-beast had returned.

For now, she was on the floor next to his other prisoner. Bluejay, a mere shadow of the powerful being he had claimed to be. This vampire drained of everything. Such was the way of false messiahs.

Draven had long since let go of any anger he held for this creature. The man simply served a purpose now. Capturing him allowed Scott to set his plan into motion.

He sat very still, waiting for the connection between him and the minister to re-establish itself, the man's flesh inside him long since digested and voided, but the spiritual essence still remaining. He wondered how much longer it would last and became anxious at the thought. What if it had only been temporary? What if it was gone? Patience, he told himself, patience. Earlier, he had been connected to the man-beast as he'd ripped the large man's head off, then ripped the pimp in half, gorging himself on the dripping innards. But then something unexpected happened. The man reached out, as if with Scott's own powerful hand, not to rip the scared teenager's face from her skull, but to cradle it. Images had come to him of a little girl riding excitedly up and down on his knee.

Ride me, Daddy! Ride me!

And then the frustration came again as the man-beast left the other two untouched. He'd wanted them too, but the minister let them go. Then the connection faded.

Even now, as he waited, there was still nothing. The lifeline between them had grown weak. He needed more. Needed to bring the minister here. Where the trap waited.

He leaped to his feet in rage. He wanted it now. He'd waited too long, had come this close. So easy for him to take his rage out on one of his prisoners if he wanted to. Break the woman's neck. He reached for her, blinded with anger.

When it hit, it slammed into him like a sledgehammer. Knocking him to his knees. The feel of enormous hands that felt as if they were his, but were not his, breaking through rib cage bones, encircling the unprotected heart. Wet and hot in his grasp.

He closed his eyes and felt the power coursing through his body as if it was his own.

As it would be soon. Very soon.

CHAPTER TWENTY-TWO

Paul Blackburn lived in Macabee, a few miles west of the Allenside center city church where he served as board chairman. His front lawn was compulsively cut the proper height, the bushes trimmed just so. Even in the dark, it looked like a property out of House Beautiful.

The two figures walked up to his front door; one gave three sharp raps with the door knocker.

"Who is it?"

"Police, Mr. Blackburn. We need to talk."

"Police? Do you know what time it is? Can't it wait till tomorrow?"

"We apologize for the hour. We wouldn't bother you if it wasn't important."

"It better be important." The sound of locks being undone preceded the door opening.

Stan Marles pushed into the door, hoping for the element of surprise. He got it, the edge of the door knocking Blackburn backward, his arms cartwheeling, until he fell, conveniently, into a chair. The detective was on top of him before the man could summon up the proper indignation.

"Where's your wife?"

"What...? I..."

Marles hesitated only a second before pulling out his gun. "I said where—?"

"She's not here. She's visiting her sister."

"I just have a few questions."

"What the hell do you think...?" At the sight of Louise Calabrese coming up behind him, Blackburn shut up, fear now in his eyes.

"That bank robbery where Barbara Hardesty and others were killed," Marles continued, his own heart beating hard in his throat. "What do you know about the two sleazebags that shot up the place?"

"Well, of course, everyone knows—"

"I thought you might know something the average citizen doesn't."

Blackburn's eyes darted toward Louise, then back to Marles. "I'm going to have your job for this."

"Sure. Right after I let it slip how you used church money to fund a drug deal."

Eyes darting again. Sweat on his upper lip. But still he bristled. "How dare you—?"

Marles shoved his gun against the other man's throat. "I don't give a fuck whether you admit the truth to me or not. I'll still get as much satisfaction blowing your goddamn brains out."

He pulled the gun back, giving the man room to talk. Holding his breath. Visions of his police career flying out the window dancing in his head.

"What do you want?" Blackburn asked.

At least they'd gotten past the first step. "Right now, I could bring you in for embezzlement," Marles said, "drug trafficking, and maybe bank robbery and murder with a little luck."

"You can't prove a thing." Stan had to admit the man had guts.

"How hard can it be? Get a warrant; search the church books. Shouldn't be hard to find."

"I don't know what she's told you, but you're not going to find anything in those books."

"Maybe, maybe not. You sure you want me taking the time to find out? All that publicity?"

A pause. "Are you here to harass me or is there something you want?"

"We're looking for someone," Stan said. "We think you can help us find him."

Blackburn's eyes shifted, again, to Louise, who had yet to say anything, then back to Marles. "You can't prove a damn thing," the church board chairman repeated, sitting up. "And you sure as hell aren't going to be able to get a warrant. You're lucky I don't call your superiors on you for breaking and entering. Whatever this woman's told you, let me tell you something about her. She's a pathological liar who I wanted to fire a long time ago, but the minister of our church for some reason—"

Louise was past Marles so fast he didn't realize she'd moved until she was on top of Blackburn. She grabbed the board chairman by the balls, squeezing his scrotum through the pajama bottoms he wore. He gave a high-pitched squeal as he fell back into the chair, Louise following him, still holding on. "Maybe we can prove it, maybe we can't," she hissed. "Who cares? Rumors will be enough to hurt you. That and me telling everyone I can how one particular pillar of the community liked screwing the minister's wife behind the poor man's back."

"I was drunk when I said that. Surely you didn't believe—"

"How about I just tear these balls off you're so proud of?"

She squeezed, and he gasped. "Please ... let ... go..."

"Give me your gun!" Turning to the police detective. "I said give me your gun!"

Stan hesitated then gave it to her.

She replaced her hand at his crotch with the nose of the gun. "I had the opportunity to kill you before and didn't. Don't give me a second chance, you son of a bitch."

Blackburn looked wildly at Marles. "Why don't you stop her?"

Silence. Save for their prisoner's breathing.

"See, Stan," Louise said, "I told you he wouldn't talk."

Marles shrugged and headed for the door. "I'll be waiting in the car."

"Wait!" Blackburn shouted. "Where are you going?"

"Goodbye, you slimy bastard," Stan heard Louise say, followed by the sound of the pistol cocking.

"Wait! Don't leave me here with her! You're right. It's all true. Everything you said."

Marles stopped, turned. She still held the gun against the man's privates. "All of it?" he said. "Even the part about Reverend Hardesty's wife?"

"Yes."

Hearing the man admit to what Louise had told him earlier did not give him any satisfaction. "I ought to let her kill you."

Louise rose from the chair, the gun hanging loosely now, and crossed to Stan's side. "You understand. I had to hear it from him," Marles said.

"I know. It's all right."

"What … what do you want from me?" Blackburn in tears now.

Marles took the gun from Louise and pointed it at their prisoner. "Put some pants on over those pajamas. You're coming with us."

Outside, he led the man to the back of the car. "Get in the trunk."

Their prisoner climbed in with surprisingly little resistance. Once the trunk was shut and Marles was at the driver's-side door, he looked at Louise. "I can't believe I just did that."

"You did good," Louise said.

"I thought I was supposed to play bad cop."

"I could tell your heart wasn't in it."

"Where's the gun I gave you before?"

"I left it here in the car. I'm not sure I like the idea of carrying one around. Too tempting." Louise opened the passenger-side door. "Let's get this bastard to the church."

"I hope Blake shows up there."

"He will. He has no place else." She looked at him. "What is it?"

"Nothing. Churches make me nervous."

"Yeah, well, get over it."

They got in the car and drove back into the city.

Blake found the pusher dealing dope to some sweating kid in a back alley. The kid begging, the pusher grooving on the high the power gave him. Blake arrived just as the kid was sticking the needle into his scarred arm, his eyes rolling back into his head as he dropped the hypodermic onto the dirty ground, the pusher kneeling, picking it up, admonishing him with, "Hey, kid, be careful. I might be able to use this one again."

The pusher didn't understand what was happening to him as Blake pressed him against the wall and reached into his chest, breaking through the rib cage, grabbing the heart and ripping it out. Blake watched the light in the bastard's eyes fade as he bit into the red-hot muscle, its scarlet juice filling his mouth, his throat.

Letting the corpse drop, he turned to the kid, already into his high. His eyelids blinking in front of dilated eyes, probably trying to decide if the thing he saw before him was real or part of the rush.

Such a waste, Blake thought. The young man's arms already riddled with scars. His face wasted and drawn. One day soon this kid would be robbing someone to get the money for his habit, if he hadn't started doing so already. Maybe he'd start doing a little pushing himself, hitting the schools and playgrounds. Not caring about the young lives he would wreck.

Without really thinking about it, he reached out and took the young man by the throat, lifting him off the ground. The punk grabbed the beast's wrist to no effect. So easy to break his neck. All those future lives he'd be saving.

Blake caught a flash of movement before something knocked him to the side, forcing him to drop the junkie.

He turned and something hit his shoulder. The pain made him roar, and then he saw the thing that was attacking him.

Another beast like him, shorter, but just as powerful, as it slammed its body into him, holding him in place just as Blake had done to the pusher.

"That's how it starts," the other creature hissed, a voice that sounded ragged, ancient. "You justify it, just this one time. Soon, you're the judge and jury on every little point, soon you're rationalizing every death. Yes, this one should die because of what he might do one day. Then, after a while, it's the taste of the meat you crave, and nothing else matters. Think about it. Are you sure that's the direction you want to go?"

The figure backed up, letting Blake go. "You're new at this, I know. There's been no one to teach you. No one to help you understand this power you have. Up to now. Now you've got me.

"Go on, talk, if you have something to say. Never crossed your mind to see if you could talk like a man when you're the beast, did it?"

Blake hesitated then tried to speak, his throat rough. "Who … who are you?"

"I'm going to tell you, don't worry. And from now on, I'm going to be your teacher. I'm going to tell you what you need to know. What can hurt you. Even kill you. Important shit like that. But not here. I've got a place nearby." He turned to the addict, lying unconscious on the ground. "Looks like he'll live. Fucking junkie. Probably will end up trying to rob some poor old woman. But we don't know that for sure, so…" He looked at Blake. "Stay as the beast so we can make better time. Follow me."

Hardesty did as he was told, the two of them sticking to back alleys. The "place" the other referred to turned out to be the occult store on the corner of 8th and London. As minister of the 7th Street Disciples Church, he had always been wary of the place and had urged his congregation to stay away.

Once inside the small shop, the owner said, "I'm going to change back, but you stay the way you are a little longer. I want to show you something. In case you're thinking of taking advantage of me in my human state, I'm gonna warn you, I can change back faster than it takes you to move two steps, and then tear out your throat before you're able to take your third."

The other willed the change, revealing a tiny old man, full gray-white beard and crooked teeth giving the illusion of a wolf even in human form. His back slightly hunched, a partially caved-in chest on spindly legs, with thin arms. He quickly pulled out a shirt and pants from behind the store's counter and pulled them on.

He laughed as Hardesty gaped. "Surprised? Don't be. We come in all shapes and sizes." He pointed to something small sitting on the same counter. "Pick that up."

Blake saw a bullet sitting there. "Why?" he croaked.

"Because I said so. You want to start learning what you need to know or not?"

Blake reached out and grabbed the bullet.

A pain like fire searing his flesh shot through his fingers, and he dropped it, stumbling backward. He held up his hand, saw singed flesh.

"That bullet's made of silver," the little man said. "Silver and fire are the only two things that can destroy us. I keep that close by, so I never forget that I'm not invincible. Now watch this."

Crossing over, he picked the bullet up himself without apparent harm. "When we're in human form, it can't harm us. Unless someone shoots us with it, of course. I became a lycanthrope the same way you did. I was once a man. Until one night a werewolf attacked me. Before then, I was ignorant. I thought God had put me on this earth to rout out evil in His name. I thought the lycanthrope was evil and should be hunted. But the one who did this to me was only trying to defend himself, live his life. My comrades killed him. Those same comrades tried to kill me after the change occurred. Fortunately, I got away. But many like me didn't. Now I survive as a living testament of my own prejudice.

"So, remember: silver and fire. But silver only kills if it gets inside the heart or the brain. I'm sure you've noticed you have very fast recuperative powers. You can regenerate parts of your body, if necessary. But a wound from silver and fire takes a lot longer to heal. So, stay away from them. Now you can go ahead and change."

Blake willed it, and he felt his muscles shift, reform, the process smoother now, until he stood naked, the old man holding out another pair of pants and a shirt. "Here, I think these'll fit you. My name's Jeremiah, by the way."

He felt light-headed, and his knees wobbled, but he put the clothes on quickly. Then he waited, still confused, rubbing where his fingers still hurt.

"You've probably got a second-degree burn there," Jeremiah said. "Sorry, but sometimes the best way to learn is through example. Then you never forget."

"That's how he died," Blake mumbled.

"Who?"

"Kenny," Hardesty said. "The one who ... did this to me. He would have killed me, but he swallowed the silver cross I was wearing. He choked on it."

Jeremiah smirked. "He more than choked, I'll bet." The old man leaned against the counter. "Did you think there were no rules concerning what you've become? Nature always has rules. It's a pain in the ass sometimes, but it keeps you humble.

"Something else. Some people who get this power are able to adjust, even grow, and become better people. But this power doesn't always work out for everybody. Some people just can't handle it. It destroys them. We don't know which one you are yet. But if you hold on to this power long enough without getting yourself killed, I suspect you'll do fine. With the proper guidance," he added, pointing to himself with a wink. "It's important you gain wisdom, and wisdom usually comes with age."

"How old are you?"

"Old enough to know what I'm talking about. I've seen my share of generations pass by."

"Generations?"

The old man smiled, nodded.

"Don't others notice you living so long?"

"You stay on the move. Relocate. Means being the new one in town a lot. I moved here about ten years ago. We do die, eventually, like any other of God's creatures. Me, I'm getting there. I've probably got less than a hundred years to go now."

"A hundred...? What about friends?"

"If you're lucky, you find one or two understanding humans in your lifetime. Maybe you find love, though you'll have to go into it knowing that one day you're going to watch your partner die. We've grown small in number, but there are still more than you might think. We're a dying breed, I'm afraid. I don't think you're going to find any animal rights activists trying to get us labeled an endangered species.

"It's time for you to learn what it is you've become. Once I was like you. Young, stupid. Used my new power for all the wrong reasons."

Jeremiah moved closer, his eyes shining. "There are two kinds of werewolves. Those like you and I who were changed by the wolf's saliva entering our bloodstreams. And there are those who were born that way, of werewolf parents. I have learned in my years as a wolf-man that the lycanthrope are a noble race. But as the werewolf faces extinction, there are those, a minority, who are desperate enough to keep the race going by attacking humans, turning them into us. That wasn't Kenny, though. In attacking you, he was trying to protect his mother. He loved her very much."

Guilt ate at Blake's insides. In trying to help Margaret and her son, he had only ended up destroying them.

"Don't waste time with guilt," Jeremiah said, as if reading Hardesty's mind. "Guilt can be good for you sometimes, but it's not going to do you any good now. What you need to do is get control of what it is you've become. That's what I'm going to help you with.

"Someday you may decide to be only a wolf. With our race dying out, many of us are already choosing that. Me, I like being the half-breed. Others decide they don't want both worlds. But becoming the wolf completely means giving up your human half. I'll explain later. You've got enough to think about for now. It's time to run again ... to be the wolf-man. While there's still darkness left. But this time I'm going with you. There's more to being a werewolf than meat and blood. Go ahead. Change."

Blake felt suddenly dizzy. His head hurt. His legs were shaking. Before he knew it, the old man was at his side. "What is it?" he heard Jeremiah say through the haze.

"I ... I don't know..." He began to sweat profusely. He might have collapsed were Jeremiah not holding him up.

"This isn't because of the change. Something else is doing this." Jeremiah held his hands against the minister's chest and head and paused as if listening. "You've got something else going on inside you. Something growing, spreading—"

Blake pulled away. "No, nothing. I'm all right," he said.

"No, you're not. You're ill." Jeremiah stared at him. "How much time do you have?"

When Blake didn't answer, Jeremiah said, "If you don't want to tell me what it is..." He paused, then shrugged. "Go ahead. Change."

Without further urging, Blake removed his clothes then

willed the change. The beast once again bursting through its prison of flesh.

"Come on," Jeremiah said. "Time to teach you a thing or two."

Out the door they went, into the still, dark night. With dawn still hours away.

Plenty of time.

CHAPTER TWENTY-THREE

Bluejay was always talking. But not now, not after what Draven had done to him, the pain making him pass out a long time ago. Maybe Scott would wake him later, before the minister arrived. The woman was still unconscious, tied up and stuffed into a corner of the room where she couldn't be easily seen from the entrance.

Earlier, he had felt Blake Hardesty plunging his hand through the drug pusher's chest, felt him feed on the heart as if it as if it had been him who was eating. Then the connection had faded again, so that he did not get to experience what the minister-beast did to the junkie. Since then, he'd been waiting. For the dawn to come, and with it, the man-beast. But with dawn fast approaching, Scott heard noises upstairs. Footsteps. Hushed conversation. Not the minister, and more than one person.

He stayed where he was. Silent. Listening. When he finally did move, his footsteps made no sound.

Louise hesitated at the entrance to the church.

"What is it?" Stan asked, looking at her, his hand grasping Paul Blackburn's arm.

"Nothing," she responded. But she was sensing something. Or was she?

She willed herself to move and led the way into the building. Blackburn gave no resistance, as if he had given in to the inevitable.

Louise expected her sense of foreboding to go away once she was inside, but it didn't. She tried attributing it to the destruction the sanctuary had suffered. But her instincts told her some new disease had infected this place.

"You still think this is the best place to find him?" Marles asked.

"Yes," she responded, despite what she was feeling.

"Best for what?" Blackburn said, the first words he'd spoken since being let out of the trunk.

"Shut up," Stan snapped.

"This was his favorite place." Louise said. "Despite what's been done to it, I still think he'll come here."

The feeling persisted. Making her want to look over her shoulder.

"Let's do it then before I change my mind." Stan gave Blackburn a shove.

The plan they had come up with was relatively simple. Tie their prisoner up and have him waiting at the front of the sanctuary for Blake when he arrived. They didn't know whether he would arrive as man or beast. But they hoped the distraction of seeing Blackburn would give them the element of surprise. To do what with, Louise wasn't sure. She remembered what she had seen in the face of the beast as she'd come out of her dream. Surely, there was enough of the man left inside that she could talk to him, get through to him somehow.

She followed Stan Marles as he guided their prisoner to the front of the sanctuary. Much of the damage remained, but, at least, the police paraphernalia had been removed.

"I demand to know what you're planning to do with me," Blackburn said, some of his bluster returning, even with the nose of the detective's gun still pressed against his back. Louise had the rope in her hands, and she began to loop it around the board chairman.

"This is kidnapping, you know," Blackburn argued. "This is—"

All three heard the noise at the same time. A footfall on a creaking floor.

"What was that?" Stan said, turning, as did Louise.

Taking advantage of the distraction, Blackburn pushed Louise into Marles. Not tied yet, the rope slid off easily.

"Shit," Louise said. as the fleeing man ran through a door

behind the choir loft that entered the baptistery.

"Where does that go?" Marles said. "Can he get out of the building?"

"No. There's no back door... Damn it."

"What?"

"The basement. It's a storage area. We stopped using it a long time ago because it was always so damp and filled with mildew. It's not very big—"

"Is it large enough to hide in?"

"Shit, I didn't think about that. Blake could be—"

Paul Blackburn's scream interrupted her. High-pitched, building. Then, abruptly, cut off.

Marles, gun poised, headed toward the door Blackburn had just gone through, Louise following close behind.

He almost fell over the quaking body. Blackburn's throat had been cut, blood pumping out onto the floor.

"My God, did Blake—?" Louise started.

"I don't know." They heard a thud. "Where's the way down?"

"Over there. A trap door in the floor. See, it's open. He must have gone back down."

Marles peered into the opening, seeing only darkness. "Stay here."

"I should go with you."

"Here." He handed her his cell phone. "Call 911. Hurry." Peering into the dim light below, he began his descent.

Louise watched him move out of sight, then, waited, the phone in her hand. She heard nothing. "Stan?" she called out.

"Oh my God. Louise, make that phone call now!"

She lifted the phone, then turned when she sensed movement behind her. Later, she would realize that the open door had been left as a trap.

She managed to shout Stan's name before a huge hand clamped itself over her mouth from behind, then turned her around so that she was looking into dead, dispassionate eyes. Tiny eyes. Strong fingers pressed against her throat, cutting off all sound, all oxygen, the only noise that of Stan shouting, "Louise!" growing more and more distant as she lost consciousness.

Blake arrived at the back entrance to the church as dawn crept in. There had been no more killings the rest of the evening. Only stories told by Jeremiah, introducing him to the legacy of which he was now part. His first lesson, how to better control the change from man to man-wolf to only wolf. And how to stay as the wolf when he wanted to, running and playing and experiencing a sense of freedom he had never known before. Jeremiah had promised more lessons tomorrow. And, best of all, the chance to meet others of his kind in a couple of days.

For the first time since embracing the change, he was not fueled by rage. He felt something more. A connection. To life and nature. To God, maybe, more than he had ever felt in his work as a minister.

But, for now, he needed to think, to sleep, to allow his dreams to take over and, perhaps, give him answers to the many questions swirling in his brain.

He sensed something as soon as he entered the sanctuary and became immediately wary. Different smells. Coming from downstairs. The smell of blood. Hot and fresh in the air. The familiar odor of generic cigarettes.

And other smells he recognized that brought him back to that horrible night and his daughter's dead eyes. He brought the man-beast forth. Strong, powerful. Filled, once again, with righteous vengeance. The lessons learned from Jeremiah forgotten for the moment.

As he headed toward the basement.

Louise heard her lover approaching and struggled against her bonds. But the chains held, and the gag stuffed in her mouth kept her from doing anything more than making futile noises in the back of her throat. Stan Marles hung to her left, bound in the same fashion as she, unconscious. Margaret Haas lay trumped up like a steer, unconscious as well, stuffed into a corner of the room several feet away.

The fourth captive, whom she did not recognize, sat, bloody, perhaps dead, on a chair facing the direction from where Blake would soon enter. The way they were positioned, the way the room was so dimly lit, he would be the first one Blake would see. Meanwhile, their captor hid against the opposite wall, the trap ready to be sprung.

If only she could warn Blake. But the best she could do was little squeals, the cloth pushed too far back, her mouth too dry.

She heard Hardesty approaching.

Frantically, she continued to struggle.

Seeing the man they'd called Bluejay sitting in front of him brought back the sight of him feasting, with the others, on his bound daughter. Bluejay holding a knife against his mutilated daughter's throat.

The knife going through her throat...

The memory fueled his rage and drove him to act. Made him completely unaware of anything else in the room as he leaped, landing almost on top of the unmoving form. He wanted Bluejay to recognize him before he tore him apart, grabbing hold of his face, turning it toward his own...

... only to see the eyes already dead. Open, but seeing nothing.

Confused, Blake turned to see Louise Calabrese chained against the wall, her arms held upright, her ankles bound together with duct tape. Stan Marles was chained next to her in the same way, unconscious.

He went to her, willing his hand to be normal for the moment as he tore off the tape around her legs and pulled the thick cloth from her mouth, then did the same thing for the detective.

Louise gave out a deep racking cough, long strands of saliva streaming from her mouth as she tried to talk. "Behind you..."

He turned, but not fast enough to stop the chain from encircling his chest. A simple matter to break, he thought, until the pain hit like fire, the poison of silver on his skin, like the pain when he touched the silver bullet in Jeremiah's shop, but more intense.

He screamed, an animal's shriek, and was yanked backward, falling to the ground. Felt more pain as another silver chain encircled first one ankle, then the other. Then the chain was quickly removed from his chest, tearing sections of flesh, only to be wrapped around his wrists then finally once more across his forehead, keeping his head still against the pain as the end of the chain was connected to a pole running into the floor and up to the ceiling.

A terrible weakness came over him, making the pain subside, his body change against his will, until he was a man again. Looking up, he recognized his attacker before he finally lost consciousness.

His moment of victory was finally here.

Scott ignored the shouts of the woman behind him. So tempted to begin his work, the beast-man helpless before him. But he had been very patient up to now, and he could continue to be patient a little longer. The moment had to be right for the next step in his plan. He had thought this out carefully, the werewolf lore he had learned serving him well. Everything he had learned during this past, glorious week coming together.

He placed his hand on his prisoner's chest. Felt the heart pumping beneath, the blood rushing through the veins.

Soon, he told himself. *Very soon.*

Louise found the most disturbing thing about her captor was his silence. He had not put the gag back in her mouth, but she'd finally stopped shouting after it was clear no one outside would hear her. The whole time the big man ignored her, even when she tried talking to him. After making Blake his prisoner, he sat in the chair himself, staring for hours, unmoving, at the minister lying spread-eagled on his back, bound and naked. Unconscious. He left the room only once, taking away the body he had used to trap Blake with. He'd returned a little while later, wiping his lips.

Her attempts to plead with him had accomplished nothing. So now she only watched, waited, trying to keep the terror, more intense than she had ever felt in her troubled life, from overpowering her. From affecting her ability to try and figure a way out of this situation.

Several times she thought Marles was about to wake up, low mumbling noises coming from where he hung. But then they would stop, and he would not stir again for a while. As for Margaret Haas, she still lay trumped up like an animal in the corner. Not moving. Louise feared she was dead.

Time passed inexorably. Louise's arms ached down to her armpits, but she understood now that pleas for relief would do no good. After a while, her arms began to grow numb.

Their plight seemed hopeless. No one knew they were here. The chains were impossible to break; even with their captor only a few feet away, seemingly lost in his own world, she doubted she could get enough leverage to even kick him. And something told her it was best not to even try.

More time passed, and sheer exhaustion caused her to pass out. When she woke later, she wondered what time it was. Was it possible it was already dark outside?

Detective Marles began coming around. Then Blake, who had not moved all day, started to stir.

Their captor rose from his chair a moment later.

The minister was moving. The urge to transform probably drawing him to consciousness. But the silver chains would keep it from happening. Draven was sure of that.

He rose from the chair and removed his clothing. From the pants pocket, he pulled out a long knife.

Blake was dreaming of the beast again. Offering him its gift. Cutting the body open, eating the flesh, organs, engorging itself.

This is my body given for you.

Drinking the blood.

This is my blood, shed for many, for the remission of sins.

Only now it was his body being consumed.

He felt himself being pulled out of the dream. Into the waking world of the basement, his body spread out on the floor.

The beast of his dream, having made the trip with him this time, now stood over him.

"What are you doing!" Louise screamed. Marles mumbled something next to her, eyes fluttering open.

"Please, no!" she begged. But he didn't seem to hear her. Not even her scream. Or Stan whispering next to her, "My God!"

As the knife in the big man's hand began to cut.

Blake's own scream blended with Louise's. Nightmare becoming reality.

Scott Draven ignored the minister's screams, the woman's pleas. They were somewhere else, not here, not now. Not in this world made up of the knife and the flesh, the blood and the organs. Revealed to him as he spread the flesh aside. A blessed feast. His dream of ultimate power about to come true.

He began his communion. Carefully at first. Not wanting to touch the heart. Not now. Later, when the moment was right, when he felt sure the power was his completely. As even now he began to feel the power coursing through his body, fresh, new knowledge flooding his brain. Such knowledge, such power. Everything he had hoped for and more.

He continued to do his work carefully. When he drank the blood, he did not cut the carotid artery. Making it last, savoring it. Ignoring the way the body thrashed against the chains. Making the meal sweeter somehow.

When he was finished, when he had partaken of most of what his blessed victim had to offer, he rose, saw that the body's lungs were still working, though laboriously, the heart still pumping, though weakly. Now would come the true test of the knowledge he'd gained. To see if his plan worked.

Standing naked before his prisoners, he howled at the ceiling. At the world. At his father, he of the glowing cigarette. Felt the hot ash on his skin as if the old man was here with him, testing him. Never let them see the pain, boy. Never let them see the pain.

Oh, blessed Father, take me. Make me your warrior.

Into your hands I commend my spirit.

Then he ran, up into the sanctuary, and out into the night.

Louise had no tears left at the sight of her destroyed lover. She had pulled against her bonds, as had Stan Marles next to her. Screamed and cried and begged.

The man had only continued to do his blood work

undaunted. Shouted like an animal at the ceiling when he was finished. Then he ran, leaving her to mourn her lover. The detective at her side speechless. In shock.

She felt helpless, powerless. All hope ripped away. All reason for life as shredded and torn as her lover was.

And so, she grieved.

Unaware that Blake Hardesty's heart still pumped. That, for him, the horror was not yet over.

CHAPTER TWENTY-FOUR

Frank Torrance opened his eyes. Smelled booze on his clothes. Found half-smoked cigarettes littering the bed. A hole in the blanket told him the one he'd been holding before falling asleep had still been lit. It now lay on the floor where, fortunately, it had caused no more damage.

He rose unsteadily, kicking several empty beer bottles that rolled along the floor. Looking at himself in the mirror, he did not like what he saw. A couple of days' growth of beard. Bloodshot eyes. Skin the pallor of milk. Clothes he had not changed in two days.

He'd never felt more hungover. Or sick. Was that vomit he smelled?

He couldn't remember what exactly he'd been fighting with his wife about before she stormed out. Had Martha taken the kids and left him? That's right, she took the kids to visit her parents. She'd be there, she told him, when he was ready to sober up and tell her what the hell was going on.

She must have really been angry to swear like that.

He took off his clothes and threw them away. Then he showered, soaping himself three or four times to rid himself of the stench. Once finished, he cleaned the room, opened the windows, and aired the place out. He wanted nothing of the man he had turned into these last few days left in this room, or in this house, when Martha returned.

Finally, feeling like a semblance of his former self, he headed on down to the station. He'd taken some time off, but to hell with that. He'd find something there to do.

Maybe he'd find Stan Marles. The image of the thing he'd seen lifting Margaret Haas off that bed flashed through his

mind; this time, however, he resisted the urge to grab for a beer.
He left his house feeling better, like a police officer again.

Draven had not realized how painful it would be the first time.
His muscles cramping as they began to shift. He cursed the
librarian, whose wealth of knowledge on lycanthropy had not
included this.

He could not help but cry out. His muscles expanding. Skin
stretching. Hair forcing its way through the follicles. Blood
filling his mouth as his teeth grew, splitting his gums.

And the memories. So much pain, so much tragedy, grief
and feelings of guilt contained in this man. Now as much a part
of Scott as they were of the minister.

But when the change was complete and the suffering
subsided, he had gotten what he wanted. He was the man-
beast. The werewolf. He stood only one step from God now.
The Father. He of the glowing cigarette. Alive in His son, Scott
Draven.

He reached up to the sky in holy thankfulness, ready to test
his new form.

Turning, he saw on old man staring at him. Grizzled face,
rheumy eyes. An unworthy sacrifice.

But, still, his first victim.

Louise had no sense of time passing. Stan Marles was awake,
but the two said nothing to each other, still chained to the wall.

She didn't care, though. Because nothing mattered now.
Their captor might as well have torn her body apart. For the first
time in her life, she wondered if she had been wrong to believe
in God. If by doing so, she had made her life nothing but a lie.

She closed her eyes in despair. The man she loved lay dead
and mutilated in front of her.

And then she heard something. A low moan.

Opening her eyes, she saw Blake Hardesty begin to move.

The movie theatre had been nearly empty for the night show.
Only twelve tickets sold. But, to Frank, the scattered remains
littering the auditorium made the number seem higher.

Captain Guthrie had come along for this one, bitching and moaning as usual.

"Jesus Christ," Guthrie muttered, running his fingers tiredly through his thinning hair. "Why me? Why me, Lord?"

Selfish bastard. As if all the violence of the past few nights had been created just to cause problems for the captain.

"This doesn't fit," Torrance said.

"What do you mean?"

"The other attacks weren't like this. In the convenience store, the owner wasn't touched, just the two who beat him up. Officer Austin and the prostitute were allowed to live, but not Diamond and his goon. The men in the back of the bar were attacked but not those two girls being raped. He killed the perpetrators, not the victims."

"So, the guy changed his mind. He's a psycho. You sound like that fucking Marles, questioning everything. I see one similarity that matters. People dead. Torn apart."

The technicians arrived to do their work and the two men left the theatre. Outside, Guthrie turned to the detective. "Have you seen Marles lately?"

"No, I haven't."

"I want you to find him."

"I thought he was off—"

"You wanted something to do, didn't you? Find him. Tell him to come see me. Better yet, you bring him to me."

Guthrie looked around and shook his head. "This used to be such a nice city." As the captain walked away, Frank wondered how long before they'd be announcing his retirement.

Louise stared in awe at the unbelievable thing happening in front of her. Marles, chained next to her, watched as well. She understood now, as she watched Blake's body repair itself, that his captor wasn't finished with him yet. New organs grew where the man had ripped out the original ones. Intestines stitched themselves back together, then moved back into their proper place. Shattered bones remolded, reconnected. Muscles returned to correct shape and size.

Finally, new skin formed to join with what remained of the

old. The entire time, Blake was delirious with pain, his head lolling back and forth, his eyes moving up into his head.

Finally, the transformation ended, Hardesty now unconscious. But whole again.

Marles finally spoke. "That guy will be back again, won't he? To put him through it again."

"Yes," Louise said.

"How many times?"

"Until he feels he doesn't need him anymore, I guess."

"We've got to stop him."

"How?" She yanked against the chains binding her. "We can't break free. Blake can't help us. Nobody knows we're here. And the church is closed down. Nobody has any reason to come here."

"My boss is going to wonder where I am."

"But they're not going to look here, damn it!"

"What do you want me to do, Louise? Give up hope? Tell him to kill us the next time he shows up?"

"At least I wouldn't have to watch Blake go through that again!" Her voice came out ragged. Marles stared at her until she looked away. "I'm sorry. I ... I just don't think I can stand it anymore."

More time passed, Marles grateful when Louise fell asleep. His own body ached, but he fought to keep himself from passing out. He needed time to think, to try and figure out a plan.

He had not told Louise about the four silver bullets he'd purchased from a specialty shop that now sat nestled in the chamber of the pistol he still had hidden on him. He'd managed to get off two shots from the other, police-issued gun he'd carried before the big guy overpowered him and took the gun from him. But his captor had not checked him for other weapons. And if he was in the process of turning into a beast like the one Blake had become, then shouldn't silver work on him the way the proprietor at the occult shop had described?

He just hoped the opportunity would present itself so he could find out.

He waited. His mind still working but unable to come up with anything.

Eventually, he heard something upstairs.

The sound of their captor returning.

Things had not gone the way Scott planned. At first, it had been glorious. His first taste of flesh as the beast, the first hot blood pouring down his throat, even better than what he'd expected, better than his sojourns with Bluejay and his group. Better than his own solitary nights out looking for victims.

No more was the simple search for knowledge that had driven him before sufficient. Now it was the act of the kill itself, the power inside him, the draining of one's life into his. He was close now to learning everything he needed to know. He had found what he was meant to be. What destiny had planned for him.

First, the man in the alley. Then the bickering couple walking home from a late dinner.

Then the massacre at the movie theatre.

But then, unexpectedly, had come the pain. Starting in his head, then spreading throughout his body. Bringing him to his knees.

And voices suddenly calling to him. The voices of his victims. Hounding him inside his brain.

Finally, the change came, unwilled by him, returning him to human form before he was ready. Forcing him to limp back to the church naked, vulnerable. Almost broken. The darkness hiding him so no one saw. Upon entering the church, he flew into a rage, he who had always been so good at not showing his emotions in the past.

Never show the pain, boy. Never show the pain.

Obviously, one feeding was not enough. But he had plenty of time. Once the regenerative powers of the werewolf had taken full effect, as he knew they would, he would commune again. Another feeding before his next sojourn tomorrow night.

He was thinking more clearly now, but the rage still consumed him. What to do with it? Now that he was back to being just a man. At least until it was time to feed on the minister again.

For now, he decided, he would settle for the two prisoners

he had chained downstairs. The woman and the cop. He'd been so consumed with his main target he'd hardly been aware of them before; now he wondered why he had bothered to keep them alive this long.

He would particularly enjoy watching the light leave the woman's eyes.

He took a couple of steps.

And then the pain hit again, worse than it had been before, seeming to split his head in two, driving him to the floor, where he passed out.

And lay for almost twelve hours.

CHAPTER TWENTY-FIVE

Frank Torrance spent the day looking for Stan Marles. Making phone calls, checking both Stan's and Louise's apartments, as well as Blake Hardesty's house. He even talked to neighbors. By the afternoon, he was afraid something had happened to him. He began checking hospitals. Nothing.

As he stopped back at his home, Torrance thought of Blake Hardesty's church. He didn't think Stan would be there, but he might as well check. There was no other place to look. First, he'd change clothes and grab something quick to eat before he went back out.

The house seemed too large without his wife and children. The empty rooms reminded him how much he missed them. Maybe he'd try calling them before resuming his search. It would mean a lot just to hear their voices.

Torrance had his cell phone in hand when he heard, "Excuse me." He turned to see an old man standing in the entrance to the living room.

"Who are you?" Torrance demanded. "How the hell did you get in here?"

"We need to talk. Now."

"Do I know you?"

"We don't have much time, and I have a lot to tell you."

"Wait a minute, don't you run that little occult shop—?"

"I believe you've been looking for a police detective named Stan Marles."

Torrance hesitated.

"He and a woman stopped by my shop a few days ago. Asking some interesting questions."

Frank had left his gun in the kitchen and began making his

way in that direction. "I don't know what the hell is going on," he said, the gun coming into view, "but if you don't tell me—"

"I wouldn't do that if I were you."

When Torrance looked back, he saw what he first thought was the beast he had faced in the state hospital. But this figure was much shorter than Hardesty, though he seemed just as fearsome, crouched, and ready to pounce.

In a gravelly voice, the figure said, "I don't like resorting to theatrics. So, sit down and listen."

Frank did as he was told, and, in the time it took for him to sit in a chair, the old man had reverted back to human form.

"You need my help, and I need yours."

"I don't even know you," Torrance said.

The old man chuckled and stuck out his hand. "My name's Jeremiah. We've got work to do."

Draven snapped awake, bumping his head on a pew. The light coming in through the sanctuary windows told him dusk was approaching. Shit! Why had he passed out? What the hell was wrong with him?

Rubbing his head, he moved quickly, ignoring his nakedness. For a moment, he was afraid his prisoners had gotten away somehow. But upon climbing down into the basement, he found everything the same, the man and woman chained against the wall, looking at him. Cursing, he realized he'd left his knife in the pocket of his pants, which were still upstairs. He returned there, only to discover that, in fact, he had removed his clothes downstairs as he'd originally thought. What the hell was making him so confused?

But you're not the same being you were before, a voice in the back of his head told him. All those souls you've ingested, they're part of you, not just their knowledge, their strengths, but also their faults, their imperfections.

Back in the basement, he found his pants and pulled out his knife. Upon seeing the weapon, the woman began to yell. Alternating cursing and pleading. He ignored her. After he returned tonight, he would kill them both.

The minister's body was whole again. Regenerated. What

he'd hoped for, prayed for. The prisoner's eyes turned toward him. Filled with the awful knowledge of what was about to happen again.

The woman continued yelling. Stupid bitch! He'd hardly noticed her before, why did she seem to bother him now? He took two steps and hit her, splitting her lip. That shut her up. The man next to her stared darkly at him but said nothing. Draven considered cutting both of their tongues out, then decided he'd wasted enough time. He was hungry. Turning back, he knelt in front of his holy communion. A saying came into his mind.

This is my body, which is given for you.

He positioned the knife. Heard the minister whisper, "Please ... don't..."

The knife did its cutting.

Frank thought he heard a noise, the sound of something big running away, as he approached the church.

"Come on," Jeremiah said. Together, they hurried inside. Frank hesitated, shocked by the sanctuary's condition. This was the first time he'd seen it since leaving the church.

"This way," Jeremiah said. Torrance followed him through the door into the baptistery. What the occult store curator had said about the trap door being here was true. Jeremiah opened it.

"You go first. I'll follow. You know what to do. I shouldn't touch the chains. In case I need to become the beast right away."

The detective nodded, then went down. Entered the basement. His first sight was of the ruined body of Blake Hardesty, recognizable only because the face had not been touched. Turning away, he threw up.

"Frank. Frank!" Wiping his chin, he saw Stan Marles and Louise Calabrese bound to the wall by chains. Stuffed into a corner of the room was the body of Margaret Haas. Judging from the smell, she had been dead a while.

"Get us down from here." The chains were connected to two bolts high above them. Simple, but effective. Torrance pulled over the room's only chair, stood on it, then released them. He planned to work on the chains holding down Reverend

Hardesty's remains next, but Louise moved first. Running to the body, she kneeled next to it. She looked terrible, her left cheek and lip both cut and swollen. She was clearly in some pain, but she removed the chains promptly.

With the silver chains tossed away, Jeremiah entered. Marles noticed him. "What are you doing here?"

"I'm here to help. But I couldn't touch the silver. So, I brought him along."

"The silver...?"

"He's like the reverend, Stan," Torrance said. "A werewolf."

Jeremiah knelt beside the opened body. "Is he—?"

"Yes," Louise interrupted, talking with a little difficulty through her torn mouth. "See? His heart's still beating."

At her words, Frank turned. "Did you say his heart...?"

"...is still beating?"

"Yes." Louise held Blake's hand. Knowing what would be coming next. Planning to stay by his side the whole time to nurse him through the agony of regeneration.

"It should start soon," Jeremiah said. "Stay back."

"I'm not leaving him," she said with conviction.

The old man did not argue. Instead, he knelt next to her and put his hand on Blake's forehead.

They didn't have long to wait. It started with Blake's shriek of pain.

Draven ran, the change complete. He was the beast now, the wolf-man. More powerful than the night before. Stronger than any living—

He stumbled when the pain hit, greater than before, again starting in his head, then through his entire body. He fell to the ground, fighting his body's urge to return to human form.

It wasn't supposed to be like this. What was the matter with him?

For the first time, he considered the possibility of poison. But how? When would somebody have had the chance to poison him? He searched his mind, trying to distinguish between the memories that were his and those of his victims. Finding it more difficult than he thought it should. Slowly, but surely, he found the ones that belonged to the minister. Sorted through them. There must have been something he missed before. He searched each one until...

When he found the answer, he roared with anguish. It had been there all along. If he hadn't been in so much of a hurry to take hold of his new power, he would have found the poison—the cancer—that had been a part of the pastor.

And that was now part of him!

Fighting to hold on to his beast form, he turned and ran, returning to the church.

Where he planned to kill them all.

She cried with him, suffered with him. Watched in amazement at the way his body regenerated. New healthy organs now in place, the bones coming together, new skin starting to appear.

She noticed Jeremiah smiling as he kept his hand against Blake's forehead. "Why are you smiling?" she asked.

Jeremiah looked at her. "Something I told him before," he said. "This power isn't for everyone. Some people are crippled by it. Others become not only stronger; they become better children of God. I wasn't sure how it would affect this man's illness. Whether it would make it better or worse."

"The doctor in the hospital said his cancer had accelerated," Louise said.

"That may be. But now?"

Jeremiah's smile broadened as he smiled down at Blake Hardesty. "It appears his regeneration here has helped. Perhaps cured him. The illness that was inside him is gone."

"You mean the cancer—?"

The sudden sound of a door banging open above them caused them all to look up.

Followed by a loud animal cry.

"He's back!" Stan shouted.

"Hurry, my love, hurry," Louise urged, as new skin spread over fresh organs.

Fresh, *healthy* organs.

Marles reached down and undid the leg holster beneath his left pants leg. Pulled out the gun that contained four silver bullets. He heard the trap door being flung open, something landing just outside the entrance into the room.

A beast appeared in the entranceway, howling. Their captor in his new form. But something was wrong. The thing seemed to be fighting itself. For the briefest of moments, Stan would see a human leg, a human hand. Then the shape of the beast would return. But not fully formed.

Frank Torrance stood nearest to the creature, and the thing dispatched of him quickly, slamming him into the wall. Marles tried a quick shot, but the safety was on. As he clicked it off, he saw the thing move toward Blake lying weak on the floor, Louise with her body spread across him, ready to die to protect him.

This time, he took careful aim for the head, working to steady his shaking hand. The beast not even looking his way.

Then something moved. Jeremiah, in his beast form. Leaping at the invading creature. Right into the path of the bullet as Marles fired. The bullet catching Jeremiah in the arm.

No!

Jeremiah howled and fell to the floor. The beast crouching over Blake and Louise looked at Jeremiah, then at Marles pointing the gun at him. With eyes widening in realization, it jumped out of the way as he fired a second shot. Then the creature, howling in rage, ran back out of the room as Marles fired a third time, missing him again.

Shit! Shit!

The beast was gone.

Blake, now fully regenerated, crouched down next to Jeremiah.

"I'm all right," Jeremiah said, back in his human form. He winced. "Damn, it hurts."

Looking up at Blake now, grabbing his arm. "You must go after him."

"I know."

Blake heard Torrance moan. Thank God, the man was alive.

"And you know what you have to do," Jeremiah said.

Hardesty nodded.

He rose from the floor.

"Be careful," Louise said.

Blake smiled to reassure her. Wondering if this was the last time he'd ever see her.

He closed his eyes. Allowed the change to take over. Then he left the room and exited the church.

Once outside, he started to run, following the last of his daughter's murderers into the night.

CHAPTER TWENTY-SIX

It was not supposed to be this way. He, who had once been Scott Draven, was now a new creature, born out of the joining of others. With powers never before experienced by any living soul. He should be held in awe and worshiped by these lesser beings that populate the earth. He who is God's new son, carrying out His Father's dark vision for the world. His victims he now carried inside himself made holy by their humble sacrifice.

But that was not what was happening. All the voices of his victims now cried out within him. What seemed like a thousand voices sounded in his head, his heart, his veins. Each one fighting to make itself heard. His victims' pain and unfulfilled dreams, unrequited loves and desires cut short. Pounding inside him. Shouting for release. For his attention. All that they might have been and now could never be. Their secret terrors now becoming his, driving him. Making him run. From what? From himself. The one thing in the world it was impossible for him to run away from.

And now the greatest indignity of all. Now that he knew, now that he had the power to do something about it, now that he stood only one step from God, he could do nothing with it because of the poison that was now inside him. Passed on to him by the minister. Why had he not felt it, detected it the first time he had opened him up? Because he had been too caught up in his own hubris, had been blind even as he was opening himself to new possibilities. The many voices now warring among themselves to be heard only reminded him of how he had lost touch with his own voice.

As panicked as he felt, he didn't know where he was going.

He crossed a street and was almost hit by a passing police car. It swerved, stopped. He heard shouts. A gun being fired. A bullet grazing his shoulder. He barely felt it. The wound would heal itself. But what about the poison now inside him? Could that be healed?

A call for help. The growing wail of sirens. The sound of running footsteps.

He turned and ran from the chaos. A sudden pain shooting through his body almost felled him. He stumbled, remained on his feet. Soon the sounds of chaos were far in the distance. But soon others would be coming for him. And he questioned whether he'd be able to fight them in his current state.

When he saw the church, he realized he'd been running in circles. Was now back where he'd started. Cursing, he turned again. But where to go? Out of the city this time. Away from the chaos. But what about the maelstrom inside him? Could there be a way—?

Something blindsided him, knocking him off his feet. Hitting the ground, he rolled, and leaped back up. Felt his human form trying to re-emerge and fought against it.

He looked for his attacker.

And saw the minister, in his beast form, facing him.

Blake recognized the man from that terrible night, even as the larger man's body kept changing, from beast to man, then beast again. Remembered how he had forced him to watch his companions consuming his daughter before he passed out.

The other man kept fighting it. His head shaping, reshaping. His eyes blazing, then cooling, then blazing again. A look of anguish on his face, of agony. His hand went out to the minister even as it, too, kept changing. Human, then clawed, then human again. After what he had done, was this man turning to him for help? For relief? Revenge was what Blake had been desperate for, had told himself he needed for his soul to finally rest in peace.

But that was before he had met Jeremiah and learned there was more to what he had become than rage and vengeance.

He watched this thing start toward him, then double over

in pain. It looked up at him. "You bastard!" he hissed. "You did this to me!"

Blake remembered what Jeremiah had told him.

This power doesn't always work out for everybody. Some people just can't handle it.

"You did it to yourself," Blake answered.

"You were tainted. Poisoned."

"Yes. But you chose this life without understanding what you were getting into, what the consequences could be if you weren't ready. Let yourself become human again. I'll do what I can to help you."

"No! Stay away from me!" Rising, backing away, then doubling over again.

"Please tell me your name. Let me help you."

After a moment, he said, "My name is Scott. Draven. Yeah, okay … help me. Please." He gasped. "The pain…"

Hardesty moved toward him, changing back to human form as he reached out his hand. Then Scott moved. Blake, realizing in a split-second what his intention was, willing the beast to return, but not quick enough to avoid the sharp claws that cut the flesh between his shoulder and right breast, the same place where Kenny Haas had bitten him on a day that seemed so long ago. The beast now on top of him, holding him down. Ready to strike again.

From somewhere close by, Louise Calabrese screamed, "Blake!"

His attacker looked up at the distraction, and it was enough for Blake to throw the creature off-balance then push him away. His own man-beast shape now fully formed as he rose to his feet, saw that the Scott-beast again was struggling with the change, unable to control it.

He saw the three of them fast approaching. Louise running. Jeremiah behind her, in human form, with a coat over his naked body, being helped by Stan Marles, who was trying to aim his gun.

Louise reached them first. Crying, saying his name over and over. Reaching out for him. Until Scott intervened, Blake not moving fast enough to stop Scott from grabbing her and pulling her to him. With a rip of cloth, he exposed her throat. Baring his teeth, he growled, "Stay away or I'll kill her."

Everyone stopped. "Change back," Scott ordered Blake. "Now!"

Louise struggled against her captor, but the beast's hold was too strong. Marles kept his gun out, hand shaking. Jeremiah eyed Scott with a narrow gaze, still too weak to do anything.

"I said, change back!"

History was repeating itself. Hardesty hearing Bluejay's voice saying the same thing then killing his daughter anyway.

"I mean it! I'll kill her!"

Blake, helpless. Always helpless.

Not this time.

He poised to leap.

And saw the first of the yellow eyes peering out of the darkness.

Draven saw them too. "What the hell...?" Then more eyes. Wolves, Blake realized. At least six or seven, maybe more. Watching Draven. One starting a low, fierce growl soon picked up by the others.

"Where did they come from?" Draven yelled.

"I called them," Jeremiah said. "They've been traveling for a couple of days. I suspect they're hungry."

"Keep them away from me. You hear?"

"Uh uh," the old man chuckled. "You may be able to stop us, but you can't stop them."

Blake used the distraction to edge closer. Then one of the animals leaped, causing Draven to pull back and lose his grip on her. She fell into Hardesty's arms, and then Scott Draven was running, his body doing that strange shifting again, melting and blending forms. Until he was just a man again. Naked. Helpless. Blake started to go after him, but Jeremiah stopped him. "No. He can't do any more harm." Blake allowed himself to become human again, and Louise wrapped her arms around him. Then they heard the sirens, and Detective Marles stepped forward. "I think that's me they're calling," he said. Jeremiah nodded, and Stan Marles, speaking for the final time to the man that had become the best friend he'd ever had, said, "Good luck,

Blake," and ran off in the same direction.

The remaining three stood in silence. After a moment, Blake turned to Jeremiah. "I'm not sure I understand what happened. Did my cancer really do that to him?"

"That's what he thinks. But do you remember what I said before?"

Blake thought a moment. "The change affects people different ways. These powers aren't for everybody."

"That's right," Jeremiah said. "Some people learn to handle them. And some people..." He nodded his head in the direction where Scott Draven had just gone. "Some people, they destroy. Unfortunately, not so soon that they can't do some damage."

"What about me?" Blake asked in a subdued voice. "Is it going to destroy me too ... eventually?"

Jeremiah winced as he slapped Blake on the shoulder, but still he smiled. "Hell, no, you're gonna be fine. In fact, I think you're gonna be better for it." He placed both hands on Blake's shoulders, more gently this time. "Thanks to your regenerating powers... Well, I think you'll find you won't need to worry about your cancer anymore."

Louise looked at him, eyes wide, then hugged him fiercely. "A miracle," he heard her whisper. "Thank God. Thank God."

"Where's Frank?" Blake asked.

"Hurting, but okay," Louise said. "He was awake when we left him. He stayed behind to start cleaning up the mess, cover our tracks."

"Margaret?

"Dead, I'm afraid."

Blake sighed. She had been a help to him, after all.

"Enough," said Jeremiah. "We have things to do."

The wolves moved closer. Ten of them, it turned out. Waiting, watching.

"I said they were coming. To meet you and to help you continue your lessons. But, perhaps, there's more. A decision to be made tonight."

"Decision?" Louise questioned. Blake looked at her.

"Come on," Jeremiah said. "We have one more journey to make."

Scott Draven ran to get away, but the voices followed him. Their pain, his pain. His victims exacting their revenge on him now. For cutting their lives short, for leaving their dreams unfulfilled. Tears blurred his vision. When was the last time he'd cried? Not since he'd been a child, when his father had started using the cigarette on him.

Scott ran onto Madison Street, into the center of Allenside. Into the surrounding headlights of police cars. "Stay right there!" a voice shouted. From inside his own head? No, from close by. "Don't move!" He kept shifting, changing, but he barely noticed. He only wanted to get away from the voices...

Two shots were fired. One hit him in the arm, but he paid it no heed. He was screaming now, but not from the gunshot wound. Turning away from the headlights, he turned down an alley, then saw a familiar figure step into his path.

Stan Marles blocked the man-beast's escape, bringing up the gun, grabbing Draven by the arm, pulling him close until they were face to face.

Up until the events of a few days ago, the detective had never had a moment when he needed to fire his gun. He'd always known he was a terrible shot, confirmed by his barely passing scores at the shooting range. Not to mention recent events.

Now he had one bullet left in his gun. One silver bullet. Into the heart or the brain, Jeremiah had told him.

Draven stared at him, his eyes showing his desperation for relief.

Marles made sure this time, shoving the barrel into the thing's open mouth.

Before he fired.

As Scott Draven lay dying, unaware of the uniformed figures surrounding him, he thanked God silently for his release from the voices. The silence a blessed thing, allowing him a sense of peace he had never known. He waited for the bright light he'd always heard about, then saw it, and with it, a figure approaching, coming for him. "Holy Father?" he asked, his voice simple and child-like again. The figure clearer now. Come to take him. *Into Your hands...*

He saw the lit cigarette then, glowing for eternity. His eternity.

The silence then shattered by the sound of screaming.

His own.

CHAPTER TWENTY-SEVEN

The three of them rode on the wolves' backs, the rush of air not enough to drown out Jeremiah's howling, from the pain of his wound or joy of the ride, Blake could not be sure. They didn't stop until they were out of the city and had reached the hills from where they could see Allenside's city lights and, beyond them, nearby Latham.

"I talked before about a choice," Jeremiah said, as they looked out over the cities. "The lycanthrope is a dying breed. Perhaps God intended it to be that way one day. Who knows? But as I told you before, some choose to live their lives as animals. You can make that choice now. If you wish."

Blake turned away from the old man, his sense of grief never as great as at this moment. "It's not fair that I should have a choice. When others didn't."

"Life is what you make of it, my friend."

"But look at what I've done, supposedly in His name. How can I make up for it?" He looked at the old man. "How can I ask God to forgive me?"

Jeremiah smiled and reached out to cup his hand under Hardesty's chin. "He already has. Now the question is, can you forgive yourself?"

He already has. The force of the words overwhelmed him. Filled him. He'd used these words himself from the pulpit so many times before. Telling people that if they were truly seeking forgiveness, then God was willing to give it. That if they chose to live full and righteous lives from that point forth, then they would truly earn it.

He turned to Louise. "You understand, don't you? Why I need to do this?"

"Take me with you," Louise said.

"What?" Blake stared at her.

"Make me like you."

"It would mean hurting you. I can't..."

She touched him. "I don't want to be without you."

The wolves stood around them silently. Soon they would sleep before their long journey home. Jeremiah watched.

Blake took a moment to stare into his lover's eyes. Then he put his arms around her, brought her close so that she didn't see him will his hand to change, the sharp claws striking once, rending cloth, exposing flesh of which he partook. Feeling her essence fill him. The ultimate joining. She fell against him, unconscious. Blake held on to her firmly, looking at Jeremiah.

"With shared pain, there is growth," the old man said. "She'll be all right. After she wakes, you can help her learn. As you will be learning. After that, your change will be complete."

The wolves, as they surrounded them, seemed to move as one. "Don't worry. They'll wait until she's awake and ready." Jeremiah embraced him then pulled back. "Be well, my friend. Who knows, maybe I'll decide to join you one day before I die."

The old man changed then ran, not looking back as he went. Then Blake settled down with his newfound friends to rest and wait for his lover to awaken.

A week later, Stan Marles sat at a table in a bar, working on his third beer, courtesy of Jeremiah, who sat across from him.

"They promoted me. Can you believe that?" Marles waved his glass. "I guess the new boy did all right after all."

Jeremiah smiled. "It would appear so."

"I'm happy Frank quit. I never thought police work was his thing. Now he can spend more time with his family. Must be nice to have a family."

"Yes, it is."

Marles took a drink. "I guess Blake never found out about his wife and that creep, Blackburn."

"Perhaps, on some level, he knew all along. And had already forgiven her."

"Maybe." After another drink, Marles said, "I miss him."

Stan finished off his beer and decided against another one. "Do you know, I haven't been to church since I was a kid?" He looked at Jeremiah. "Do you go to church? Do you think you might go with me some time? I get nervous..."

Outside, the dawn was still hours away.

Meanwhile, far away, the pack, having set up its new home for the coming season, slept, its two newest members lying nuzzled against each other.

Dreaming peaceful dreams.

About the Author

Jeff Johnston is the author of over 30 short stories in the horror genre, as well as stories in the genres of mystery, fantasy, and even religious/spiritual. He has also written numerous articles covering theatre, film, and other topics. BLOOD WORK is his first published horror novel.

As Jeffry W. Johnston, he writes dark and edgy mystery/thrillers for teens. His works includes the Edgar-nominated FRAGMENTS, which was also chosen by YALSA (Young Adult Library Services Association) as a Quick Pick for Reluctant Young Adult Readers. His other teen thrillers are THE TRUTH, also a Quick Pick selection, as well as an In the Margins Book Award Winner, and FOLLOWING, a Junior Literary Guide Gold Standard Selection.